THE COUNTY

ZANE HOROWITZ

The County

Copyright © 2024 by Zane Horowitz.
All rights reserved.

This novel is entirely a work of fiction. The names, characters, and incidents portrayed in it are the work of the author's imagination.

No part of this book may be used or reproduced in any manner whatsoever without written permission, except in the case of brief quotations embodied in critical articles and reviews. For more information, e-mail all inquiries to info@mindstirmedia.com.

Published by MindStir Media, LLC
45 Lafayette Rd | Suite 181 | North Hampton, NH 03862 | USA
1.800.767.0531 | www.mindstirmedia.com
Printed in the United States of America.
ISBN-13: 978-1-965340-20-2

CHAPTER 1

AFTER THE TWO BOYS DIED side by side, Sam escaped out the side door into the drizzle of the cold December night. Exhausted, he bent over, hands on his knees trying to take a few deep breaths. His anger and frustration had been growing but this night it tightened its choking grip on him, draining what little breath he still had out of him. He had tried to speak several times to tell someone he was going out, getting some badly needed air, but he was so choked by his anger he could no longer get the words out. After shaking his finger rhythmically four times at the side door he finally just expelled the word "out" in a guttural exhalation of anguish. He needed space to breathe, but now more than ever he longed to be free of this place. He pitched himself down onto the rickety wooden bench outside the side door, banging his head on the metal bar behind him as he dropped limply into the seat. Bright sparks floated inside his eyes as his hearing disappeared into a deep monotone tunnel. He rubbed the back of his head with his hand. It was wet; *was it just his sweat, or worse?* He grimaced when he pressed his scalp and felt a lump. He checked his fingers, *no blood at least.*

The old bench was the spot used by those stepping out to smoke, and it reeked of old stale butts strewn on the wet cement below his seat. He hated that smell, but there were few places to find solitude from the pit. He leaned back, coughed at the suffocating stale smell, and turned his head upward. Above him, not too far across the field, four giant spotlights that lit the yard and the parking lot beyond set up an eerie yellow glow as the dense valley fog was descending. He thought he could smell the faint scent of logs burning in chimneys somewhere nearby, he remembered that comforting odor from years ago. *People at home, staying safe and warm*, he thought. But here he was in the County, his home for the last six years, and he did not feel safe. He developed that heightened sense of always needing to be alert for the trouble that would invariably find its way inside. This was a sense he rapidly learned at the County, something the survivors had.

The bump on the back of his head made him think back to the day of the murder. That horrible murder he never forgot. It had been a chilly day like this his first December at the County. *Senseless*, he shook his head. He leaned back and closed his eyes, years later tears still came, and he felt the tightening in his jaw. Unconsciously he was involuntarily making a fist as if he wanted to smack somebody hard. Water dripped steadily somewhere close by and he tried to use its sound as a form of hypnosis to blot out tonight's tragedy, and the memory of that first December. He was still not able to cope with that one particular death inside the County. It too was a blow from behind, like the bump he now had on his head.

He thought he heard sobbing muffled in the distance and opened his eyes to see where it was coming from. Surprised, it now seemed darker outside, in just a few short minutes the fog had become denser against the Klieg lights obscuring the sky, and he felt a chill. The wailing was coming from inside the building not from far away as he first thought. *Or was that a siren?* Sam could barely think straight, but knew if he could just hang on a bit longer, he might be getting out of this hellish pit soon. He inhaled slow and deep and tried to use the smell of the fireplaces, the rushing of the water dripping, all to conjure up some hope. But the stale reek of cigarettes and washed off debris won out; he coughed while trying to hold a deep breath. Sam could not have imagined then that once he did escape, in just a few months he'd be thinking about ways to engineer his return to the County. Soon enough Sam would be behind its walls again, perhaps this time for life. The County did that to people.

Fish stepped out the side door of the main building, "I thought maybe I find you here. You doing Okay?" As he stared at Sam he noticed how spent his young friend looked. His shoulders slumped, his once eager smile now a passive blank face. Whatever spark was once in his eyes had turned dull, sad, and now moist with unfulfilled tears.

Sam sighed, finally able to speak without choking up, "I don't know what okay is anymore. We both just watched two kids die in there. Another gang just kids again. Nothing we could have done to save them, at least that's what I keep telling myself."

"We don't get to choose; we can't fix the unfixable most of the time. Sometimes it's people that are unfixable, and sometimes it's just that the County is, and perhaps always will be, unfixable." Fish sat on the bench next to him, turning to look him in the eye, "Well, you just try to think about the day when you get to walk out of here. For me, it's gonna be quite a while." Sam watched the fog swirl and for a second expose an opening with the full moon above. Fish tried to reach through Sam's despair with logic, "I've heard the experts say the longer you institutionalize a person, in a place like the County, the harder it is for him to adjust to life on the outside. Still, it's possible, you're still young. Lots of others have adjusted to the outside after three or so years inside. Or at least that's what I assume when they don't come back."

"What about Snider, he's here for what? A dozen years? That's as close to forever as it gets. You think he's adjusted?"

Mac Snider was the longest resident in the County. Practically a legend. Most people did a maximum of six years, but Snider was on his second stint. Everyone always assumed that Snider was just plain mad, but no one knew what he was like when he first got here. Not even Fish. He may not have started that way but after 12 years inside your mind begins to change. In a way, though, with all he had to put up with, he was sort of a mad genius. Sam was thinking that with only a fraction of Snider's time he could make it out okay. He was thinking about lining up a job in the mountains. His family would support that if he got out, and it could be the beginning of a new life. Sam would first have to cleanse himself of all the bad habits he had adapted to survive inside the County, and try to relearn things the right way. Some of his self-imposed rules he would keep, the bad ones would have to go.

Sam wondered why was he still here. How would he judge his time after his years in the County? That night there were only those two deaths in the pit. Only, not that death is to be taken lightly, but because once inside you either got used to the deaths, or it drove you mad early on. Maybe that's what happened to Snider, always wise-cracking, dark and sarcastic, that was his armor for survival. Two deaths for a night were not unusual, especially in December with Christmas coming. But Sam knew these two tonight struck a nerve deep within him. These two kids were stabbed in the chest and bled out. If someone just wanted to send them a warning, they would have got a short jab in the back, but a direct knife to the heart was different. It would not be the Christmas visit their parents would want to get when an officer would ring their doorbell later that night. The season of supposed joy and good tidings on the outside just meant more pain and suffering for those in the County. Fighting increased and suicides were bound to go up by January. Sam had seen them all over those years. There were predictable patterns that he now knew the rhythm of.

Sam's mind drifted. Fish was the philosopher, just like tonight always rambling on about the reason behind things. Sam had started to tune him out recently. Fish was always unassuming with his advice, even though he wasn't in that long of a time, just two years more than Sam, he seemed wise beyond his years. But Fish's attitude had been upsetting the administrators, and both he and they knew the only answer was to get rid of him. They were just looking for an excuse, preferably a simple mistake on his part, to make him gone.

"You got to believe a man when he tells you things," Fish was saying as Sam refocused from his dazed stare back to Fish's words, "at least give him the benefit of the doubt. Now that doesn't mean that he is necessarily telling you the truth. Sure, everyone in here is capable of lying, but you got to start from somewhere and look for the clues to support or deny his story. I know it's easy after a short while here to start assuming that everyone is lying all the time, and has some ulterior motive in mind. But you should make it your secondary agenda to discover that. Listen to him. In some way what he says and how he acts will get you to the truth. The new ones have the hardest time learning that, and the experienced ones, like yourself, need to be reminded because the County makes it all too easy to forget it."

"Especially this time of year," Sam interrupted, his anger still not controlled. "You think for Christmas people would be on better behavior? But here there are no seasons. Just more damn senseless violence, it's just getting worse. I put up with it for so long telling myself I was making a difference, but I no longer believe any of that. Is that what we get as our punishment for trying to follow the rules? Who's rules? Theirs? Your rules? Why is senseless death always the answer?" He thought back to the day of the murder six years ago in December when he was hardly at the County for half a year. *I can't believe I did not get out then. Wilson was smart. He knew it was time to leave.* Sam felt for the lump on the back of his head again. It was beginning to throb, still there; just like he was still in pain and still here.

"You're getting too hard-boiled for your own sanity," Fish said, then firmly as if slapping him to his senses with his words, "If you're hoping to get out, and you don't wise up, we'll be sitting here spending next Christmas working the pit."

"Ha! I don't think so, my friend," Sam yelled back at Fish, for the first time clearly angry at his friend. "This time it's truly a parting of the ways. I need to find a way out this time. This can't be my fate!" Sam felt for the bump on his head again, and winced, but he would not have time to ponder about it long.

It was then they both heard the siren.

CHAPTER 2

THE COUNTY, OR CENTRAL CITY County Medical Center as it was properly known was not a prison, but all too often to many of its residents, it felt like one. This County was one of the oldest of the many county hospitals in California. The university bought the County when it was a time-worn almost forgotten hospital that had deteriorated and was in disrepair with closed wards. In a remarkable deal worthy of the behind-the-scene political wrangling; it only cost them a single dollar, on paper at least, with a promise to restore it to working condition. It was often said they overpaid. Despite patchwork fixes here and there since 1973, in feeble attempts to keep their promise, the university only renovated the County so much. It was scrubbed clean but smelled like too much bleach, even in the cafeteria. There were water stains in corners on the spackled ceilings and the original color of the walls faded into an amorphous beige. The floors were the most unappealing choice of linoleum, still with random stains here and there. The lobby looked like the room you wait in while mandated to appear for jury duty. And it was hot. Despite the Central Valley getting to over a hundred degrees in the summer there was no central air-conditioning. The most concerning part was that equipment was woefully outdated, sometimes missing. Once something broke and needed repair it seldom happened.

The pit, as in most county hospitals, was the Emergency Room, or ER. To comprehend why it was called the pit you had to go back a few years. Back then when it was really just an Emergency Room, as it was originally only a single room, the County instituted a policy akin to the inscription on the Statue of Liberty: All who entered would be cared for. It was a good policy and still is. However, the County could never imagine the hordes of people striving to find medical care. As the city of Central City grew, private hospitals emerged siphoning off those patients with insurance to pay for their care; one day they went from being patients to being customers. Those hospitals were all new with the latest equipment, scanners, staffed with specialists, and their ribbon-cutting ceremonies heralded the best in innovation, science, and technology, a fact they began to advertise in the newspapers and on TV so they would attract more customers. Those other hospitals spared no expense when they built cancer centers, cardiac units, stroke teams, and maternity wards. Lagging far behind, as there was never any money to help the County, more and more uninsured patients became its bread and butter. While other areas of the County hospital suffered as well, none was as neglected as badly as the emergency room. Over the time since the university bought the old county hospital, no one added as much as a brick to the Emergency Room.

The part of town just outside the County was from another era. Deteriorating early century homes, and closed business flanked its neighborhood. Meanwhile as Central City's population grew, housing tracts dotted what used to be farms and hop fields, stretching outward from Central City. People moved there from the older parts of town. The highways had lanes added to bring traffic from those new homes to downtown Central City, where many people still worked. The crime in the core section of Central City rose, and the old County ER was where the police took their suspects that they arrested who needed medical care, or sometimes the police were called to the ER to arrest someone from the growing number of gang fights. Even a new jail was constructed nearby to deal with the rising crime. But the Emergency Room was ignored. And so, the pit was where all the problems were. From time to time some disaster prompted cleaning up the edges of the pit, but relentlessly its problems kept growing. Most of the little fixes were all window dressing. Soon after the University bought it, a few more rooms along the hall were converted from other uses, to expand its original space, but it did not take long for the number of patients to outpaced this fix. No longer just a room but a hodge-podge of rooms, it still was called the Emergency Room, or simply "the pit". While the pit and its problems were as plain as day to everyone who worked there, it remained largely invisible to all those who had the power to solve them.

Four years later when Fish arrived as one of the first new interns it still appeared to be the same dilapidated county hospital. The University didn't even bother to change the hospital's name after it's nominal attempt to clean up the

County. The arrival of eager young interns, like Fish however was the hidden essential major improvement over the old style of care. It just wasn't obvious from the outside, or for that matter the inside either. The fresh interns did not know what they were getting themselves into and they did not have experiences to compare the County to. Rarely did these interns come from universities of a pedigree stature where things might have been cosmetically different. But they all were ready to work long hours, and tolerate whatever the system threw at them. Sam was no exception. In 1978 just two years after Fish began working there, it was only by luck Sam would see the County firsthand.

CHAPTER 3

SAM HAD THOUGHT THE DRIVE up the Central Valley to the County would be easy. That December when he was still a medical student and had never even heard of Central City. He got an interview there at the last minute, and figured he could be up and back in the same day. The weather in LA was mild and California was not Buffalo where he grew up. There would be no December snow or ice, so the drive would be a snap he thought. Driving from LA deep into farm country to the Central Valley didn't look far on his pocket map of California that he had picked up at the airport when he arrived. The day turned into a series of problems. It started with the Tule fog.

Sam was antsy to get going, it was one of only a few interviews he managed to get, and couldn't sleep the night before. He sped out of LA in pre-rush hour darkness in his rental car, and caught the interstate over the Tehachapi mountains. It was still 6:40 in the morning, he watched the dawn over a crystal-clear blue sky in the mountains, small patches of snow at the highest peaks. Not a sight he could see in Buffalo; it was wonderful. He drove down the north slope of the mountains, through the Grapevine, and was startled to descend into a pea-soup fog he had never encountered before. Just minutes later, once down on the valley floor he could no longer see the front end of the car. He rolled the window down to listen for the sounds or other cars, the cold wet air harsh against his cheek, whistled in his ear. Dressed in his only suit with no warm jacket, the cold fog chilled him. At times he rolled the window back up to reclaim some warmth as he continued to drive north on the highway. He drove fist tight on the steering wheel all the way through the Central Valley towards Central City. Luckily, almost no one was on the road. *I must be the only idiot driving in this.* He feared he would run into a car or truck stopped in front of him, the ride was slow and nerve-racking. *Did I really need to see this last place?*

That December Sam had been doing a medicine ward rotation in L.A, working in the interviews when he could in between. He was approaching the end of his "interview trail", the furious months of November and December each year where the senior medical students try to get interviews at hospitals where they wanted to do their residencies. After multiple missed phone calls from his roommate, also a medical student back home, left at Sam's rooming house, finally he connected with Sam. Someone in a place called Central City left a message on their answering machine. Sam's roommate played the tape for him over the phone. They had an opening for an interview, but Sam had to be there tomorrow, Friday afternoon. Sam figured why not? They must have been on his growing list of hospitals Sam called during his lunch hours, checking them off his list each day, but never hearing back from any of them. Out of over fifty calls they were the only ones to call him back.

Sam had three days off and was up for a bit of adventure after a month on medicine wards in a community hospital in Pasadena. There he just admitted stable well-dressed little old ladies who were dizzy. WADAO they were called; weak and dizzy all over cases. They got extensive medical workups, consults from every subspecialty service, and often no one found something specific, but they went home with a bunch of new meds never-the-less. While all the patients were polite to him, and he was courteous to them, he was growing bored with it all. *I am spinning my wheels and not actually helping anyone. There must be a better way somewhere.* He hadn't looked at any County Hospitals yet on the interview trail so maybe this would be something different.

Despite three years of medical school, Sam was following predetermined expectations and still did not know exactly what he wanted to train in. "Internal medicine," was what his advisers had said, "Master the basics and you can go anywhere from there." The ward in Pasadena was definitely not convincing him that was true. But he did not see himself living that life. Neither could he sit behind a desk in an office, counselling patients in 15-minute intervals. By this late day in December, it was now too late in the year to turn back on that choice. He could maybe sneak in one more application if this last-minute interview worked out. He anguished over the thought of next three years working as an internal medicine resident on the wards. It just didn't seem like the right choice, but he was on the interview trail, like a treadmill he was stuck on, and needed to push forward.

THE COUNTY

As noon approached the fog-shrouded fields of the Central Valley of California gave way to clusters of small towns. The dense Tule fog was finally starting to thin a bit so he could see more than just a few feet ahead. The clearing haze revealed a series of towns with small frame homes with a car parked in their front yards, an old couch on the porch here and there, an occasional corner store. As each small town passed out of view, the stillness gave way to empty fields, an occasional barn, then the next small town. As he entered Central City the homes were closer together. They showed greater and greater signs of disrepair, cracked paint, and peeling old siding. There was more torn furniture in yards than on porches, and rusty cars, primer paint exposed, propped up on metal milk crates with their hoods open. The main street Sam drove was flanked by once majestic trees, but now they were leafless in winter. Glimpses through front windows of a few homes showed red and green Christmas lights flickering on a tree still alit mid-morning.

Sam searched the storefronts in the few strip malls on the side of his route for a place where he could eat quickly, but found none that looked inviting. Many businesses had metal bars across their windows, others were boarded up with plywood, covered in stylized gang graffiti. Outside uncollected garbage cans overflowed on the curbside, lids missing. Small groups of men sat on hoods of cars in parking lots outside bottle shops, drinking from paper-bag hidden bottles. As Sam slowed as he passed them, trying to find a place for some food, they stared at him. Sam was dying for at least a hot black coffee to ease the chill of the long fog enshrouded car ride. There were no restaurants, no banks, no department stores, no pet stores, no dry cleaners. None of the businesses that suggested any semblance of a city lived in. Sam wondered if the whole city was like this. Finally he saw the large red brick hospital building looming above the blandness of the city.

CHAPTER 4

BY THE TIME HE REACHED the hospital parking lot it was too late to stop to eat. Sam went straight up to the fourth-floor office that he was told to meet in. Once there he was ushered into a conference room, and immediately Sam had a sense it was all going to be the same as the ward he was working on in Pasadena. Sam in his black suit and white shirt looked exactly like the other five men in black suits already seated there, except theirs looked well pressed and new. Sam's second-hand suit seemed to not fit him, a size too small perhaps, and his unpressed shirt was a dull off-white, and started to itch his neck. He just did not feel comfortable or confident dressed up for show. He had tried to clean up his appearance as best he could, shaving off the beard he grew each Buffalo winter, and got a conservative looking haircut. He looked youthful, as did the others, but he was shorter than the five other men. They appeared more like college athletes, lean and self-confident in their garb for the game that was about to be played. They were really interviewing against one another.

Sam's anticipation of out-shining them sank, and he began to fidget with his pen to keep his hands busy, pretending to be eager to take notes during the presentation. He heard the usual blah blah blah dog and pony show presentation about the training program. After the interview then there was a walking tour around the wards, bleak as they were. They smelled a whole lot more rank than the hospital wards in Pasadena. Some of the other men in their black-suited uniforms made snide comments out of earshot of the resident who escorted them around. Kip Drysdale, their resident tour guide appeared just as bored as the interviewees were, checking his watch every few minutes. In his dry monotone he told them about the residency they might join, as if he had said this spiel a hundred times unenthusiastically before. He was just about to let them all go for the day when the group of six men, finally stopped in the ER.

Drysdale finally happy to stop talking and pass the task onto someone he knew would be happy to take over introduced the group, "This is Dr. Fish, one of our star interns. He can probably give you more of a view from ground level."

Fish seemed eager to talk. As he turned around from where he was writing, he stuck his pen in his rumbled blue scrubs, and addressed the group, "Just call me Fish," he said shaking each of their hands, as Drysdale slipped away down the hall, happy to be done with yet another group of students. Fish was working a 24 hour shift that day and Sam decided to asked him what he thought of the program. Drysdale had few answers for Sam during the tour. Fish proceeded to rambled on for several minutes, as Sam would learn Fish was prone to do. Fish motioned with his hands as he spoke, first to the right then the left, highlighted both the good and but also the bad about the place, something the other programs Sam had interviewed at had not done. There was something about Fish, he looked like a mountain man, short, a bit overweight, with a bushy mustache and a long beard. He talked with excitement, and in his wandering style soon got off track, yet he had a certain gleam in his eye, clear he enjoyed what he was doing. He finally said, "If you want to see what this place is really like you need

ZANE HOROWITZ

to spend a night in the pit! Don't buy the car unless you've driven it around the block once." So, with that Sam agreed to come back later. No other program invited him to see behind the curtain to what it was all about. "Lose the suit and tie," Fish said, "dress in something you might want to throw away later."

After leaving Fish in the ER, Sam ate dinner at a drive through burger place and booked a room in one of the many cheap motels near the highway figuring he could not handle driving back in that fog. The drive up was too stressful, he would wait for the next day. He dumped his suit jacket, tie, and good pants in the trunk of his car, and changed into some jeans he was originally planning to wear just as soon as the interview was over so he would not be stuck in his dress-up clothes all the way back. He barely got back to the County ER at 6 pm and went to the front desk.

"I am here to meet one of the docs for his shift," Sam told the clerk.

"You have his name?" Sally, the desk clerk asked.

Sam was embarrassed that he had talked to this guy for an hour and never got his name, "No, he's got this long beard, talks a lot, and is about my height."

"Oh, yeah, that's Dr. Fish. You can go back in and find him."

Fish was standing outside Room One, gloved up and ready, when Sam walked up. "Good timing kid, glad you did not bail on us, we got a code coming in. We could use some help." Thirty seconds later the ambulance doors opened and a paramedic crew rolled in with an older man on the gurney and rushed directly into Room One. They were doing chest compressions.

"This guy went down in the old Eclipse cafeteria waiting for a meal. We got there in about 5 minutes, he was already blue, no pulse, so we started CPR. He had V. Fib and we shocked him a few times, but no go, still in V. Fib. Not enough helping hands to do an airway so we're bagging him and continuing CPR," the paramedic told Fish the story.

"Kid, get up there and do some chest compressions. I need to take care of his airway. After I am in, let's do a quick look and see what he has on the monitor." Fish pointed Sam to the patient.

Sam looked puzzled. He thought he was just going to watch Fish see patients for a short while, not get his hands dirty. "Me?" he asked with a perplexed raise of his brow, pointing at himself.

"Yeah, yeah, get started. You just press down and release every second. Count in your head if you need to. Try to sync with the song Staying

Alive from Saturday Night Fever." An orderly kicked a stool with his foot along the side of the bed and Sam stepped up and began chest compressions, the two-word refrain playing in his head.

Fish pulled out some equipment from the head of the bed, a curved metal device with a light, and inserted a plastic tube in the man's throat. He then took the defibrillator paddles and pressed them on the man's chest. "All clear!" he yelled. "Stop Compressions!" He motioned to Sam to back up, so Sam backed away, arms high in the air to show he had heard the all clear. Fish pushed a button on the paddles and the man's chest heaved upward a few inches. "Resume CPR," Fish immediately said. He checked the monitor. It had an ECG beat on it, slow but distinctly an ECG complex. He felt a pulse. "Great got a pulse back. Let's keep him on 100% oxygen, get a blood pressure and a chest X-ray."

Sam had only done CPR for all of 30 seconds but it was the most exhilarating 30 seconds of his medical school career so far. *Did I save someone's life?* he thought. Of course, there was Fish running the code and a room full of nurses and orderlies all around him, working in unison. *But hey I was part of this.* It was pure adrenaline running through his body. His first hit; like a drug user mainlining speed. This one was a freebee. All future doses will be trying to recreate this initiating rush in his brain. Those he would pay for with his soul.

There was several more maneuvers that needed to be done after the code, lines set, a Bird ventilator brought in. Fish called the ICU team, and they seemed to know him well and agreed right away to take the new case. Sam just stared at the patient, and at Fish. His mind was still racing, his hands were actually trembling a bit. The patient was admitted and the gurney with the man on it, and a clear complex on the ECG monitor, was pushed down the hall to the elevator.

Fish looked at his wide-eyed recruit and asked, "So is that the kind of medicine you want to practice? We spend a lot of time covering the ER in this internal medicine program. Let me give you a tour of the pit. The Emergency Room is a complex of eight rooms. This is Room One. The lower the room number you get put in the sicker you are. Someone's chance of dying in Room Six, for instance, is impossible, here in Room One if you lived, it was a miracle. We just performed our first miracle of the night."

CHAPTER 5

FISH GAVE SAM THE GRAND tour of the pit. Room One was the resuscitation room. It was the largest room, and the only room designed to hold only one patient. Many times, overcrowding forced the doctors to put two patients in because there was nowhere else to go. "Everything you needed to save someone's life is hanging or stacked against the walls in Room One. We have begged for more equipment but seldom received any. So, while the cardiac unit gets a new external pacer, the ER won't. If the eye clinic got new slit lamps for exams, ER gets their old ones, in need of repair. If a new drug was available the pharmacy committee would release it selectively, and the pit was not what the suits in administration considered the select few." Room One, stocked as it was, was what they had to work with. Fish explained they did save lives, many of them. They "cracked" chests, and "slit" necks, and "tubed" airways, and "cutdown" ankles, and "buzzed" hearts, and basically entered the body through every orifice, sometimes making new ones. But it was not Room One that caused the pit to be a problem. Most of the interns relished the excitement of the cases treated there.

Room Two did everything Room One did, except it did it three times over. Although just slightly smaller in size than Room One, it held three beds and these were likewise held for the sickest of the sick. If a resuscitation was going on in Room One, then there were usually three people in Room Two just a breath away from needing to be resuscitated. And sometimes that is where they took that last breath and crossed the line. The problem with Room Two was that it did not have as much life-saving equipment stacked against the walls as Room One. It was necessary to always run back and forth across the hall to Room One to retrieve some needed instrument or tray when the patients started crashing in Room Two. People always seemed to crash in Room Two. In Room One you were assured the vigilance of two nurses and at least three doctors, but in Room Two there was one nurse and one doctor for all three patients. "Only an ER doc skilled at juggling multiple tasks will master the art of working in Room Two. Don't expect to get to that point until after a year or two here," Fish explained.

Room Three, likewise, held three beds, and those patients assigned to it seemed to be at least stable enough not to crash. Little old ladies with heart failure, gunshot wounds to the leg, asthmatics, bleeding ulcers, and the like were assigned a bed in Room Three. "Room Three has two features that make it special. First, it is the OD room. When a patient comes in after an overdose or suicide attempt, he is placed in the corner bed in Room Three, tied down sideways to the gurney, and has his stomach pumped." Lavage, it was called, was a cleaning out of one's insides, to remove the offending toxin. It also removed dinner, beer, and everything from soup to nuts. "The ODs were almost always screamers as they fought to resist having their stomachs lavaged, and sometimes the process made them vomit up around the tube. All this made Room Three noxiously loud to the ear and fetid to the nose."

"If a puking OD isn't enough to send you running for air the other unique use of Room Three is. In addition to ODs, there are I&Ds.

Incision and drainage to open up an abscess. Depending on the location of the abscess changed how foul-smelling the organism in it was. The junkies have little abscesses on their arms, good for starters. If you passed that you could drain an axillary abscess in someone's armpit; pretty rough stuff. And then there's the peri-rectal abscess; as malodorous a bag of pus as there ever existed. Oh, abscess patients, like ODs, are prone to screaming."

"Now as we continue down the hall, you might hear a bone-chilling scream as if someone was having the life beaten out of him. No doubt it came from Room Four. Orthopedics is what's in Room Four. It seems a prerequisite to becoming an orthopedic surgeon is a complete insensitivity to pain. The patients, that is, not their own. Here in Room Four are all the torture devices discarded by the Spanish Inquisition." Fish walked into the room and pointed to several pieces of equipment he wanted to show Sam. "Finger traps to hold up your forearm in the air while the orthopedist manipulated your broken wrist. Steinman pins drilled through your shin bone to drag your fractured femur out to length in traction. Perhaps one of the Inquisitor's all-time favorites is the Halo device. A Halo is necessary for a fractured spine. Four holes drilled into your skull and the Halo is fixed with screws to your head. Then an erector set of four steel towers are assembled and strapped with leather harnesses to your shoulders. Despite its horrendous look, and the fact it required a twist drill to tap a screw hole in your cranium, it is the least painful of the orthopedic procedures. It just always bothered me to see a surgeon with a Phillips head screwdriver twisting with all his might just above a patient's ears."

Rooms Five, Six, and Seven each held five beds. "Collectively Rooms Five and Seven directly across the hall from each other are known as Observation. We see patients who are not so sick in them but usually that means that the patient lingered waiting for lab tests to return, a consultant to get free enough from their other duties to see them, or a bed to become available should, perish the thought, someone decided that you should become an in-patient at the County." Room Six was an all-purpose room. There was discarded equipment from the eye and ear, nose, and throat clinics for "special" exams. The equipment was outdated, all too frequently didn't work, and unless you took the time to learn how to use it correctly you usually did more damage to it than you got out of examining the patient. There was one special piece of equipment in Room Six that required no special introduction; the proctoscope. The proctoscope was a 12-inch hollow plastic tube with a light on the end of it, used for looking up your rectum. This was usually done with the patient hanging onto a table upside down with his bottom up in the air and his head down at a sharp angle. Unlike proctoscopes in doctor's offices in which the patient is "cleaned out" first with enemas as a prep, the ER docs did unprepped proctos. If by some chance you survive the odor of Room Three, you could push your nostrils to the limit in Room Six.

"Room Eight was originally for ambulatory patients, but was recently converted to a radio room to hear paramedic calls." When that change was added to the emergency room the name Room Eight disappeared forever. Room Eight remained a mythical place where you could send someone, however. Since that time the expression "room eighting" a patient meant to send him into oblivion. When a drunk became combative a suggestion was usually made to "room 8" him. That usually resulted in that person being parked way down at the end of the hall where he couldn't be heard or seen and he could curse or scream or puke to his heart's content.

"Unfortunately," concluded Fish at the end of showing Sam all the rooms, "We have more patients than rooms and we start stringing them out down the hall, and around the corner. This place can get pretty busy, especially at night. Every so often, when and if it calms down, it pays to do a walk around to check that you have not forgotten anybody."

Sam spent the best night he ever had following Fish around the pit. It was exhilarating. Sam had thought he would just be watching how things went for a few hours then going back to his motel. Fish let him do a lot of hands-on patient care, even though he was just supposed to be an observer. The place tingled with excitement, and with drama. He watched Fish take care of not just internal medicine patients, but gunshot wounds, broken bones, little kids with fevers, and people in the throes of mental crisis screaming at the staff. There were overdoses, cardiac complaints, strokes, and people bleeding from all sorts of places. Fish let Sam start some IVs, and hold someone's arm while Fish applied a plaster splint in Room Four. When it got real busy Fish let Sam put a few sutures in someone's leg because there was no one else around to do it. Sam was thrilled. He had never done sutures, plastering, let alone CPR before. What a ride that night was! More and more adrenaline; like throwing gasoline on a fire.

Sam ended up talking with Fish, who had plenty to say, and staying until change of shift the next morning at 7 am. Nothing like this happened in Pasadena, or any other residency he had visited so far. As he talked with Fish in between cases, off and on all night, he found out that as an intern he would spend at least three months in the ER, seeing everything that came through the door, no holds barred, no crisis too difficult to let a new intern attack. He would be pushed to think fast, and work hard. This was the first time Sam thought he felt pride in what he was doing, in what he thought he could see himself doing in medicine for a long time. *I was never cut out for the office or the ward*, he thought as he said goodbye that morning. He thanked Fish and told him he hoped he would see him again.

Sam went to the hospital lobby where he bought a cup of coffee and got a pocket full of change, and found a bank of pay phones. He called his roommate back in Buffalo; it was Saturday morning and his roommate was in trying to study for an exam on Monday. Sam talked so fast on the phone his roommate wasn't sure he was acting normal, but Sam asked him to go to the medical school dean's office first thing after his exam Monday, and file a completed application for Sam for the program at the County.

"Are you sure?" his roommate asked, "You sound a little punch drunk high. Don't you want to sleep on it for a day first? It's not like they have a stellar reputation you know."

"No. Put the application in. Send a copy of the Dean's letter they have on file for me. If you need to, sign my name for it," Sam spit the words out at his roommate in a quickened urgent voice.

Sam found his motel off the highway and went in and slept for four hours. He showered, ate another drive through burger and black coffee and got back in the car for the drive back to Pasadena. He didn't want to be caught in the Tule fog after dark. As he drove up the steep incline of the Grapevine before dusk, the fog had lifted, both back in the valley behind him and in his head. He thought he knew now where he wanted to train. He made it to the guest house he was staying in near the hospital in Pasadena. It would take all his will to walk back in the door at the little community hospital Monday after his weekend outing at the County. Its strange magnetism started to work on him.

Sam finished his medicine ward rotation in Pasadena, but he didn't land any more interviews. He made more cold calls during his lunch breaks to programs around the state, but it was at the end of the interview season and there were no last-minute openings. He flew home just days before Christmas to see his family and to tough out the worst of winter in Buffalo. Maybe he would grow his winter beard back now that he was done faking the clean-shaven look he needed for interviews. Fish had a beard so it must be acceptable to work with one in the County. You did not need to pretend to be something you were not there. Sam still needed to finish the last five months of medical school. But all he could remember and talk about from his trip out West was the night in County.

CHAPTER 6

BACK AT THE COUNTY, FISH had moved on to his next rotation in January, the medical intensive care unit or ICU. The third weekend in January is known as the weekend that people finally realize that the holidays are over, that the relatives they never got along who had made their lives miserable were still something they would have to deal with. That money they spent unwisely on gifts, would have to be paid for soon. Whatever New Year's resolutions they made this year would fall by the wayside once again. That winter was here to stay. It was the weekend people became overwhelmed and acted on it. Some called it suicide weekend.

Late that Saturday night Fish was called by the ER where an intubated patient was his first admission. A young man had overdosed on a common antidepressant called Elavil. Catchy trade name implying it would somehow elevate your mood, but it was extremely dangerous in overdose. The intern tried to arouse him with a coma cocktail, that included another catchy-named drug, Antilirium. Unfortunately that just made the patient have a seizure, so the intern gave him a giant dose of Valium and intubated him. The nurse was bagging the overdose patient in Room Three to breath for him through the newly placed endotracheal tube when Fish arrived. They needed to lavage him first before he was admitted. They had no ventilator available in the ER so Fish took over from the nurse bagging him by hand, giving him slow steady breaths while he was trying to figure out what to do. Upstairs in the ICU there were four patients on four ventilators in the only four beds they had. This fifth patient had no bed and no ventilator. While Fish and a nurse took turns bagging the patient, Fish used his time not bagging to desperately make phone calls for help. His first call was to his chief resident. The resident had not encountered a problem like this in three years in the County but said he would come over to the hospital from his sleep room across the street to try to wean one of the other patients off a ventilator to get one for the new admit.

Two hours later the chief resident felt he was able to wean an old emphysema patient enough so he could be taken off his ventilator, but not enough to have the tube taken out of his trachea. He was left with a T-piece, simply oxygen flowing over the intubation tube with no ventilator attached. It was like breathing through a big fat straw. They brought the overdose patient upstairs to the ICU. Once the ventilator was cleaned it was hooked up to the new admission, and the ICU nurse was told to watch the now ventilator-free emphysema patient carefully. They squeezed the new ICU patient into a space between the others, with five patients in a room designed to hold only four.

Fish wrote some orders, rechecked the ICU patients with his resident, and the resident went back to the sleep room. Fish stayed in the ICU, he couldn't sleep even if he wanted to, he felt responsible for the five patients now crowded into this little space; they were his miniature ward. It was 1 a.m. About 15 minutes later Fish got called back down to the pit for another overdose patient in Room Three. A depressed divorced woman, only identifiable but the name

Maggie, had just stopped breathing all before Fish was able to find out her last name or what exactly she overdosed on. The police were sent to search her home while Fish prepared to first intubate her, then lavage her in Room Three. At least she was not seizing like the last case. The ER nurse continued to bag her to breathe for her during the lavage, which washed some small pill fragments out of her stomach into a collection bag on the floor. The room still reeked of stale beer from the last lavage.

After the lavage, the police got back with an empty bottle of Milltown; they placed Maggie on a 5150. A 5150 is a 72-hour psychiatric hold. The County now could hold Maggie against her will legally for up to 72 hours. She wasn't breathing on her own and Jenni, the nurse bagging her for the last half hour looked up at Fish annoyed and said, "Well are you waiting for an engraved invitation? Call for a ventilator so we can get this lady up to the ICU."

The lights went off in Fish's head. It was 2 a.m. There were already five people in an ICU designed for four. In a way, they were sharing four ventilators among five people. Maggie was now number six. Something had to be done. Fish called his resident and asked him to come in again. Fish then called the night medical supervisor Dr. Jablonski. Dr. Jablonski was a psychiatrist who now performed administrative duties. He was the youngest on the administrative ladder and therefore got night administration. This was usually an easy job as few administrative problems could not wait until morning. Fish was now asking him to borrow two ventilators from another hospital. Borrowing two ventilators was not likely to be accomplished easily or inexpensively and were not the administrative challenge that Jablonski wanted to deal with a 2 a.m. Fish was persistent and persuaded Jablonski to come into the hospital to see if he could find a better solution.

Jablonski was a rotund man, always flushed in the face, and always seemed out of breath from carrying his better than 300 pounds around with him. He always emphatically expressed himself to those he now was able to command by the nature of his junior administrative position. To the nurses, especially the young ones, he was always condescending and used expressions loaded with innuendo. Interns and staff were mere peons to him, he thrived on the small position of power he was able to obtain. When Jablonski arrived in the ICU at 2:45 there were now six patients who had tubes in them. Five clearly needed ventilators. Jablonski had barely been there two minutes when the emphysema patient coded and stopped breathing.

"Bag this guy!" Fish ordered Jablonski.

"Don't tell me what to do, it's your job to manage these patients up here." Jablonski looked panicked. "I can barely move around this room. You got it packed too tight with patients." Jablonski had not practiced clinical medicine in over ten years. It wasn't his job to get his hands dirty. That's why he went into psychiatry first and then administration.

"Well then bag that lady over there. She is your patient after all," Fish yelled back pointed at his newest admission. All memories of how to bag breathe for someone else had vanished in ten years of treating depressed patients. Depressed patients like Maggie. As he looked down at Maggie, he recognized her. She was his patient! She had just gotten divorced from the city editor of the local newspaper. Jablonski became anxious and started to sweat. He knew her husband was a man of considerable influence who had editorialized against some of the spending programs at the county hospital. Jablonski started bagging wildly.

"No! Not like that. Squeeze the bag completely every five seconds. No! That's too fast. Slower! You'll hyperventilate her that way, and I don't need both you and her hyperventilating and spasming out right now." Fish yelled at Jablonski, "Count to yourself 1-Mississippi, 2-Mississippi,

3-Mississipi, 4-Mississippi, bag-Mississippi. There now you got the rhythm."

Fish ran the code and ended up bagging the emphysema patient the rest of the night, and Jablonski out of fear for his patient kept bagging Maggie all night. Fish had to keep waking up Jablonski who was falling asleep on his feet with the call, "Bag-Mississippi" By morning Maggie was coming out of her Milltown haze. The chief resident came in and he was able to transfer one patient out to the VA hospital. Maggie was able to be weaned off the tube. An exhausted Jablonski slumped into a chair at the nurse's station and fell asleep.

Jablonski was awakened at 1:30 that afternoon by someone calling his name. Maggie was dressed, rifling through her large designer handbag, and standing over him ready to be discharged. "Dr. Jablonski, Dr. Jablonski, wake up, Dr. Jablonski," she cleared her throat loudly, "Oh, did I wake you Dr. Jablonski? I'm sorry. But I just spent the most God-awful night in this hospital. I was in a room with three men. You should know I always insist on a private room. I'm going to have a little chat with my husband about the deplorable conditions in your hospital." She added with a sigh of aloofness, "I'm ready to check out now because I need some better-quality rest." After another

THE COUNTY

fruitless check in her bag she added in a sweet falsetto voice, "I seemed to have lost my bottle of Milltown. Could you be a dear and write a new prescription for me so that I could get some sleep tonight?"

Jablonski didn't know what to say. He was still dazed. He reflexively reached into his jacket pocket and pulled out an already signed prescription. The drug company salesman for the newest drug for depression had agreed to have made up a pre-written prescription pad with his signature on it, their company logo on the back. All Jablonski needed to do was fill in the patients' names. It was a brilliant timesaver for prescribing, the drug company rep had told him! He really did not need to think anymore, which at this moment he was incapable of doing. Jablonski tore off two of these and handed them to Maggie and told her to fill in her name on the top. Maggie collected her things and left the ICU. Jablonski, still exhausted fell back asleep in his chair.

At 3:00 Jablonski was awakened by Fish screaming at him. Fish had been up all night as well. That would not have made him irritable but when he heard that Maggie was discharged with a new prescription, he lost it. "You asshole! How could you give that lady more meds to OD on? Did you know she has had six ODs in the last year? All I presume all written by you. Are you incapable of learning anything from last night?" Then unable to stifle his harangue, "That's the problem with all you psychs. You write these scripts in your office and go home at five. Then in the middle of the night when the patient lies awake wondering if life is worth living, do they call you? No, you are on an answering machine by then, so they OD instead, and I have to take care of them all night. I would think that after last night's experience you would maybe learn something? But it's clear that once a Candyman, always a Candyman. Huh, Jablonski? Get out of my ICU!"

Jablonski realizing the entire ICU staff was now watching and he was not going to let this tirade go unpunished. "Your ICU Dr. Fish? I didn't know you made a substantial contribution to the University and they put a gold plaque on the door with your name on it. You are nothing but an intern. I am the ranking administrator tonight and I will decide what my private patients need."

"Night? The sun has long ago risen on your fiefdom Jablonski. It is three in the afternoon. Go to bed. And please stop handing out crap like it was candy unless you want to build a bigger ICU, which we need anyway, and we can put your name on that plaque."

With that Fish turned and left. The nursing staff applauded.

Jablonski was steamed, "Get back to work all of you. You're a bunch of clucking chickens. Just wait, your smartass Dr. Fish will get his." Jablonski, like the elephant he was, would never forget. But he did ask for the extra rooms to be added, mostly so he would never get called in the middle of the night again. Two adjacent rooms were converted into ICU spaces. They were dubbed Room Nine and Room Ten. There were no plaques on their doors.

CHAPTER 7

MATCH DAY IS A STRANGE phenomenon that few outside medical school understand. It was the most anxiety provoking day of Sam's life, as it was for every medical student about to graduate in the country. Similar to the basketball or football draft where the participants had no control and were selected by the teams where they would be obliged to play for. At least the medical students had a small degree of choice by submitting a list. All those students created a list of hospitals in order of their choices where they wanted to do residency. They could only list hospitals they were asked to interview. The program directors at each of these hospitals did the same, listing the students they wanted in their preference order after they had interviewed them. All of these lists were due in by February. A computer had sorted out the choices from the lists and matched every student to all the hospitals. Well, not every student. Some students near the bottom of the list did not match, and their dreams were dashed as they had no internship for all their hard work for the last four years. Probably every student was as stressed as Sam thinking that would be their fate as the clock ticked slowly towards noon. For the last few months, Sam feared he might be unmatched, his life as a doctor over. He had only five interviews, and he thought of all the places he went. Only the County was different, inspiring the little bit of hope he hung onto. At noon on the third Friday in March every student in the country was handed an envelope, inside the name of the hospital and specialty they matched. The rest of your life was determined by a little card inside an envelope. That Friday morning the school had set out all the cards, lined up alphabetically on a series of long tables in the gym. Some students arrived hours early, pacing nervously while they waited. Others arrived just in time, perhaps some panic in their eyes hoping they were not too late. No one was allowed to touch the envelope with their name on it until noon when someone would ring a bell giving them the signal to tear open their futures.

Sam was expecting to open his envelope and find nothing inside. He did not think that Fish would have spoken to anyone who mattered in the decision process after his night with him. The decision would ultimately be made by some of the chiefs he spoke with in the offices upstairs earlier that day. The same ones who had given him the dog and pony speech, and walked the fading beige halls of the wards with him. He didn't think he made much of an impression compared to the other students that day, because he hadn't. All during that day he thought he had wasted his time, maybe risked his life driving up the Central Valley just to do the interview. But up until that point he had only four other interviews, and he was convinced the call to his answering machine in Buffalo was just them trying to fill a last-minute opening that someone for good reasons had dropped out. He couldn't imagine that they were interested in him. Average grades, average national test scores, no publications. Nothing to make him stand out. But the County was not looking for any of that, and in fact someone had asked Fish what he thought of the only applicant that day who volunteered to spend the night.

THE COUNTY

So it was that three months later, when the bell was rung and students rushed forward to tear open the envelope, when sounds of joy, of relief, of disappointment, and of heartbreak all were mixed into the buzz that rose from the gym. Sam hesitated when the clang of the bell was sounded. At first terrified, a knot in his stomach, Sam could not even bring himself to pick up the envelope. Finally, when it was nearly the las one still untouched on the long table, he picked it up trembling. Taking a deep breath, Sam opened his envelope that Match Day and pulled out the card inside. He got his number one choice—Central City County Medical Center, or as he would come to call it, the County.

Something else happened that day, too. Sam's mother was thrilled for him, but she had been hiding something from him, his father and brother. She had been having stomach cramps for half a year, and had lost several pounds while Sam was away on the interview trail. She was the epitome of the suburban mom, straight from Leave it to Beaver, Ozzie and Harriet, or I Love Lucy. Everyone's mom in Buffalo had her hair done like Lucille Ball who after all was a hometown Buffalo success. That night the whole family went out to celebrate at their favorite restaurant where they all ate a large dinner together. His mom only picked at her food, but no one noticed. Later she started throwing up when she came home. She waved their concerns away not wanting to spoil the celebration. Everyone, including Sam, thought it was just bad food from the restaurant. But only she was sick.

By Sunday it had not let up and Sam convinced her to go to the Emergency Room. They all sat for a very long time in the waiting room as they ran some lab tests and started an IV on his mom. He went up to the front desk several times to ask if there was any news, but the clerk just told them to "be patient and have seat." The doctor never came out to talk with Sam or his dad, but the nurse said that she was only dehydrated, as she pulled out Sam's mothers IV to discharge her. They signed a piece of paper that told her to see your doctor this week. Later that week at Sam's mother's doctor office she was sent for a barium swallow and that's when they found the problem. She had stomach cancer. Sam may have been an average student but he knew this was bad, treatment was awful, surgery, radiation, chemo, and the prognosis was still bad even after all that.

"I don't have to go to California, mom. I'll just ask for a year off, maybe and stay here." He was thinking maybe he should not have

THE COUNTY

matched after all. Maybe he should have wished for an empty envelope.

"I'm not having it, Sammy," she'd said, in that calm but determined way she had of laying down the law all those years as Sam was growing up. "You're going to California. That's all you have talked about for the last year."

"I'll go next year. It can keep. I can stay and help you out, get you to the doctors. Maybe I could do some research around the school, so I look better in the match next year."

"You don't know that will work. No one does. Didn't you tell me if you violate the match rules, you won't ever get hired anywhere? You made a commitment and we keep our commitments! I need you to go and follow your dream. I'll be just fine. You need to do that internship. You worked so hard for so long, and this kind of opportunity does not knock twice. Please, do that for me, Sammy."

Sam told his mother he would. What else could he do? He did not want to upset her any more that he knew she must be feeling inside. She soon had her surgery. Sam waited for hours in the waiting area anxiously worrying, dreading what the doctor would say. She spent a week in the hospital after her surgery. *Maybe I can tell her later that I'll stay home.* Sam came in every evening after his classes. But she looked better by the end of April. Then chemotherapy took a lot out of her, nausea and vomiting after each session. She lost weight and looked pale. After a month of that the radiotherapy started three times a week, strapped to a special table so she could not move a muscle so the radiation beam would not hit the wrong place, she put up with it. Sam had driven her to each appointment. She was looking worse, not better after she came home from each session. Each time he wanted to tell her he was staying in Buffalo, but couldn't see upsetting her over it. By the end of May she bounced back, she started eating again. She once again told Sam he had to go and do as he had promised; *we keep our commitments*. With her therapy done and less than a month to go before Sam started residency, he finally convinced himself it would be okay, and told her he would go.

He had been thinking of backing out all along. His mother was right about what he had told her and that weighed heavy on him too. If you violated a match agreement you were toast, a burnt match they called it. Likely he never be able to work again in medicine if he did that, especially now with only weeks to go before he started. Deep inside he did not care, he wanted to stay home and be with his family, especially his mother. *California be damned.* But each time he tried to have the conversation with his mother she put her foot down. 'You going Sammy! Don't disappoint me! You made a commitment, now keep it!" She was looking better by this point. All those enriched nutrient milk shakes they fed her, she regained a few pounds, and she got a little sun working in the garden in late Spring. She no longer looked so ghostly pale. She looked more like Sam had remembered she looked last summer, only a little thinner, when all was well. Sam thought she will pull through this.

The week after Memorial Day the school held its graduation, and Sam said all his goodbyes to his classmates, who were all off to their new internships in different cities. Sam tuned up his old car that he had had since high school, and got new tires. He sorted through all his belongings, but only packed two suitcases, a clock radio, and two boxes of medical books. Whatever else he needed he would have to get in California.

It was an especially tearful goodbye in the driveway with his mother and father.

"Promise me you won't worry about me and do a great job out there," his mom said, looking spry in the sunny mid-June morning on the day he left. She could not be prouder of Sam.

"I will. Promise to come visit as soon as you feel up to it," Sam said as he hugged her.

"Of course. With all your talk about California I need to see it for myself. Remember to call us each night you stop. Be safe, and make us proud."

Sam got into his old Toyota, drove south out of town and followed the shore of Lake Erie. After lunch at a drive through burger place in Ashtabula, he continued all the way to Toledo, where, as he had promised his mom, he called that first night. She once again reminded him to keep his commitments, but as she spoke her voiced cracked a bit, as she knew she couldn't keep reminding him of that every call. She went out on the back porch to look at her garden, and pulled her favorite old sweater around her shoulders as the cool air of the evening caused a chill. Something changed in her voice, she tried not to show it to Sam on the phone, but her inflection and persistence were not as confident as she had tried to be through the cancer treatments. That part was over, Sam was gone, and she thought she may never see him again.

CHAPTER 8

FISH WAS DOING THE LAST rotation of his internship that June, back in the pit. The first morning Fish was back in the ER he was sitting writing a note when Della Damone, the new obstetrics research fellow walked in without saying anything to him. She had been at County for a year putting together a research grant. She needed to build her reputation with research, and getting a grant, even a small one, was the way to start. She was good with numbers, with data, with equations, but people, not so much. Her work did not require her to be in the ER before. It was a place that disgusted her. Now she was out to recruit new patients for her clinic. She brought a basket of fruit for the nurse's station, less to thank them for looking out for potential patients for her clinic, and more out of transactional intent. A subtle bribe, she was not above employing it to get ahead. She tacked a poster on the bulletin board in the doctor's room of the ER. You could not help but to notice when she entered a room. Della was tall and thin. She had sharp angles to her face reflecting an uncommonly muscular jaw. Her hard piercing black eyes with short cropped black hair made her look like a military recruit. She looked through people with a sense of determination, as if you were not there and did not matter.

"Well, what brings the research fellow down to our den of disarray?" Fish asked.

Della glanced down at him, not anxious to strike up a conversation with some intern, she dryly replied, "Read the poster."

Fish not easily going to let her get away held out his hand, "Dr. Fish. Everyone calls me Fish though."

Della did not shake his hand but felt compelled to reply, "I'm starting a two-year research study on obesity in pregnancy. I've got a federal grant to study overweight pregnant women. I intend to prove that being overweight is significantly detrimental to both mother and child. So, if you have any overweight pregnant woman that you see down here who qualifies, please send them to my clinic." Every time she said the word "overweight" there was a caustic disdain that pitched in her voice, almost as if she wanted to spit out the word. The gaunt Della Damone not so secretly hated fat people.

Now here was an interesting twist. It was sometimes said that certain men were drawn to the field of obstetrics by their disdain for women. They were able to express their dislike of the opposite sex by performing surgery on them. Here was a woman drawn to the study of obese women by a similar disdain. Della had struggled with her own weight problems through a lonely childhood. She turned those isolating days inward and excelled at math and science, at a time when woman were discouraged from those fields. Annoyed that her college advisors had suggested nursing as a profession, she dug in deeper and showed them. She took all the pre-med courses and got solid A's. She became a vegetarian and lost all her weight, and it became a compulsion of hers to stay thin. She got into medical school and wanted again to defy the status quo, to show them all, and be a surgeon, but in the 1970s this was a hard path to plow. She did well in her rotations but was constantly told that if she really wanted to operate like a surgeon, then gynecology was where woman could find such a career. After failing to get any interviews in any surgery residencies due to the similar prejudices of the surgeons running them, she capitulated to reality and did an OB/GYN residency. Now she was seeking to lift herself above the others, to show them once again, by being a researcher. She found a grant she could use to propel herself above her peers, and she would show them all. She now had a mission to prove that unhealthy obese women are a menace to the health of their unborn children. The coldness in her voice and her curt speech suggested that she preferred the accuracy of science to the nuisance of patient care. Human interaction, even with a colleague such as Fish, took too much of her time.

Fish sensing this coldness with her first words, withdrew his hand that she did not chose to shake, and said, "Excuse me, I think I have a patient to see."

Fish went in to see a middle-aged man named Sid with abdominal pain. His belly was big and greatly distended, but Sid was not overtly overweight, the excessive build-up of gas and stool in his intestine gave him a protruding abdomen. After talking with Sid who said he not had a bowel movement in over a week, and examining his newly large belly, Fish thought probably a bowel obstruction, but maybe if the patient was just constipated he could fix it himself with a decompression from below.

"Okay, sir I think we can help you. Don't worry." Fish said trying his best to act professional. He turned to the nurse and said, "Could you transfer this gentleman to Room Six and get a procto tray set up in there?"

Fish thought he had better have the surgeon stand by during the procto, in case things turned sour. He saw Snider down the hall and asked him if he could stand-by for the procto. Snider was on for Trauma call, but as a favor to Fish agreed to hang around. Snider was in an unusual talkative state. He was tall with a thin mustache, but what was unique about him was his strangely spiderly long fingers, a gift for someone who was a surgeon. Pointing his stringy long index finger at Fish he launched into a story, "Did I ever tell you about the time I had to decompress a bowel obstruction down here years ago? That case is why I hate to do these in the ER, so I am not sure why we should do this one now. We were all set to take him to the OR when we get bumped by a trauma case. So, I decided to procto him down here and see if he's got a tumor or something. Well apparently, just inserting the proctoscope dilated him enough to relieve the block, and out shoots a ton of foul swelling loose bloody stool. I mean it was squirting across the room like Old Faithful covering the walls, the floor." Tapping one thin long finger to his temple he went on, "But I had my good old Snider wits and reflexes about me and stepped out of the way." Then Snider got to the part he relished telling over and over, "We had this eager-beaver med student who, not to overuse a pun, was brown-nosing her way so she could get a letter of recommendation from her rotation here for a surgery internship. She had been trying desperately to peer over my shoulder during the procedure, and as I stepped sideways and she gets it right in the face. Boy, was she surprised. She starts heaving her guts out. And now the whole room is covered with puke and shit and blood."

"Who was the student?" Fish asked trying his best to suppress a laugh.

"She was here way before you started Fish. She was one tightly wound piece of work trying to impress the attendings all the time, named Diamond or something like that. Anyway, I save the guy a trip to the OR. What a mess. I don't think anyone could come back into Room Six for at least a week."

Fish was holding his chest and finally got control of himself. "Listen try for once to be tactful in there." He held his arm out to prevent Snider from rushing right into the room, "No

THE COUNTY

jokes, no unprofessional crap, ... and don't make me laugh in there."

Snider and Fish explained the procedure to Sid, who probably did not understand it but just nodded. They put him on the procto table, head down, buttocks up in the air. They insert the proctoscope with the usual deflation of the rectum of gas wafting passed them. They proceeded up, 8 centimeters, 12 centimeters, 16 centimeters, and finally at full insertion at 20 centimeters they found some dark spots in the colon.

"Take a look. What do you think?" Fish stepped aside to give Snider a look. Snider came in cautiously prepared to duck if needed. Snider stared through the eyepiece for a minute, manipulating the end of the scope right and left and up and down to get a complete view. Finally, he let the scope go, and with just the hub dangling out of the patient's rectum he walked around to the front of the procto table and hurriedly told the patient, "We did our best, I think the only way we can get at the blockage is with surgery. Dr. Fish will consent you and tell you the details."

"That's buried to the hilt, and there is something higher up causing the problem." Snider said to Fish walking out of the room, "We need to take him to the OR. That's what

I should have done in the first place. Never do a procedure in the ER that should be done elsewhere. That's always been my rule, not sure why I let you convince me otherwise. I'll make the arrangements."

Fish sternly pointed a finger at Snider, "You could have at least removed the proctoscope before talking to him. You think he can comprehend the ramifications of needing surgery with that stuck in him and his head upside down? Can you once be a tiny bit professional?"

"You asked me to stand-by, not take over. So it's still your patient."

Snider then grabbed a nurse by the elbow as he left, "After Fish pulls the scope, start an IV, and get that guy's belly prepped for surgery. I'll let the OR and the anesthesia resident know." He turned and left.

Fish went back in to the room to try to repair the situation, First, he carefully removed the proctoscope, rolled the man back over and got his head up. Sam offered him a tissue to wipe his sweat-drenched face.

"Please tell me what's going on?" Sid pleaded; his eyes looked even more sunken that when he came in.

"Listen I have to apologize for Dr. Snider. Honest he's an excellent surgeon, just brusque with patients. I understand your discomfort, but we'll give you some Demerol. Again, I'm sorry for any discomfort we caused."

"OK doctor. Please, just show me where to sign, and then please, please just put me out."

CHAPTER 9

ON WEEK LATER DELLA DAMONE was in her obstetrics clinic with the first patient of the day. "Okay honey, just slide your butt down to the end of the table," Della Damone was telling an obese woman in her clinic.

"I can't. My knees don't bend." the poor woman lamented.

"Maybe you should lose some weight," Della said loud enough for her nurse to hear but not loud enough for the woman to overhear. Then in a loud and demanding voice, "Keep sliding down to the end of the table Mrs. Lenox, and put your feet up in the stirrups. We got to check on how the baby's doing deep down inside there."

Now the tables in the OB clinic were constructed out of wood and were hollow inside. The metal stirrups were ill-fitted in their sockets from years of use. They tended to rotate out of kilter with each other. It was impossible to place one's legs in them symmetrically in the spread-eagle fashion necessary for a pelvic exam. The lighting was poor and consisted of a single 100-watt bulb on a gooseneck lamp which had to be dragged into position between the patient's legs once she managed to contort herself into the desired position on the pelvic exam table. Better designed pelvic tables were available but in typical County logic, if it wasn't broken why spend money to fix it?

Della inserted a cold metal speculum, failing to warn the woman of the shock she would feel.

"Whoa!" The woman screamed and sat bolt upright. When the large young woman sat up the center of gravity changed to everyone's disadvantage. The table at first slowly, then with sudden speed began tipping over the end the woman's legs were up in stirrups. Over the end where Dr. Damone was sitting on a low stool, a gooseneck lamp between her legs cramped into the little space remaining in the corner of the examining room. Without a warning sound there was a crash and the low popping sound of a bulb being crushed. Dr. Damone's brief scream was muffled and then you couldn't see her anymore. She was buried beneath a table now sitting upright on end. The large woman's legs, still spread wide open in the stirrups, were now wrapped around Dr. Damone's head holding a gooseneck lamp with a broken bulb against her face. The woman was wedged against the wall screaming, "Whoa, Jesus! Whoa, Jesus!"

The nurse screamed, "Oh my God, Dr. Damone. Dr. Damone. Are you all right? Oh my god, I think Dr. Damone's unconscious! Call a code. Someone call a Code Blue! My God, I think you killed Dr. Damone!"

The code team arrived from the ER with Fish in the lead. "Holy shit! What the hell is going on here?"

"Help Dr. Damone she's trapped under Mrs. Lenox, the table broke and everything collapsed on Dr. Damone. I think she's out."

"OK. Call the ER. Tell them I need four, no make that six strong orderlies down here stat to help me." He reached under the pile and grabbed Dr. Damone's wrist. "She still has a strong pulse." Let's see if we can tip this table upright while we're waiting. Fish, the nurse, and a receptionist pushed hard against Mrs. Lenox but neither she nor the pelvic table wouldn't budge. She was wedged in tight against the wall.

THE COUNTY

"Oh, Jesus I'm bleeding down my legs. Jesus Don't let my baby die, please, please, Oh. Please, Jesus!"

"Baby!" said Fish, *oh, shit of course she would be pregnant. Dr. Damone's the pregnancy clinic fellow.* He shook his head. *You would think with all that federal grant research money you might buy a reinforced GYN table*, he imagined yelling at the unconscious Dr. Damone.

Two orderlies showed up from the ER. "Sorry Fish but we're all they could spare they have a gunshot wound coming in and they said they could use you back ASAP."

"Damn we need more help! OK. Let's give it all you got. Put your backs in it and PUSH!"

The table began to tip upright with Mrs. Lenox on it.

"Jesus, Jesus, save me. Is my baby Ok? Jesus have mercy."

"Please, we're trying, keep pushing guys. We're almost over the top."

Crash! The table righted itself. Fish went to check on Dr. Damone. One of the stirrups pulled loose and fell on her feet. He held her head along both sides. "Someone get me a C-collar. We're taking her back to the ER. Someone please call the on-call OB STAT to check this lady for injuries and vag bleeding."

Fish placed the polyurethane plastic collar carefully around Della's neck keeping it still so as not to move it in case she had a spine injury. The orderlies lifted her like a log and placed the unconscious Dr. Damone on a gurney. Fish checked her lungs with his stethoscope. *Still breathing.* He checked her pupils with a penlight, they were equal on both sides. *Good.* He pressed her abdomen. It was rigid and her pelvis was unstable. *Damn, bad news.* "OK let's roll. We're going back to the ER Now! Can you call someone to help this poor lady and check her baby. I have to go with Dr. Damone, she's in critical shape."

Just then Dr. Corkerin the chief OB resident showed up with a smug expression on. "OK, Ok. What's all the commotion about."

The nurse jumped in," Mrs. Lenox fell on Dr. Damone and she may be miscarrying!"

Corkerin pulled out a doppler stethoscope from his white coat. "Gooooood," he said, his head bobbing rhythmically, after listening to her belly for a few minutes, "Strong fetal heart tones." He handed the earpieces to Mrs. Lenox to hear.

Mrs. Lenox listen for a second, her head bobbing up and down with each heartbeat too, and she smiled, a tear rolled down her cheek. "Thank you, Lord," she said, "I always had faith in you."

"Ok. Let's get her up to labor and delivery and get an ultrasound on her." Turning to the nurses Corkerin added, "Ladies, please, after you."

Fish ran pushing the gurney carrying the unconscious Della Damone back to the ER. He rounded the corner and pushed her into Room One. The surgical team, with Mac Snider was waiting there for him. *Great, for once no delays today!*

CHAPTER 10

"**SORRY FISH YOU GOING TO** have to take her out in the hall. We got two GSWs about one minute out." Snider said knowing he could not cover both critical cases.

"This is Dr. Damone," Fish pleaded, "She's got a crushed pelvis and a rigid abdomen. We got to get her to surgery."

"OK. Listen just pull her out in the hallway, get some vital signs, a couple of lines in her, and a chest and pelvic x-ray, and well evaluate her as soon as we see what injuries these gunshot wounds have." Snider told him, "We may need to call in a back-up surgeon. Let's just see what we got with these gunshots."

Fish pulled the gurney out in the hallway just as the first ambulance stretcher rolled by him into Room One. A trail of dripping blood followed the path the stretcher took and two paramedics ran right through it. A fireman was perched on top of the gurney straddling the patient doing CPR. The paramedic talked rapidly catching his breath, "We got called out to a gang fight in progress in the south area. Lots of Saturday Night specials going off in some turf fight in the old South mall. We were held on the perimeter until the police cleared the area, but most of the shooters just ran away. When we get to the west parking lot this guy was down, took a few 22 slugs to the chest but was talking to us. We just lost a pulse backing in here. We got two IVs running wide open and I got to get his partner out of the rig and I'll be right back." He ran out.

"Okay what have we got on the monitor," Snider shouted, " V. fib. Okay everybody back! Let's buzz him."

Snider pressed the two defibrillator paddles across the young man's chest and pushed the button. Nothing happened—the machine had lost its charge.

"What the …, out of juice. Didn't anyone check this today?"

"We did," the nurse shouted back defensively," But we had a long code this morning and we must have buzzed the guy fifty times. We probably drained the battery."

"Shit. OK. Let's crack him."

Snider pulled the plastic sealant off a thoracotomy tray and gloved up. Snider went into reflex mode. He took a wedged-shaped scalpel and cut open the young man's chest along the line of a rib from his sternum to the side of the bed he was standing on. "Spreaders!" He shouted. A nurse handed him the large metal instrument which looked like a car jack. Snider inserted the spreaders between the ribs and turned the vise to open them up. He exposed the heart. It was dark blue and beating fast and irregularly. With a scalpel and a delicate forceps, he picked up the thin opaque membrane surrounding the heart and made a small nick. A small amount of blood came out. Snider extended his incision downward towards the patient's feet, carefully around the heart. As he cut large amounts of dark blue blood oozed out and beneath it was the bright red heart beating slower and stronger. "He's got a hemopericardium." Snider suctioned the blood around the chest. He gently palpated the back of the heart with his long fingers. "Here it is. He's got a nick in the ventricle. Give me a 1-0 Gut stitch with a pledget." Carefully Snider began to sew the hole in the young man's heart closed. The heart seemed to be pumping stronger.

"Ninety over fifty." The nurse called taking his blood pressure.

"Keep the fluids wide open and get me two units of whole blood. Call the OR and tell them we'll be up in five and I need a cardiac setup."

"Good save doctor S…" The nurse was just beginning to say when a young man in fatigues stepped into the room screaming.

"Malcolm, that you Malcolm?"

"Get him the hell out of here!" snapped Snider.

The man pulled a gun out of his pants and aimed it at Snider' face.

"No, you get the fuck away doc."

Snider dropped his instruments in the young man's chest and stepped back fearing for his life. The fatigued-clad intruder abruptly changed his aim and emptied three shots directly into the young man's now open chest. A geyser of blood pumped up out of his chest and the monitor alarm sounded. When everyone looked up the intruder was gone.

The nurse slammed the door to Room One shut and began crying.

"Shit, and I almost had him back," Snider looked miffed.

There was a commotion heard in the hall outside and everyone in Room One froze on the spot not knowing what to think or do. The nurses all stifled a sob.

"Oh my God. Fish is out there." Snider said in a whisper. Just then they heard a knock on the door.

"All clear. We got him. You folks OK in there? Anybody hurt?"

The nurse cautiously opened the door to see the uniform of a sheriff's officer outside. Just beyond him, three more officers were beating the fatigued-clad man's head against the ground with his hands cuffed behind his back.

"He shot our patient!" the nurse cried, "He could have killed us!"

"Is anybody injured?" the sheriff spoke softly. As he glanced around the room everybody seemed to be shaking their heads no.

The handcuffed man was dragged out the ambulance entrance face down, toes dragging through the trail of blood left by the young man's wound. He was still screaming. "You bastard Malcolm, I got you. I got you good. They can fry me if they want. You're dead you bastard, you hear me, bastard."

The paramedic rolled back in with his second victim.

"This guy's just got a single entrance and exit wound to his thigh."

Snider roared out of Room One, "Fish, Fish, where are you? Are you all right?"

Fish was coming down the hall with the gurney with Della on it and two x-rays on top.

"Fish, where the hell were you? I thought you were out in the hall with that maniac."

"I missed all the commotion," Fish nervously replied, "I was down getting Della's X-rays. Are you Okay? What the hell happened?"

"Some asshole came in looking for someone named Malcolm and shot the guy in Room One."

"Listen you got to take Della up to the OR now. CT is waiting to scan her head, but her abdomen is rigid and she has an open-book pelvic fracture." He held up one of the X-rays. "I've got eight units of blood typed and three IVs in her. Please! If we can't save our own selves first, how are we going to save everyone else? Please, Snider, get her up to the OR."

"Somehow I'm not into playing God today anymore," acknowledged Snider. "Listen I'll take Della up. You go check on the guy shot in the leg in Room Three."

Snider grabbed Della's gurney and rolled off down the hall to the elevator to the OR.

Fish composed himself for a second, thinking that in a way it was lucky the gunshot victim died and didn't tie up the OR that he knew Della needed desperately. He felt an odd sense of emotion for her and said under his breath, "Dear God please save her. Please, oh please, let Snider save her."

Fish stepped over to the sink and threw some cold water on his face. He glared at himself in the mirror. There was a second of emotional and ethical horror he saw in himself. He desperately wanted Della to live but was shocked by the notion that he was glad the gunshot victim was dead, and needed to be dead to not have to make a choice between him and Della for the only available OR. Medically he knew that the open-chest gunshot wound would go up first, leaving him to try to manage Della in the ER until they were done in the OR. Too much wasted time and she would die. Now no choices had to be made. Playing God was easy with strangers, not with people you know. The intruder solved that by playing God with anger and a weapon, a one-time decision. Fish, Snider, and the others played God daily, understaffed, under-funded, under-equipped, and today under the gun. Fish splashed some more cold water on his face and exhaled. *Okay back into the fray.*

With his usual litany he stepped into Room Three, "Dr. Fish, but you can call me Fish. What happened to you today?"

A fifteen-year-old black child, thin, scared, and in pain looked up at him pointing to his left leg he just cried.

"What's your name son? Don't be afraid."

The boy stuttered, "Mmmmalcolm."

CHAPTER 11

SNIDER ROLLED INTO THE OR. He had just gotten off the phone with Westman, his attending surgeon who was now on the way up to help with the operation. Della's head CT had to be postponed, they would not worry about brain damage until they stopped the internal bleeding. Her blood pressure had fallen, and her abdomen was distending. She was losing massive amounts of blood internally. The ER called with the results of her blood count—19 %. Della had lost more than half of her circulating blood volume, she needed blood. Snider went out to call the blood bank to send up the first two units. When Snider got back to the OR sink, his attending, Dr. Westman was already

THE COUNTY

scrubbing. Westman was tall, commanding in appearance. In his middle 50's with touches of gray at his temples in his closely cropped hair. He was an institution within the institution, a general in the army of doctors at the County. As the chair of surgery, and chief of the trauma service Westman was called for every trauma patient that arrived in the ER, whether they needed surgery imminently or not. Della, by Snider's assessment, needed emergency surgical intervention. Standing at the wash sink, Westman was meticulous in the order he scrubbed his hands for surgery, first his fingernails, then each finger, the hands right always before left, and all the way up to above his elbows. He followed this certain order rigidly each time. Snider joined him to scrub as the anesthesiologist went in to check out Della.

"Did you do a pelvic exam?" asked Westman.

"No, why?" replied Snider scrubbing his arms up to his elbows in dark brown iodine solution.

"Why? Why you ask, Dr. Snider? What is the percent mortality of an open book pelvic fracture if it is open and contaminated?" He motioned ever so slightly with his chin to the pelvic x-ray hanging on a view box in the scrub area. Despite the urgency of the situation,

Westman took a moment to teach, something he prized.

"It goes up to about fifty percent," Snider replied not wanting to be caught off-guard by any of Westman's queries. He had heard almost all of them before.

"Right! And where are the potential major contaminating wounds?"

"Perineum, bowel, vagina." listed Snider by rote.

"Good, now break scrub, and go in there and check her pelvic and rectal exam. I'll finish here and do the skin prep of the abdomen."

Snider rinsed off his arms and entered the OR. The anesthesiologist had a black rubber face mask over her face. "Are you ready yet?" asked Snider.

"No, we've got her breathed down with halothane but I haven't tubed her yet." replied the anesthesiologist, referring to the process of passing a tube into her windpipe to breathe for her during the operation.

"Okay! You tube her. I've got to do a pelvic on her."

The anesthesiologist placed a curved metal blade in her mouth and lifted. Snider placed a metal speculum in her vagina and pressed down. "Suction" they both cried in unison. The anesthesiologist suctioned out her mouth, "I

THE COUNTY

can't see her cords. Wait there they are. She has a very anterior epiglottis."

"She must be anatomically symmetric because her cervix is way up there as well. No blood down here."

The anesthesiologist passed the endotracheal tube into Della's trachea and hooked her up to the ventilator. He withdrew the curved metal laryngoscope from deep in her throat. Snider finished his exam and withdrew the metal speculum from Della's vagina. The anesthesiologist greased up a thin clear plastic NG tube and began passing it through Della's nose down into her stomach. Snider changed gloves and greased up a finger and inserted it deep into Della's rectum and swept his finger all around in all directions. "Ooops. What's this NG tube I feel down here?" said Snider loudly.

"What! What are you talking about!" the anesthesiologist looked panicked.

"Just joking. Boy, you gas passers have no sense of humor at all. I'm not sure who needs more Valium, you or her." Snider withdrew his finger. It was covered in brown stool which he wiped on a test card to check for blood. He took his glove off and stretched it out over his index finger. He snapped it and it went flying toward the wastebasket in the corner but missed. The anesthesiologist hooked the NG tube in Della's nose up to suction and her stomach contents came sucking out. He too placed a drop of it on a test card to check for blood. "*Good, no blood.*" They thought simultaneously, as both their cards failed to turn blue.

Snider went out to rescrub and Westman came in his arms held up in the air dripping with water. The circulating nurse draped a dry sterile towel over his arms, and he proceeded to dry them. The nurse then held up a sterile cloth green suit and Westman stepped into it from behind. The nurse tied it from the back. Westman's mask was readjusted by the nurse. Lastly, she held out gloves for him to insert his arms into and loudly snapped them as he passed his arms deep into the gloves. "Let's do it," said Westman boldly. The nurse walked over to a tape player against the wall and dropped in a cassette marked "OPENING—WESTMAN." A few seconds of static hissed then at maximum decibel level the 1812 Overture spewed forth. On the second cymbal crash, Snider pushed the OR door open with his back and entered with his hands held high dripping wet. He proceeded through the dressing ritual of the OR getting his towel, gown, mask, and gloves applied to him by the nurse as if she were the valet of some wealthy English country gentleman. The music charged along and Snider positioned himself on the opposite side of the operating table as Westman.

"Are we deep enough?" Westman asked, raising an eyebrow towards the anesthesiologist.

"Yes sir, you may start," was the reply.

Westman handed the shining scalpel to Snider, with a slight nod, and Snider took it to mean he could begin. Snider's long fingers carefully guided the knife in one continues slice as he made an incision from just under Della's breast bone down to her belly button making a sharp C-shaped curve around it and then straight down to her pelvic area. A red muscle was exposed and Snider proceeded to dissect through it. "Not much fat on this one he said," finishing the first level of dissection." Buzz that bleeder for me," he said politely to Westman.

Dr. Westman picked up an instrument that looked like a soldering iron and pressed it to the side of the wound just created by Snider where a small pumping blood vessel was pulsating a thin stream of red onto Snider's gown. "BUZZ." He said. A nurse stepped on a foot pedal and an electric buzz was heard as the odor of burning flesh rose from the wound in a swirling puff of blue-gray smoke. The pumping blood vessel had ceased to soil Snider's gown. The scrub nurse dabbed the wound with a clean gauze and the dissecting continued down to the next layer. "BUZZ." was heard again and a second puff of burnt flesh arose from Della's abdominal wall and another pumper was stilled. They continued this process for another minute until Snider looked up and said, "Okay, I'm ready to go through the abdominal wall. Have some blood ready to give her. If she's filled up, she'll drop her pressure to her toes as soon as we release the tamponade." The nurse calmly readied two large suction devices in anticipation of what was going to happen next. The anesthesiologist opened all three of her IVs up to run as fast as they can and placed two units of blood up to run in. "Okay, here we go."

Snider incised the entire length of the wound and sure as he said would happen dark blue blood welled up and over the sides of the wound pouring onto both his and Westman's gowns and shoes. "SUCK, Get those suctions in there."

Westman plunged his hands deep into the dark bloody well that was Della's abdomen and reached for something he knew was there deep in her upper left side. "Got it." He nodded to Snider who was sucking with two large suction devices to clear the wound out so they could see. The scrub nurse knowing what came next had a middle-sized clamp in her hand extended over the table in the right position for Westman to grab. He grabbed it with his free hand and passed it gently into the wound to where his left hand was holding Della's aorta tightly between his two fingers. He passed the clamp up parallel to his two fingers and gently squeezed them down. Leaving the two fingers in place around the aorta he carefully separated them to see if the bleeding was stopped. It worked. The welling of blood had ceased and the view of the abdomen revealed multiple loops of Della's intestine that now bulged up into the wound. Snider took a wet towel and pulled the intestine to his side of the table. Westman pulled a dark oblong organ up into the wound after making a few cuts with a scissor to free it up. The spleen was beefy and had several pieces of its smooth outer wall missing. "This has got to go. It's all torn up," said Westman to Snider. "You know you never should have planned to take her to head CT first if her abdomen was rigid. You should just come up here to the OR. The neurosurgeons will always have to wait until we save the patient first. Remember that Snider!"

"But what if she had a head injury? Neurosurgery could have been doing a craniotomy on her while we did the belly." protested Snider, his judgment being called into question by his senior staff.

"The head can wait. If she bleeds to death from a ruptured spleen there will be no head to operate on. We have a golden hour in which to operate on abdominal trauma. They have four hours to get the same result with a head injury. The abdomen always takes precedence over the brain, the bones, the face, and the spine. It doesn't take long to bleed to death from an abdominal injury. Remember that. We'll have this under control in an hour, then orthopedics can come in and help stabilize her pelvic fractures."

The notion that neurosurgeons had to wait struck in Snider's mind. He shook it off and dove back into concentrating on what he had to do in the operation. That thought however would come back.

Snider and Westman removed the damaged spleen working in unison each anticipating the other's moves. Snider had operated with Westman for six years and he was nearly done with his surgical residency. He wanted to become a neurosurgeon but had been turned down by the program for two years in a row. He was biding his time in surgery waiting for a position in the neurosurgery residency to open up. Each year they had only two openings in neurosurgery and each year Snider was always their third pick. Each year he continued in surgery, and now that he was soon to be finished, he was one of the best surgical residents that had come through in years. The only problem was Snider did not want to be a general surgeon even if he was the best. Westman knew it and always pushed Snider hard in the OR. They still worked together excellently.

It was the privilege of rank that let Westman criticize Snider; Westman believed that is what made a surgeon tough enough to be a surgeon, a breed apart in his mind. Snider after all was there to learn the skills of the trade and Westman felt, like most surgeons did, that surgeons should be raised in an aura of stress. Stress would help them achieve their highest expectations. If they couldn't handle stress, they had no business being a surgeon. That was the credo that allowed Westman to have high expectations his residents for the six years he had to imbue them with his knowledge and philosophy. Any surgical resident coming out of the County was at the top of his game as a result.

Two hours later Westman pulled off his gloves and turned to Snider saying, "Finish closing I'll catch up with you in the ICU."

Snider sutured Della's abdominal wall with extra care. For two hours he did not think of her as a fellow resident but as a tray of organs that he had to fix. No emotion. No personal attachment. Just like Westman had trained him to act. Now coming back to the skin layer, he returned to the knowledge that this was a fellow physician and deserved an extra good job to lessen the scar. "Sorry Della, no bikinis this summer." He said as he tied the last knot. Down at her hips on both sides protruded a metal erector set known as an external fixator. These mini-beams and girders were drilled into the sides of her pelvic bones by the orthopedic team who came in to the OR to stabilize her pelvic fracture after Snider and Westman had stopped her internal bleeding. "No, it won't be because of my scar that you won't get into a bikini this summer Della," He said looking at the metal external fixators, "It's the ortho boys who have just turned your hips into the Golden Gate Bridge."

CHAPTER 12

FISH AT FIRST VISITED DELLA daily while she was in the hospital. He had an irrational feeling of guilt for what he perceived as delays in getting her to the OR. He tried to come by around lunch breaks, but she mostly ignored him when he tried to start a conversation. She just plowed ahead with her data and paperwork. She had her office bring a box of charts to work on to her hospital room. It did not take Fish long to realize his efforts were in vain, it was just guilt at this point that kept him trying. After a week, Fish stopped trying.

After discharge Della returned to work briefly in the obstetrics clinic, she remained driven, but her cause was now without funds or patients. She blamed everyone, but most of all she blamed fat women for her problems, her injury, and the loss of her grant. She did not blame Fish, because she barely knew what his role was in helping her. She had been unconscious during the time he came to save her, and she never asked about it. She was puzzled why this guy kept coming in once a day to talk to her, and she did not care to talk to him. She had work to do; there was no time for friendly conversation. Unknown to him, he was to become the second casualty of her accident.

Dr. Corkerin had to take over the obesity pregnancy clinic for her. Lloyd Corkerin was great with the patients, always flirting with them. He was handsome, athletic, sun-tanned, and never talked down to anyone. Everyone in the clinic loved his good-natured presence. His patients, and now the ones he took over from Della Damone, never missed an appointment with him, and they all got great care. They loved to come in and once every few weeks they could fantasize that this tall handsome doctor really liked them. Corkerin had that charm. The patients often didn't have anyone else at home to make them feel better. Way too many of them were victims of abuse, early and repeated pregnancies by strings of men who beat them and left them. Poverty and children were all they had to look forward to, except now they could look forward to fifteen minutes with that cute young Dr. Corkerin.

Lloyd Corkerin was not very good at collecting data, however. All that paperwork required to sustain the grant application that Della had worked for, that she thrived on to the exclusion of patient contact, was left half completed. Della tried first from her hospital bed, then between rehab exercise sessions, to fix the paperwork mess in her usual compulsive style. She would wake at six, eat a yogurt for breakfast, go to physical therapy to exercise, do six hours of collating patient records, return for a second round of physical therapy, then another two or three hours of paperwork after diner. She never ate lunch, remaining her anorexically thin self during the entire course of her recovery. She pushed herself harder than any of the physical therapist had seen before in their patients. Within a few weeks she was walking again. One week before her fellowship was up to be renewed her grant funding was pulled when she could not file an interim data report on time, and the obstetrics obesity clinic closed. All her patients were merged into the remainder of the obstetrical program.

After her research grant was terminated Della became more withdrawn and angrier at women. At times she was hostile to everyone, nurses, patients, and staff. No one wanted to work with her. No patient wanted to see her again after their first encounter. She was the polar opposite of Dr. Corkerin. He was charming with a laid-back style and listened to his patients; she was tense, cut people off mid-sentence, and made everyone around her feel belittled. But Corkerin treated her with all the respect he could muster, offering to help in any way since she had been tragically injured. She did not want to be perceived as tragic or injured or in need of special treatment and spurned his help. Her clinic workload became lighter as her patients refused to see her again, so she spent most of her time trying to salvage the data from her obesity clinic to write a paper or apply for a new grant. She was good at crunching numbers, and terrible at talking with real people.

By July Della was gone. No one knew exactly where she went. She wasn't practicing in town like many graduates tended to do, so everyone assumed she got another research grant somewhere. There was a rumor she went back to school to take some classes as she recovered; but she told no one; she was friendless. She became just another doc who after a year at the County just disappeared. For now.

CHAPTER 13

THAT JULY THERE WAS A change in every County, and Central City County Medical Center was no exception. A new group of untested interns arrived to replace the now-hardened group of interns who just endured a grueling year. Most of the surviving interns were now residents and had to break in the new ones to the bizarre life that lay ahead for them. Fish was one of the medicine residents who stayed on. As the new senior resident in the pit, he got to break in four new interns on their first day. He remembered how he felt when he was like that, so ready to get started, but scared to death inside.

A tall black man with short cropped hair from Duke named Wilson firmly shook Fish's hand, smiled, and introduced himself. Wilson wore a red and blue regimental tie and a white pressed shirt with a polo player on the upper breast pocket. He spoke directly with the assurance of someone who just weeks before was heaped on the accolades of having achieved a major milestone in his life—graduating from medical school. But inside Wilson was not so happy as his confident smile falsely declared. He felt he had been cheated out of better internships. Match day was painful for him, but his family supported him through the roller coaster of emotions of leaving home, moving to a place he never thought he would end up at. So here he was trying to smile, and as his older brother who he looked up to told him "make lemonade out of lemons."

The second intern was a quiet, well-spoken and well-coifed, sun-tanned woman wearing a business suit, sensible shoes, and a lapel pin declaring she had just graduated from a prestigious hospital in Boston. Next to her was a man with dark long hair parted in the middle, casually dressed in a new Go Cal tee shirt wearing a pin that said "Trust me I'm a doctor". The woman, edging slightly away from the man in the tee shirt, introduced herself, in a husky Bostonian accent, as Gina Bautista.

THE COUNTY

The tee-shirted man was Harry Martin from, most recently, Guadalajara. She was Cuban, and always got testy when people assumed she was Mexican, which Harry immediately made the mistake of doing by asking where in Mexico she was from since he thought he knew the whole country after going to medical school there. He wasn't from Mexico, but went there as a desperate last resort to get in anywhere for medical school after several years of rejection. He was happy to be back in the states, even at the County. She was not.

"OK, where is our last intern?" Fish looked around, "did we lose one already?"

And that's when Sam walked up and apologized for being late. "I was just transferred down to the ER from the medicine wards." This was a scheduling error that was about to change Sam's life. Sam waved congenially to the three new intern-mates and introduced himself, "Sam Wyatt, from Buffalo." Like the other three interns he was eager to get started. He had gotten a haircut, and shaved his winter beard off. Like the others he wore a new over-starched short white coat, pockets with stethoscopes and notepads in them. Fish recognized him, but did not let on.

Fish started his introduction, "The shifts are 24 hours, every other day, all month. Let's split you into two teams of two interns." Pointing to the two interns on his right, "Wilson and Gina on even days," then to his left, "Sam and Harry on odd days."

"You know there are 16 odd days and 15 even days in July," Harry immediately complained.

"After the first twenty-four hours it won't matter anymore," said Fish. "You won't remember if it's day or night, weekday or weekend. Unless you park in the same spot every day, which isn't a bad idea, you won't remember where you left your car when it's time to go home. By the end of fifteen days, you won't even remember if you have a car or a home. The only thing you will know is if it's a sleep day or a work day. You get four meals per on-call day free, that's if you can make it down to the cafeteria long enough to eat. There is a sleep room here but you might as well forget about it. No one ever slept at night in the pit at the County. See your patients as quick as you can and then present them to me and we'll talk about what to do. Any questions?"

"What do we do today?" asked Gina, signaling herself and Wilson.

"Well, I guess to make it even you all get to work today so everyone gets sixteen call days this month. Does that make it fair Harry?" Gina glared at Harry and immediately wanted to object for getting assigned an extra day, but stood quiet, not wanting to make trouble on her first day. Fish continued, "Consider it a first day break because you will only need to see every fourth patient today instead of every other patient like you will need to starting tomorrow."

"But if we work today and tomorrow that means we will be working 48 hours in a row!" Wilson observed forcefully. Gina nodded in support.

"Hmmm. You're right." said Fish rethinking his plan, "Why don't you guys work till midnight tonight then go home to sleep and be back at seven tomorrow? Okay. All settled. Let's lose the shirts and ties unless you want to be choked by some psych patient. Go up to the OR and steal yourselves some scrubs."

"Has anyone ever been attacked by a psych patient?" Gina nervously asked.

Fish thought back to the gunman's attack in Room One. Technically he wasn't a psych patient. Technically he wasn't even a patient. "No," he paused for a thoughtful second, "we have never had a psych patient do that. Basically, this place is safe, always a cop or two around. I just want you to realize that you are dealing with a population of people who are frustrated being here and some have short fuses. Don't inflame the situation with your own frustration, and believe me you can count on getting frustrated."

Everyone hurried off to change and the barrage began.

A 13-year-old pregnant girl came in seizing. She had never seen a doctor or told her parents that she was pregnant. She had developed eclampsia from her failure to obtain any prenatal check-up. Gina had to tell her parents that not only was their teenage daughter pregnant but that she needed emergency surgery to save her and her baby's life.

Harry had to sew up a man who tried to cut his wrists. When he took the bandages off his forearms there were thirty some lacerations in multiple rows on both arms. "You sure you wouldn't want me to just staple this back together?" he asked Fish, who just shook his head.

Wilson saw a three-year-old with a mild sore throat and was trying to explain to the mother that she didn't need antibiotics for a virus. He was telling the mother word for word what he had been taught in a lecture at Duke about viruses vs. bacteria, but the mother kept asking "So what antibiotic are you going to give me doc? Jimmy likes the pink bubble-gum stuff." After forty-five minutes of trying to convince the mother that this was the correct thing to do medically, frustrated, he sought Fish's advice.

"Both you and I know that antibiotics are worthless for a virus," Fish agreed. "I have not been able to convince a mother with a Ph.D. in microbiology that when her kid is sick, and you won't be able to convince a County mom of that either. Just ask them what flavor they want and send them on their way."

"What!" steamed Wilson, "this totally goes against everything that I've been taught. This is the way we did it at Duke and this is what I going to do here! I am not going to be the Baskin and Robbins of antibiotics!"

It took a few more minutes of back and forth, Wilson upset that medicine had deteriorated to handing out flavored antibiotics on demand without a good reason, and Fish trying hard to soothe his new intern into the reality, shameful as it was, that medicine had become. Finally, Wilson relented, "Good thing I am not going into pediatrics." He went back in the room, wrote the prescription, and the mother smiled, and thanked him. Wilson complained to Sam about his first case when they were alone together at the desk. "Do you do stuff like this in Buffalo?" he asked.

"No. I didn't do any out-patient peds. I didn't think we would be doing any of it here since we're in internal medicine. But its anyone who walks in the front door down here, so I better learn some of this fast. I am definitely not prepared to see kids. They're okay most of the time, but dealing with angry parents is not easy."

"It's just one more insult," Wilson complained to Sam. "I signed up to be an internist, to be the one to diagnose complex medical problems, not to unload the ER just because it's understaffed. I don't need to see children or broken bones, or whatever else they have down here." Wilson looked annoyed. *It would take a lot to make lemonade out of this crap* he told himself.

Sam went into Room Three and found there was a man complaining of shoulder pain going down his left arm. He weighed over three hundred and fifty pounds and had been hauling tar up to the roof in 90-degree weather. "Probably shoulder strain" Jenni the nurse whispered as he walked into the room. Sam talked to the roofer, Mr. Loffler, noticing he was drenched in sweat. His hands were covered with tar, but his face looked pale. Sam asked him to move his shoulder around in several positions, but none made it hurt more. As he raised it up into the air the man did something that saved his life. He retched three times, then vomited. "Sorry kid," he said ,"but that actually feels better." It began to fit together nausea, vomiting, sweating, left-sided pain after heavy work—the man was having a heart attack. Sam gave a wet towel to

THE COUNTY

Mr. Loffler and wiped the vomit off his pants with another towel.

Stepping back out of the room he asked Jenni, "I'd like to get an EKG."

"What for?" she balked.

"I think this guy's having a heart attack, he just vomited all over me. You don't vomit with shoulder strain."

"It's probably the heat outside, or maybe you just look like someone he wanted to vomit all over. You've just got that kind of face. Why don't you give him some aspirin and the day off from work? That's what he really wants. No one wants to be working today in this heat. They come in all the time for work releases this time of year and all you green interns think he's got something serious and order the million-dollar work-up."

"Sorry. You are wrong, I am sure this guy's sick. Please no million-dollar work-ups, I promise. Just do an EKG."

The EKG showed he was having an MI—a heart attack. Sam grabbed Fish and showed him the EKG, and also told him about how the nurse was being obstructive.

"That's just Jenni Omygod. She's worked here 15 years and thinks she knows it all, but all she knows is the shitty way they practiced medicine 15 years ago, back when this was the actual County, before the University stepped in. She will mislead you every time. She is what's known as a negative barometer, always pointing in the wrong direction. If she's not worried about a patient, be worried. If she's worried about something, don't worry. That's why we call her Jenni Omygod because that is the most reassuring thing she can say. If she panics, you shouldn't. Got yourself a gold star for diagnosing this guy despite having Jenni for a nurse. That's like running an obstacle course with your legs tied together. You might make a damn good ER doc if you keep it up." Then turning and looking Sam directly in his face with all seriousness, Fish spoke his first truth, "Remember the primary rule, everyone will be trying to kill your patient," Sam seemed to recoil at this but Fish continued, "It's your job to stand in the way of everyone who is trying to kill them."

"Thanks," Sam smiled at the praise, but was puzzled at the thought that Jenni and others were working against him.

Fish had just given him his first rule of survival in the County. He went on, "Just don't let it go to your head, always listen to the patient. Listening is our most powerful skill. Forget that and they'll be calling you Oh my God Sam someday. It's easy to get burnt out down here and start taking short cuts. And Jenni is the poster child for the Burnout Society. Be careful."

The barrage of patients continued. Gina got an amputated finger; someone was trying to see why his lawn mower wasn't spinning and reached under it while it was still on. Harry got a child who stuck a pencil in her eye, her mom was concerned about lead poisoning, and Harry had to explain pencil lead is really just graphite, just carbon. Wilson got a drunk vomiting up blood, he felt better seeing him rather than another kid. It posed a long list of diagnoses he could ponder as the cause. Sam got a patient who drank a cup of Drano in an attempt to kill herself, Gina got a 1-week-old with a fever and she needed to do a spinal tap, she had never done that before, but Fish helped her through doing it. Harry got a man with a seizure who refused to take his seizure medications. Wilson got a debilitated old lady coughing up blood who turned out to have tuberculosis, *at least that was interesting finally seeing some real internal medicine*, thought Wilson. Sam got a 15-year-old girl, now pregnant for the third time, with vaginal bleeding. *I don't know any gynecology*, he thought, *let alone pediatric gynecology*. Gina got a man in a fight the night before and was turned away from a private hospital with a broken jaw. Wilson got a teenager shot with a BB gun he and his friend were playing with that hit him in the eye, the central clear part of his eye was all filled with blood. Harry got an alcoholic with a distended belly and pain, and dark yellow eyes, Harry already knew what the work-up for jaundice and liver problems was, it was his special secret.

Sam helped Fish in Room One with a man under CPR who didn't make it, Sam remembered his night during his interview trip when Fish allowing him to do CPR, not a complicated skill at the time. Now, Fish allowed him to practice intubating the patient, inserting a breathing tube, after the patient had been pronounced dead. Sam had never done that. Sam did it twice, and got the tube in correctly both times. Fish relayed another of his many rules he would impart to Sam, his adage about codes, *"the first pulse you take is your own"*; if you're not calm and steady then you can't make decisions in a crisis. A second pearl of wisdom from Fish, and it went on and on and on all day.

At midnight Gina and Wilson crawled home. Harry and Sam stayed and kept seeing more and more patients.

CHAPTER 14

SAM SIGNED OUT ALL HIS patients the next morning at seven to Wilson, "I hope you have a better day today. It was non-stop cases all night long, but most have gone home, except the three I need to tell you about." Wilson was obviously relieved when he heard none of them were kids. After signing out Sam went up to the cardiac unit to see Mr. Loffler, the roofer, his first patient.

"Big MI," the room nurse said to Sam before he walked in, "They needed to Swan him last night and put him on Dopamine." Sam wasn't sure what that meant yet but it sounded serious.

"Is he conscious?"

"Oh yeah. He looks a little better when I checked on him this morning" Sam walked up to the bedside, and the roofer opened his eyes when he heard him come in.

"Hey, doc thanks a lot. You're the guy from the ER right? You saved my life. That bitch of a nurse was telling me off before you walked in. You must be pretty smart; they tell me up here that I had some unusual symptoms for a heart attack. At least that's what they tell me what I had. I still can't believe it."

"Well, you were my first patient," Sam felt compelled to tell him.

"No Shit, I thought everybody was supposed to kill their first patient." the big roofer laughed.

"Now Mr. Loffler, you're at the best hospital in the city. We don't kill anybody." the nurse cautioned him.

"That's not what I hear," the big man coughed, " Everyone knows what I heard growing up in Central City. I heard the County is where you come to die. My uncle came in here with a cough. Two weeks later they called my aunt and that was all she wrote. This kid here is sharp though." he said pointing his beefy finger at Sam. "He told off that old battle axe of a nurse down in Emergency. Thanks, kid you saved my life. I guess if you don't kill your

THE COUNTY

first patient, they make you a real doctor, hey son?" Mr. Loffler laughed again. The room nurse shooed Sam out of the room just as they brought in the breakfast tray."

"Shit, no eggs, what kind of place is this anyway?" the big man complained.

"Low salt, low fat, low cholesterol diet!" the nurse said. "If you ate like this all the time you wouldn't be here today"

"If I ate like this all the time I'd starve to death. What's with you people? I can't get a nurse in here who can just lighten up on the rules once in a while."

Sam was standing at the elevator waiting to go down and to go home to sleep when he heard "Code blue, CCU. CODE BLUE, CCU."

He turned and ran back inside the CCU. His heart started pounding in his chest and he felt it all the way up to the top of his head. He remembered *the first pulse you take in a code is your own*. Oh no! *The big man. He was right. When a patient tells you they're going to die, they usually are right.* Fish would ascribe to that. Listen to your patients he told Sam at least three times yesterday. Now the big man predicted that you always kill your first patient and he is going to have the last laugh. *It was my fault, what did I do wrong?* He relived every second of his encounter with the roofer, Jenni the nurse, and Fish. Sam had a vision of the big roofer sitting there in bed laughing that laugh of his with his pendulous stomach rolling back and forth. "You're not going to become a doctor after all kid, you just knocked me off," he could imagine him saying.

Sam rounded the corner and saw a flurry of activity in the big man's room, but he stood back, his hands shaking, eye wide open, afraid to go in. People ran in and out, monitor alarms sounded, a defibrillator cart was rolled in and he heard the snap of the shock wave it generated on his chest in the hallway. Sam was devastated, both numb and angry. He had been up for twenty-six hours. He couldn't cry. He couldn't talk. He couldn't scream. And he wasn't going to be able to sleep. He thought he had done a good job his first day as a doctor, and now this. *What did I do wrong*, he criticized himself again.

After about twenty minutes a resident came out past where Sam was pacing back and forth, and told the ward clerk, "Call Mrs. Feinman. Her husband just circled the drain and bought the farm."

"Feinman. Feinman? FEINMAN?" Sam cried. Sam hurried into the room that he was afraid to look in. The big man was sitting up in bed wolfing down a plate of eggs. Behind a curtain he saw an intern practicing passing a tube into what he presumed was Mr. Feinman's deceased body. The other side of the room was quiet. The big man ate his eggs and watched a small TV hanging from a pole just inches from his plate.

"How you doing? " Sam asked awkwardly, embarrassed that he had barged back in. He was so shocked to see the roofer sitting there he didn't know what else to say.

"Great" the big man replied, "I got two breakfasts this morning. They told me Feinman wasn't going to eat his."

CHAPTER 15

HARRY MARTIN WAS LAYING IN his bed trying to sleep. He was all jazzed up from what he had seen on the first day of his internship. Like Sam he was reliving his first shift full of doubts and second guesses. He thought back about all his patients. *Should I have ordered a coagulation profile on that jaundiced man? Did I start the right antibiotic on the old lady with diabetes and pneumonia? What happened to that kid with a sprained ankle who just disappeared and never came back from X-ray?* Each patient was reviewed over and over again in his mind. Harry was exhausted. He looked at his watch propped up on an upside-down packing box which substituted for a night stand. "Shit!", he said, it was ten-thirty. "I really need to get some sleep."

Harry went to his refrigerator. He opened it up. The only two things in it were a half-finished cherry cobbler from a fast-food place, and a half of six-pack of beer. He took out a beer and sipped it. He rolled the cold can back and forth across his forehead. He was beginning to get a headache. He flopped down in a reclining chair that was the only piece of furniture in his studio apartment other than the mattress that lay on the floor nearby. He began to wonder how he could even drink this stuff after all the alcoholics he saw yesterday. *These were not hard liquor alcoholics; these were poor joes like him who drank beer every day of their lives.* Many of them were in their thirties and forties. Their livers were failing, they were jaundiced. Harry had a good eye for spotting another jaundiced eye. All those patients had some degree of internal bleeding. One had fallen down and hit his head. Because he reeked of beer and vomit, they parked him in the back all night long. "*Wait,*" thought Harry. "*I never checked him after 5 a.m. No, wait! I never checked him out to Gina at 7 either.*"

Harry put down his beer and grabbed the phone on the kitchen counter to call the ER. After about fifteen rings someone picked it up. Harry didn't wait for the person to answer to speak. He just blurted out, "This is Dr. Martin, I need to talk with Dr. Bautista STAT."

Long minutes went by until someone picked up the phone.

"Harry? This is Gina, what the hell are you still doing up?"

"I've been sitting up worrying about my patients. Listen I forgot to tell you about a guy we room-eighted last night. He was drunk and we parked him in the back. But there was a vague history that he fell and hit his head. Listen, go check him for me and see if he needs to be kicked out or if he is still out of it, he needs a CT scan."

"Okay, Harry. Go back to bed and get some sleep. I'll check it out."

Harry walked back to his bedroom and fell back on his mattress. He stared at a fly on the ceiling thinking to himself that he'd just stay awake a few minutes more until Gina called him back and told him everything was okay. But Harry was too exhausted to force himself to stay awake any longer, and slowly drifted off to sleep.

Gina tried to call Harry about an hour later. She found that this was impossible. Since Harry just got his apartment the day before internship began, he didn't call in his phone number to the house staff office. No one had a record of his address or phone number. Harry meant to call it in the first day but the ER was so busy that he never had a chance. Harry never even got a chance to eat. The only thing he ate in twenty-four hours was a Big Mac he picked up at the drive-through window.

The man who was room-eighted was still snoring loudly when Gina found him in a hall by the X-ray bathrooms. She shook him gently. No response. She checked his wristband. *Yep, that was Harry's patient.* She shook him again, this time more forcefully, calling his name. No response. She pulled out her reflex hammer and twisted his toes with the metal shaft of the hammer inserted between his two smallest toes. Still no response.

Gina made a mental note to remind herself to clean her hammer. She pulled off her Boston U. pin from her lapel and stuck the needle end into the patient's hand. Still nothing. Gina was starting to worry. She took a Q-tip and poked the man's eye with the cotton end, then poked his gums with the wood end. Nothing happened. The man just snored.

Gina figured it was head CT time. Since she was near X-ray, she walked over to the tech and asked if he could do an emergency CT scan.

"How long has this guy been in ED?"

"All night"

"Was he in a car accident?"

"No."

"Gunshot?"

"No."

"Violent assault?"

"No."

"How about headache?"

"Well, I can't tell, he's sleeping."

"Listen, Honey. He doesn't meet any of our criteria for a CT scan, emergency or otherwise. You look new here. Is this your first day on the job?"

"No, second, actually."

"Well go find a resident or somebody to check your patient, if he insists on a CT scan, we can probably work him in at the end of the day."

Gina left X-ray feeling a little embarrassed. Then she thought that this was Harry's mess. If the resident didn't think this guy needed a CT scan, then she would leave him for Harry to fix up tomorrow.

Gina's resident was tied up with a heart failure patient, so she saw another patient first. Gina still didn't have a chance to speak to her resident. She decided to take a gamble. She went to the Orange sheet. The Orange sheet was published each day with all the hospital on-call assignments and their beeper number. She started on the top:

THE COUNTY

Administration	Jablonski	7555
Anesthesia	Miller	7231
Burns	Parkland	7903
Cardiology	Framingham	7001

and so forth.

Finally, she found who she was looking for:

Neurosurgery	Snider	7911

CHAPTER 16

SNIDER WAS NO STRANGER TO a page from the ER. All those years he was a surgery resident he figured if it was important, they would page him again in 15 minutes. That always bought him time to finish what he was doing. Snider was thrilled he was now the new junior neurosurgery intern. He did not get into neurosurgery this year it turns out; his third time he came in third. The new intern the neurosurgery department had chosen above him was driving from Texas to California and got into a fatal car crash two days before he was to begin his new life. Paradoxically he died of massive head injuries, somewhere in the Mojave Desert, never making it to California. The chair of the neurosurgery department, more pissed off than empathetic (after all he was a neurosurgeon by trade) called Snider, hoping he had not left town, and he would be able to be talked out of whatever job he had lined up after finishing his 6-year general surgery residency. Snider did not have anything lined up. He made a deal to become a white-water river guide with a friend for the summer, but he had nothing in medicine to move on to. Most, if not all of that was due to his personality. After six years at the County, he evolved from sarcastic to malignant. No one would hire such an asshole. Surgeons despite their skill in the OR still needed to talk to patients, and Snider failed in that aspect. He would however be the perfect neurosurgery intern, all one had to do was ask. The chair did, and now it was his first day on call for neurosurgery and the ER was paging him.

Gina, tentatively asked him, " I have a 56-year-old male who is unconscious and I can't wake him up. I think he may have a head bleed."

"What makes you think that? Does he have something on CT?"

"Well, that's part of the problem, I can't get a CT. They asked me to call you before I got one."

That is when Snider did the first decent thing in years, not on purpose mind you, but as a delaying tactic that he was the master of.

"You must be new, sweetheart. I'll just order the CT for you. Let me know what it shows." And abruptly he hung up. Gina bristled at being called "honey" by a tech and "sweetheart" by some other intern. But five minutes later an orderly came to find her, called her Dr. Bautista, and he took the sleeping man to the CT scanner. It turns out it was to the outpatient scanner—two buildings, a long hallway, across a parking lot, and an elevator ride away.

A code blue, or cardiac arrest, was called 20 minutes later to the outpatient CT scanner. Gina looked up at Fish, her senior resident in the ER that day, and asked "What do we do?"

"Nothing. The in-patient team responds to those." and after a pause, "Well usually."

"But I just sent my patient there. How many patients could they possibly have in the outpatient scanner at once?"

"Okay. Grab the airway equipment roll, and let's run down there to see if they need help. One thing we can always do is an airway, most of the internal medicine residents who respond know the CPR meds, but not how to intubate so well."

Gina ran following Fish, trying to keep up. She had thrown her interview dress shoes in the closet after her half-day shift yesterday and wore tennis shoes today. She was ready to run, but she was having a hard time keeping up with

Fish. When they entered the stairwell they saw Sam was coming back down from seeing the big man in the cardiac unit. Sam asked as they ran by him down into the basement "Where are you running to?" They did not hear so he figured he follow and ran after them as he bounded down two sets of stairs to a sub-basement he did not even know existed. They all ran about a quarter of a mile past overhead pipes and sheet metal exposed air conditioning ducts before running up another three sets of stairs into a building that was separated from the main hospital. Sam's adrenaline was pumping once again. *I should be asleep*, he thought, but he figured something bad was up or Fish would not be running off in this direction far from the ER.

"How did you know that way?" Gina expelled, out of breath, as they reached the top of the stairs entering the outpatient radiology suite.

"It's the fastest. No patients or staff to get in your way down there, and no elevators to wait for." Fish replied, "I found it one day after making a wrong turn out of the cafeteria and knew it would come in handy someday."

Sure enough, when the three of them ran through the back door everyone was crowding into the CT scanner room. And there was the sleeping man with a CT tech doing chest compressions. There was no code team from medicine. Fish and his interns were the first doctors to get there by taking the underground passage. Fish immediately went to the head and felt for a carotid pulse. He felt one, but it was slow and weak. "Atropine" he yelled and unrolled his airway equipment roll pulling out a number 3 Mac blade laryngoscope and a number 8 endotracheal tube. "Do one of you want to tube him?" he said looking from Sam to Gina.

Gina knew it was her patient, but hesitated. Sam said "Yeah, I will." With pure muscle he forced the mouth open, insert the blade to the hilt, and pulled upward toward the ceiling. With his other hand, he slipped the breathing tube between the sleeping man's vocal cords. It all happened in just a few seconds. His practice session with Fish the day before came in handy. Sam had tucked a bag mask under his armpit simultaneously and once the tube was in place, he swung it around and began to bag the patient watching his chest rise.

"Can we get some O-two on this?" He asked.

Fish asked the tech, "Did we finish the scan?"

The tech replied, "Yes I can print it out, it looks like there was something there as it was scanning."

THE COUNTY

Fish ran the code, "OK, do we have a pulse? Blood pressure?"

It turns out oxygen was the thing most needed and the pulse came up even without the atropine. Unless one of the docs choose to inject it, it was not given since the tech knew he could not give it anyway since he was not a nurse. There was no nurse in the outpatient x-ray department. Why would there be?

"OK. Time to move we need to get him all the way back to the ER!" Fish said.

"No sir," the tech interrupted. "Our policy is we need to call 911 if we have an unstable patient. Since this building is separated from the main hospital, we cannot take him outside and roll him through the parking lot like this. We need to transport by ambulance. That's our policy."

"That will take too long. This guy needs the ER then the OR. This scan shows a head bleed. Is there an elevator down to the basement?"

"Yes, but it's just a service elevator for construction use, not patient use. When we bring in new scanners and parts that way."

"Today we are using it for this guy! Gina, grab a copy of the scan and get back to the ER as soon as you can. Oh, and page Snider to meet us there, STAT. Sam you're with me, keep bagging him"

"Sir, you can't do that. He needs to go by ambulance" the tech said forcefully to try to make his point, "and we can't use a construction elevator for patients, and we can't just roll him through the basement which is not a patient care area. That's at least three rules we'd be breaking." The tech said firmly.

"Well, I am in charge. I am making the call, and we are going to do it my way," Fish shot back more firmly. "Do you have a clean sheet or blanket to throw over him? Unlock the gurney's brakes because I am ready to roll. Gina, get the airway roll and the scan. We are out of here." With that, Fish kicked the brakes on the gurney up, pivoted the direction the wheels were facing, and was off out the door.

Stunned on-lookers, mostly patients waiting for outpatient scans, looked shocked. The x-ray department staff looked shocked. Gina for a split second also looked shocked, and even a bit tearful realizing that her patient she picked up from Harry was now dying. But she grabbed the airway roll and the celluloid scan and followed Fish and Sam to the service elevator and pushed the down button repeatedly.

In what seemed like forever to her the wait for the elevator was only a minute. Just as the doors were closing behind them, she reached out to stop it and shouted to the tech, "Call the

ER, tell them we are coming, and to open the resus room now!" She withdrew her arm and the elevator disappeared into the basement.

The sprint through the basement was easy. Their running footsteps made an eerie echo off the walls and tiles. Sam was bagging the patient and the exhaled air was the rhythm they ran to. No one was down there and it was a straight shot back to the elevator that would take them up to the ER. Gina was able to run ahead near the end and get to the elevator first, where again she repeatedly pushed the up button over and over. This time the elevator opened instantly. She held the door and Fish and the gurney with the sleeping man rolled in. Fish felt for a carotid pulse once in the elevator, his head bobbed up and down ever so slightly as his head unconsciously moved in time to the now bounding pulse. Sam kept bagging the man at a steady pace through the endotracheal tube he had placed in the patient's mouth. Fish could tell his was counting in his head to remember to keep it regular.

When the elevator doors opened on the floor to the ER, Snider was waiting there along with an orderly and two nurses. Snider grabbed the CT scan out of Gina's hands and held it up to the overhead fluorescent lights. "Damn, he's got a subdural. OK, we need to do this fast, two minutes here to get lines and send labs and a type and cross and we are up to the OR." He looked at Gina, who now was the only one without something to do, and asked, "Can you shave his head in less than two minutes?"

Gina, not knowing what to say just nodded once. This time she did not hesitate.

Into Room One they all rolled and like a precision team, each nurse took an arm and inserted an IV line, drawing bloods. The blood was handed off to the orderly who applied patient labels to all of them and ran out to the front desk. Sally, the desk clerk looked up and said, "There is someone from medicine calling from x-ray somewhere wanting to know about the code blue. Is this that guy?" Apparently, the medicine code team had just shown up at the right building after getting lost. In that time Fish's team had run a quarter of a mile in each direction, intubated the patient, and got the wheels moving to get the OR ready. Before the clerk could get an answer, she turned around as the patient and the team with Snider in the lead rolled back out of Room One, back to the elevator to the OR. Snider yelled, "Get me two units of blood to the OR" as the cluster of nurse and orderlies passed the desk. Just as suddenly as they appeared, the elevator doors closed behind them, and the ER for a brief moment was silent.

THE COUNTY

Sam was even more exhausted than when he finished his 24-hour shift three hours ago. He just looked at Gina and said, "Well, that was different."

Gina was upset, it was her patient now, but laid the blame squarely where she thought it belonged, "That was Harry's mess. He forgot to sign that patient out at change of shift. He should have got a CT when the guy first came in too." Gina already didn't like Harry from the day before when he asked her where her hometown in Mexico was and forced the decision to have Gina work an extra day.

Fish looked at both of them, "No blame game stuff. Just take care of patients. We won't call Harry if he's likely asleep." Turning to Sam, "Which is where you should be, but thanks for helping. But go home now. Gina, back into the fray, to work, the pit calls."

CHAPTER 17

HARRY AWOKE AND IT WAS light out. July in California and the sun set late. He squinted at the blinds in the window of his bedroom. He did not know what time it was. At first, he thought he needed to go back to the ER because it was morning again, but he found his watch on his upturned box that served as his night stand. It was late evening and he knew he had better get some more sleep as he was due back in the ER at 7 am. He pulled the covers over his head but couldn't fall back asleep. All sorts of thoughts and questions raced through his head again. *Should I call the ER and find out what happened to the guy in the back hall? Yeah I really should call. What if they're busy? I don't* *want to bother Gina again; we did not get off on the right foot.* He thought better to wait and find out in the morning and he drifted off to asleep.

When his alarm went off at 6:00 he was already running behind. He showered, put on his scrubs, ate a chocolate bar he accidentally left in his white coat pocket, and found his car keys. When he got to the ER, he heard the first words out of Gina's mouth that no one working in the ER ever wants to hear, "Do you remember that guy you left me with last night?" Gina then unloaded all her pent-up anger on Harry.

Harry just kept saying, "I'm sorry," as Gina ranted on. He was already feeling bad about the patient, but now he was being bawled-out by a fellow intern, someone who was supposed to be his friend. His devil-may-care attitude had been taken down several notches. Gina was still steamed when she finished, but she just wanted to go home, and finally let up on Harry. He said his final "I'm really sorry," and she left.

Sam was already in the process of taking his sign-out from Wilson who seemed more upset than Harry. "I had four people with back pain, three wanted pain meds, and the last one did not want to go to work for his night shift and needed a note, then walked out of here like he was hustling to go somewhere. Fish was okay with just giving them a six-pack of pain pills,

T-3s, just to clear the board. What garbage, I was not practicing medicine the way I was taught to do, doing a complete history and physical. I even wanted to get an X-ray on a few, but Fish said the X-rays are generally worthless unless there is a history of direct trauma. Then there was a mom who brought in four of her own kids and a cousin who all got sick throwing up at a picnic. Ich, kids again. Fish said the history and physical are worth more than all the labs in the world, and did not want any. He gave them Compazine suppositories and send them all home. What did I do for those kids, nothing I have been trained for? I finally have one real medicine patient to sign out to you, but I am okay staying at least until he gets an X-ray. This 45-year-old guy with progressive trouble breathing and weight loss. I heard rales and decreased breath sounds on the right, and on exam I percussed some dullness posteriorly. I think he has a new effusion and wanted to tap it. Make a diagnosis. He just went down for a chest film."

"Listen, Wilson, I am happy to follow up and do the tap. I over-stayed yesterday and Fish warned me to go home and sleep at the end of each shift. So, it's okay. Go home, get some rest, you are back in the morning after all. You can't live in the hospital. That's why we have a sign-out system."

"No, I'll want to wait for the chest X-ray, it shouldn't hold me up for more than a few minutes while I finish some notes. I just want to see if my suspicion by my exam pans out with the film."

Wilson was right, *he should trust his clinical skills*, he thought. The chest X-ray showed fluid three-quarters of the way up his right pleural cavity, the space around his right lung. Sam tried to reassure Wilson he would do the procedure. It was clear Wilson was tired, and the procedure would probably take at least an hour or more to set up and do. Wilson wouldn't let it go. It was his case, a real medicine case for once, and he was not going to sign out a procedure of all things to another intern. So, in an effort to help Wilson, Sam consented the patient and moved the patient to Room Seven. Wilson went to talk with the new attending, Brent Plumber, to get his approval for the procedure and see if he wanted to stand by and watch him do it. Brent's style was quick and to the point, a looser-control attending. He certainly wasn't as long-winded as Fish. He okayed a lot of what the interns wanted to do if it made sense, without any long discussion. He perceived most of his job as verifying the behavior of otherwise good interns, and only stepping in to avoid disaster. They needed to learn from being in the moment, much like he was taught.

"Have you done a thoracentesis before?" Brent asked about the tap to drain his lung.

"Yeah, I did a few medicine wards at Duke. Lots of little old ladies with heart failure and fluid on their lungs. They needed to do this once or twice a week when I was there." Wilson replied.

That was good enough for Brent. When he asked if you knew how to do something and you said yes, he assumed you did or would say so. But it was only the Fourth of July weekend, and no matter how good their medical school was, even at Duke, nobody was so good that they did not need some oversight. Your highest chance of being killed by a medical error was on the Fourth of July. Brent Plumber, having a full ER to run, sized Wilson up as someone who likely knew what he was doing. He told Wilson, "Take the patient to the back and get it done."

Room Seven was as far back and out of sight as someone could go to get it done. That was the only bed available when Sam moved the patient. It did not have the best lighting to do a procedure such as this. Wilson had bragged just a bit about his experience. In Duke he only just assisted on those thoracenteses as a medical student, not done one from start to finish. But the mantra was see one, do one, and teach one. Wilson was confident he was ready to do one.

THE COUNTY

Mr. Duffy was the patient who needed his lung tapped by Wilson. He was a chain-smoking wiry man, craggy-faced and bald. What wisps of hair he had around his temples were prematurely gray. His face was wrinkled by time and circumstance, making him seem years older than the forty or so years he actually lived. It probably was his work. He had worked as an exterminator his whole life since high school, spraying all sorts of poison on all sorts of critters. Usually smoking his next cigarette right after each application, his fingers were still wet with the pesticides he used. Wilson thumped with one finger over the knuckle of another finger on his other hand, as he moved down his patient's back checking for the dull thud that meant there was fluid in his chest. Lots of reasons for Duffy's chest fluid went through Wilson's brain, but almost everything he could think of was some type of cancer causing the fluid accumulation. Only inserting a needle, tapping the fluid out of his chest, and sending it to pathology would let him know which type. Wilson repeated his exam convinced now that it exactly matched the X-ray. It was dull to percussion nearly everywhere on his right chest. He prepped the patient's back with betadine, a brown antiseptic solution, and taped a sterile barrier over his chest. The thoracentesis kit had a single large evacuated container, a one-liter bottle with nothing in it, with the air vacuumed out so that when a needle was inserted through the rubber membrane on top the fluid that flowed through that needle spurted into the empty bottle. A vacuum evacuated container worked much faster than by gravity alone. All was going well as Wilson adjusted the goose-neck lamp over his shoulder, put on sterile gloves, and injected a small bit of local anesthetic over the top of one of the Duffy's ribs. The needle popped through into his pleural cavity easily and Wilson advanced a long plastic catheter through the metal sheath of the needle, as far as it could go into the space between the chest wall and the patient's lung. *That was the tricky part.* Wilson did not hit the lung, a frequent rookie mistake, he was feeling really confident as the empty container filled. Straw-colored fluid flowed out of the catheter into the evacuated liter bottle, filling it under 10 minutes. Mr. Duffy sat his arms crossed on a rolling dinner tray table facing away from Wilson. He was comfortable and Wilson asked him how he was doing a few times during the drainage. He indicated it was all okay, giving Wilson a thumb's up sign each time. But given the size of the patient's fluid collection around his lungs, the one bottle Wilson had was not going to be enough, and he had brought only one with him to the back of Room Seven. The flow slowed as the fluid neared the top of the bottle.

Wilson called out, "Can I get some help please?" to see if anyone could bring him another. No one answered. Wilson yelled louder; still no response. Room Seven was sufficiently isolated from the main action of the emergency department that a nurse rarely came back there. Brent wasn't coming back to check on him either. Wilson knew he would have to unglove and go find another bottle himself. He told Duffy, who seemed to understand, to stay still and that he would be right back. All Duffy wanted to know was if he could get a smoke when it was done. Wilson told him absolutely not. Wilson went to the stock room and opened all the drawers and found an evacuated vacuum bottle. Wilson could not have been gone more than five minutes. When he got back to Room Seven Duffy was lying back in bed, smiling for the first time since coming to the ER, smoking a cigarette, his nasal oxygen still in his nose.

"Oh, that feels great doc," he said, "I could barely inhale one of these for weeks before you fixed me."

"No, no!" Wilson said, "there's a tube still in your back," as he frantically dialed the oxygen off at the wall. The last thing Wilson needed was a fire.

"I got tired of waiting, and pulled it out"

"What? You can't do that. Turn over let me see it."

When the patient turned over there was a little hole in his right chest still oozing a bit of blood and the plastic catheter and metal sheath were lying on the gurney beside him. Or at least he thought so. After a closer look Wilson immediately concluded that the catheter on the bed was now too short. Much shorter than the one he used to drain the fluid. Wilson swung the stethoscope off his neck and asked his patient to take a few deep breaths as he listened. The breath sounds were fine. *Where was the other half of the catheter?* It dawned on Wilson that after pulling up the sheets and looking on the floor that the only place it could be was still inside the patient. *Crap*, he thought, and put a gauze pad over the hole tapped a bent paper clip pointing to the opening, and went out to the desk to ordered an X-ray.

Wilson walked into the real Room Eight, the radio room, to wait for the X-ray and to sort out what he was going to tell Brent, and what he would say to the patient. Harry was in there leaning over holding his head with both hands. He jerked up when Wilson entered. Wilson

THE COUNTY

could tell he was upset. "What's up, man? Are you okay?" he asked. Inside he felt the same way, but maybe not this bad.

Harry told the story about the sleeping drunk from last night, with the follow-up that Wilson did not know yet, ".... and then they took him to the OR and did a burr hole first got out some blood and then he needed a craniotomy. He is still in the recovery room, intubated on deep sedation. There are no ICU beds to transfer him to. He has been in post-op for hours and likely to spend overnight there. I went up to see him and he is completely out of it. No movement, no withdrawal. I am screwed. I messed up on my first day. This is going to be the first case at Morbidity and Mortality conference next week, and I will get raked over the coals."

Trying to sound positive Wilson told Harry, "Well, it's probably not as bad as all that. He is still alive? Isn't he? Have they repeated the head CT?"

"Good idea." Harry brightened and ran out. "I'll check in X-ray to see if they ordered one post-op."

"Wait, I'll go with you. I have a film of my own to see."

Harry found the second CT on his patient, and it looked like all the blood was now gone.

Sure enough, when Wilson looked at Duffy's chest X-ray there was a dark paperclip pointing to an opaque strait plastic tube inside his chest. About half the fluid was gone, and the lung that had reinflated behind it looked hazy. Wilson was trying to convince himself that there was a tumor there. Hoping that if he needed surgery for that, they would remove the catheter tube along with a cancer. Wilson checked with Benny, the radiology resident sitting there calmly reading X-rays that morning. He looked over the chest X-ray carefully, but said he could not tell for sure, but maybe a CT could help.

When Wilson went back to talk with his patient, to tell him he was going to get a CT, he was gone. The nurse told Wilson he said he was going to go out to smoke after she yelled at him that there was no smoking in the ER. Wilson ran out the front ambulance door to find him. He kept screaming outside the ambulance entrance, "Mr. Duffy! Mr. Duffy!" But he was gone. Wilson searched the waiting room, the bathrooms, and every other room and hall, but Duffy was long gone. Wilson tried to find Brent to tell him what had happened, but Brent was tied up in the ortho room with the orthopedic saw whirring so loudly he could not hear. By this time Wilson was too stressed and tired to do anything else, he had been up for 27 hours and it was time to go home and sleep. He told Sam he was officially signing out to him this time and went home.

Later Wilson checked on the final radiologist's read of Duffy's chest X-rays—no cancer. He checked the fluid results—no cancer. It was a transudate, just clear fluids from some heart failure. Wilson thought he would never see Mr. Duffy again, or worse he would turn up and sue him. He felt some empathy for Harry, both of them now being in the same situation with first day errors. As it turns out, Duffy came back many times during Wilson's internship. He always said, "there's the doc that saved my life. He even let me smoke after he drained my lung." Wilson would shake his head no, no, no in the background, and wave both is hands furiously in front of him, not wanting anyone to think he would do something like that. But Wilson kept the sheared-off catheter a secret. It never bothered Duffy, and Wilson never had the nerve to tell the patient after he kept thanking him every time he saw him.

Harry more or less survived his first-day foibles as well. Harry was nervous about every patient he took care of after that. It took a month but the craniotomy patient woke up. He had a tracheostomy placed after a week on the ventilator, but by the time he was discharged to a skilled nursing facility four weeks later, it too was removed. He could speak with a bit of a slurred phonation and walk with a wide swinging leg motion on his right. The repeat head CT that Harry looked at that night was impressively free of brain swelling, in fact, his brain looked shrunk if anything. And that's what ultimately saved him. By having chronic brain atrophy there was enough space so that when his slowly progressing subdural started to press on his brain he did not feel it. That and a blood alcohol four times the legal limit made him sleep through the event and show no outward signs of injury. A review of his chart, which Harry did several times before the Morbidity and Mortality conference, showed multiple ER visits for alcohol intoxication, bar fights, facial trauma, and head trauma. After the ER visits piled up, the reflex to immediately get a head CT on him waned with each visit, and the evolving tactic was to give him a few hours to sleep it off and see what happens. Harry lost the medical Russian Roulette game because the night he was on was one where the patient was not going just sleep off his drunk; he actually had a brain bleed.

None of this would matter when Harry had to face the chief of surgery, Dr. Westman, in the

M and M. Westman was the opposite of Snider. He did not yell. He did not throw instruments in the OR, as many surgeons did when they were upset. He was a calm scholarly gentleman. He always wore a plaid bowtie when outside the operating room and spoke softly, and people always listened. In the Morbidity and Mortality conference, the doctor and his judgement are dissected in front of an auditorium of his peers. Owning your mistakes in a bad case while humiliating was designed for all to learn, and all to hope that it never happens to them. It was an essential passage of medical training, Westman just asked probing questions until the truth came out, there was a bit of tch-tch in his soft voice as his head shook once side to side, when you ultimately walked yourself into a bad decision in the case. He peered over the top of his half-frame glasses and stared at you for just that extra second that made you feel so very small. Then he said, "so let's continue, after that error what happened?"

The pendulum swung eventually on the use of CT scans from the ER. In time studies were done to create a set of rules to justify their frequent use. Then the ER went overboard ordering CTs on just about every case anyway despite these rules. No one wanted to be in Harry's position. Soon the CT scanners themselves were moved closer to the ER, not down long hallways far away. When patients left the ER, they also went with a nurse and airway equipment if they were unstable. And some even got intubated first to protect them from running a code in the X-ray department, acknowledged as the second worst place in the hospital to run a code blue. (The debate continued whether the worst was the cafeteria or the parking lot) But even as some procedures got better, bad things will always happen in the ER, often at night, predictably on the Fourth of July, and an intern never got over the phrase, "remember that patient you left me last night?"

CHAPTER 18

THAT FIRST MONTH OF JULY went by and the interns probably learned more than ever before in their lives and saw more suffering than they knew existed. It was their first impression of real-world medicine. In 30 days, they each worked at least 360 hours, a 90-hour work week on average. They saw mundane cases like sore throats and sprained ankles. They saw complicated medical cases like heart failure, asthma, diabetic coma, and gastric bleeding from ulcers. They saw the ravages of alcoholism with cirrhosis and seizures. They saw subtle trauma like Harry's drunk who fell down and had a slowly evolving subdural, and major trauma like auto crashes and gunshot wounds. As it turns out, there were lots of gunshot wounds! They saw people in the throes of severe mental crises with decompensated schizophrenia, domestic violence, and suicide attempts, some fatal. There was no textbook to help them through the enormity of what they could see and treat in a day, but there was Fish, and the other senior residents who had just a year or so more experience to guide them. The last morning of July at change of shift Fish took the team to the cafeteria to buy everyone coffee and talk. It was a surprisingly quiet morning for the ER, so they could spare the group for a while.

Harry was first in line and reached into the bakery display and pulled out an oversized slice of Boston cream pie.

"How can you eat that for breakfast?" Gina, making a face, asked.

"How can you not? I love this stuff. I could not get this in Mexico and here it is every day on the bakery carousel calling my name. I had a lot of churros down in Guadalajara, do you eat those? They're damn good too."

"No, that's not a Cuban thing." She frowned at Harry thinking he would know better by now. "I don't know if Boston cream pie is really a Boston dish. I lived in Boston for eight years, college and med school, and probably only ate that once. Just called them chocolate cream pies then. I'll stick to my Dannon yogurt, thanks. Although I get tired of their four basic flavors. You know how many calories are in that pile of cream?"

Fish called from the back of the line, "I'm paying, gotta clear my meal card for the month. Never get down here much, so I got a lot of backed up food credit. Treat yourselves." With that Harry grabbed a second Boston cream pie and a carton of chocolate milk off the rack.

Wilson said to the group, "I miss my mom's Southern breakfast. But a stack of hot cakes and a rasher of sausage works for me. More of a midwestern breakfast, really. But best you'll do out here in California I guess."

Sam only filled up a Styrofoam coffee cup with black coffee.

"Go and treat yourself to something more," Fish encouraged him as he picked up a bagel. "You guys all worked hard and deserve at least one good breakfast this month."

"I never was a big breakfast eater," said Sam, "My ideal breakfast is when my dad had to make a pickup for the store over the bridge in Canada early mornings and took me along. A cup of hot Tim Horton's black coffee hit the spot on a cold Buffalo morning."

The sat at a long cafeteria table on the wobbly orange plastic chairs. Gina wiped the table off with a napkin before she put her food down. "This place always has the weird bleach odor. Enough to spoil your appetite. Would make for a great fad diet," she said.

"So, what do the four of you want to do with your lives now that you have tasted some real medicine?" Fish asked after they all sat down.

Harry spoke first, "Maybe rheumatology? Arthritis patients don't die on you." He shoved another piece of pie into his mouth and washed it down with a gulp of chocolate milk trying hard not to talk with his mouth full. "The office hours are 9 to 5. I won't get rich, but I won't get sued either. This whole month all I did is worry about missing something on every case and having to face another M and M, or worse some lawyer coming down the hall to serve me a subpoena."

"Well, we are all in internal medicine right now, aren't we?" asked Wilson gesticulating with a half a sausage on the end of his fork. "Why must we be something more than that? People regard the internists as the smartest in the hospital, the sharpest knife in the drawer. Broad-minded enough to solve all problems. Know all diseases. The surgeon may get the glory, but as an internist, I will get all the respect." Wilson emphasized his conclusion by putting the rest of his sausage in his mouth, and smiled chewing it.

"All right, fair enough. What about you Gina?" Fish asked next.

"Can't say for sure. I like taking care of sick people, patients who need my skills, but I can't see myself living in the hospital." She stirred the peaches from the bottom of her yogurt, "I have a cardiology rotation later so I want to see what that's like."

"Cards is good, challenging,' Fish said nodding, "Lots of new procedures coming up. Now is the right era to join that specialty. You'll work hard and there will be long hours though. The old boys in it still think it's a 9 to 5 job, but its changing fast."

"I just need to get past those quote 'old boys' to get my foot in the door," Gina replied.

"And you Sam?"

"Is ER an actual job?" Sam asked.

"It's a job, but it may not be a career. There is no such thing as a board-certified ER doc, like a board-certified surgeon or internist, or cardiologist. There are maybe a half-dozen new residencies popping up mainly in county hospitals around the country like Denver General and Bellevue, but not in university hospitals."

"What about here?" Sam asked, "Wouldn't this be a good place to train to do that? I've mostly run from really sick patient to really sick patient all month long. It's been a great education."

Fish was quick to jump off on his favorite topic, "Since County is a hybrid of both this would be a great place to have an emergency residency, but I am pretty sure the administrators don't want it. Anyway, right now, you can always work in the ER but no one will ever say thank you or show you one iota of respect. Not like Wilson is talking about." He wiped some cream cheese off his mustache with the back of one hand, and went on, "Right now, the hospital bigwigs assume the ER is a place for misfits and washouts. They will always expect you do more at off hours and nights, and then criticize you for it. The patients will yell at you, the specialists will yell at you, and the hospital administrators will yell at you. And like I said before, everyone will be trying to kill your patient, but you. Since no one has any insurance if they come to the ER, no one pays their bills, so the hospital won't invest any money in improving our equipment or staff. And most of all, you have to be super thick-skinned, not second guess your split-second decisions. Know your stuff and be damn sure of yourself. That's the watchword in the ER—it's not a crime to be wrong, but it is to be unsure."

"I could certainly do that. This last month, whoa, what an incredible mix of patients." Sam almost stood out of his seat just talking about it.

"But, what about you Fish? You may have a year on us, but ultimately won't you have to choose a specialty, too?"

"Actually, it's two years. I did a surgical internship first. It was a typical pyramid system. They started with eight interns and worked them to death on-call every other night for the whole year. At the end of the first year, they eliminate two interns and move forward with six residents. Nothing like the sword of Damocles hanging over your head constantly to put the fear of God in you to work harder or be cut. Another year of every other night on-call, where, as the expression goes, you miss half the pathology because you only work every other day. At the end of the second year, two more residents are cut. Down to four, and over each of the next three years anyone could be cut until they only graduate one, or maybe two. Sometimes the chair will even hold one of those back to do another year based on his assessment of your ability to be a surgeon. Sometimes it's just to solve a short-staffing issue because they don't have enough residents that year. Anyway, I got cut after the first year and stayed here last year for a repeat year one in medicine instead. I have both medical skills and a few surgical skills, and agree with Sam. Wouldn't it be great if we could just train docs to be here in the ER and make critical care decisions and do procedures and diagnose new and complicated medical problems?"

The whole group nodded. Sam was drawn in. Fish continued, "In fact, my vision is even broader than that. What if we had a handle on training everyone in the emergency system along a continuum? Starting with the 911 dispatcher who takes a call and can give you first aid instructions, or even talks you through CPR. Then train the paramedics so they did not have to call in and ask permission for every drug they want to administer. They would be able to act reflexively based on protocols. We certainly could give them more drugs to use, maybe even pain meds for broken bones. Next, the patient comes into the ER where we train you to stabilize them. We would need all the tools the hospital has but they would need to be dedicated to us, our own radiology department, our own CT scanner, our own rapid labs. A full residency of docs dedicated to just doing emergency care, not a rotating roster of internists, family medicine, and the occasional subspecialist who are a fish out of water down here. And finally, we also would be in the ICUs, since we are at our core internal medicine docs, so there is a seamless continuity of care all the way through. If I could run a program like that, I'd be happy. But it does not exist, but one day I hope I can make it happen." Fish looked away into the distance a bit. The interns all sat entranced. This was a blueprint for medicine into the next century, and no one yet appreciated it. But Sam most of all, wanted to believe him. He had been nodding in agreement all through Fish's rant. First impressions count, and Sam's first impression of working in the ER was that it could be a career for life, and if he could point back years later, he knew it got started that day in the cafeteria listening to Fish.

CHAPTER 19

SAM'S SECOND ROTATION WAS IN the medical ICU. Rooms Nine and Ten had since been added as the step-down units, each had four beds with no barriers between patients. It was out of necessity that they mixed male and female patients in those rooms. The ICU itself was across the hall, it too had an extra rooms added since Fish was an intern, through a doorway into another former double room. The main ICU was now three interconnected rooms each with three beds. Seventeen beds in all, a change from just four beds in two double rooms from the prior year. This meant more patients for the intern and resident, and a lot more work.

The attending was a pulmonary specialist named Jamison. Dr. Jamison was tall, athletic and clean-shaven, curly-haired, skinny as a pole and looked like a basketball player. Jamison started early before rounds the first day with his new interns, including Sam, and explained the history of critical care, "ICUs are in a state of rapid evolution, as are the specialists who care for patients in them. Last year, all these rooms were just double occupancy floor beds. The need for a special place with critically ill patients came with the invention of the ventilator. Don't know if you know this but the very first ICU was set up by a group of Scandinavian anesthesiologists."

He paused and looked at each of the two new interns to make sure they were still listening. "When a polio epidemic broke out in 1953, the Blegham Hospital in Copenhagen were still using the iron lung, and no one had thought about using a ventilator outside an operating room. Two docs there, Ibsen and Lassen, suggested using the ventilators that were used only during surgery, and kept all their polio patients in one unit to be watched carefully. They were able to reduce the fatality rate in half. This was the very first Intensive Care Unit."

"But we have had ventilators in the US for many years now since then," Sam added, "Why are the ICUs only a few years old?"

Jamison continued, "What made the practice of ICU care in the U.S. practical was a small portable ventilator. An Army pilot named Forrest Bird invented a portable device to deliver oxygen. After tinkering with some early prototypes, the seventh version he invented was able to be mass-produced. It was called the Mark—7. As it evolved over the 1970s it was the simplest portable device, it was just called a Bird, after its inventor." Jamison showed Sam the pale translucent green box the size of a toaster that was breathing for one of the patients in the ICU. It had only two dials and a pressure gauge and on the green box was word Bird. It could be set for only two variables, how deep each breath was and how many breaths per minute you wanted the patient to have. It hung from an upside-down metal U-shaped arm on a rolling stand so that it could be rolled down to the ER for a newly intubated patient.

"But as portable and simple as the Bird is," Jamison went on to the next patient and showed the group a big box ventilator about the size of an outdoor air-conditioning unit. "This is the modern work horse of our ICU. Unfortunately, it also cost a lot more money and hospitals don't buy that many, figuring the much cheaper Bird worked in most situations." Jamison flipped the top cover over on the big box and there were a dozen or more dials and switches. With it they could control the rate, depth, how long each breath was held for, something called positive pressure, and even waveform. All highly technical manipulations that were advancements over the two-dial Bird ventilator. But it was big and expensive, and the County did not have many of these specialized units to use for the ICU.

Sam was to soon learn that ninety percent of taking care of patients in the ICU was ventilator management, learning when and how each of those dials and switches were used to help different types of patients who could not breathe for themselves. After surviving their ICU course on a ventilator, when the time was right and the patient had improved, the breathing tube could be removed, the patient was extubated, the reverse process of intubation. Given the need for ICU bed space, the extubated patient was moved across the hall to Rooms Nine or Ten. These were called step-down units, because care for these patients was a step down from the one-on-one intensive care of a patient on a ventilator. Rooms Nine and Ten was where the interns mostly lived, where Sam got to know his new patients that morning, who for starting out as a new intern, they were slightly less critical cases.

Kip Drysdale, the senior internal medicine resident, managed the nine beds in the three rooms that made up the ICU proper. Every morning, everyone rounded on all 17 of the patients in the ICU and step-down units, so that anyone could respond to a crisis in any patient, not just their own patient. This was a program of comprehensive rounds that started with a suggestion by Fish.

Sam found out during rounds there were three very large men all intubated at the same time, one in each of the three rooms that formed the main ICU. There were two other patients alongside each of them in each of the three rooms, but the large men would be the most difficult to care for. The little Bird ventilators had met their match with these three, and each of large men needed one of the larger box ventilators that were more sophisticated. Ever since the Jablonski incident with Fish, where he had to bag a newly intubated overdose patient all night, the hospital had invested in more ventilators, but only four were the high quality big box for long-term complicated patients. The Medical ICU had control over the box vents. There were probably a dozen or more portable Bird vents for the ICU, post-operative units, and elsewhere, but since the hospital only had four of these box ventilators sometime in the middle of morning rounds, Jablonski would come by to ask the ICU team, as he put it, "when we were going to get the fat men off the vents?" He was of course no one to talk, the pot calling the three kettles so to speak. But here was this external pressure to free up at least one of the three box vents in case one was needed in an emergency. For two weeks Jamison resisted. The patients were getting better, but not enough to come off the vent. That's when the ER called.

CHAPTER 20

SAM WENT DOWN TO THE ER with the team, Jamison, the attending, and Drysdale, the internal medicine resident. The case they were called to was puzzling. Barbara Warren was a young woman just 20 years old, who came in overnight with a fever and a diffuse red rash. She initially thought she maybe had the measles, but she knew she had all her immunizations from public-school. She worked in an office and was still dressed in her business clothes; she did not appear to be a typical County patient. She had become increasingly light-headed at work and by the time she got home she could barely stand up. She called her mom who lived nearby, and her parents drove her to the ER. Barbara had just got a new job in this office and had no medical insurance yet. The County was the only place they knew would see her. Other hospitals always asked for cash upfront at registration. Her parents stood near the bed with that "worried parent" look on their faces. Things had only got worse each time someone came in to ask more questions. Her labs were a mess, too. Low platelet count, high white count, renal failure, mildly elevated liver tests, but all of her work-up for a possible cause of infection were negative. The doctors asked questions about her travels and any sick co-workers, but there was none. The resident in the ER already had given her IV fluid boluses but these were not good enough to bring her low blood pressure up, so he added dopamine and called the ICU team.

Once Jamison looked her over and the team brought her up to the ICU, a central IV line was placed, and through that, a new device called a Swan was inserted by Jamison into her heart. Sam watched as Jamison explained its purpose. "This new device in critical care and cardiology is a Swan-Ganz catheter, named after the two doctors who invented it. It was thin and had a small balloon at the end. The idea was to get it into the heart from the subclavian vein and take pressures and measure forward flow to calculate cardiac output. With those numbers we can gauge fluid and dopamine resuscitation." After they ran the first set of determinations it was shocking, for a 20-year-old girl, Barbara Warren had the cardiac output of an 80-year-old with heart failure. *What was going on?* Antibiotics were started.

Kip Drysdale paged the infectious disease specialist. A woman named Dr. Kane responded and came to the ICU to look over the new patient. She was very comprehensive and even did a pelvic exam, where she removed a large tampon. She cultured it, along with the girl's blood, urine, and her sputum. She was writing a note when she got up and walked over to the ICU team and said, "I think this is Toxic Shock. I have never seen an actual case, and you are not going to believe this, but it's on the cover of the National Enquirer magazine. It may be related to some brands of tampons left in too long. The rash in the pictures looks identical to your case."

Jamison looked skeptical, "What are you talking about? Is this a real disease or a new alien scare from the tabloids?"

"No, it's real, the Enquirer is not my usual source for this, but it just so happens it ran a story the same week that a CDC report came out about a new entity affecting only young women. To date, they don't know exactly what causes it. It could be a staph infection or some new organism, and no, not aliens from space."

"What else do we need to do for her? We already have double antibiotics, Naf and Gent going, both should kill staph."

"I think I just performed the critical maneuver. I pulled out her tampon and removed the source of the problem." She looked at Jamison and then to Drysdale. "My guess is neither of you would have looked there."

Jamison titrated up the dopamine and ran the Swan numbers again. They looked a little better. But he was not convinced about the Toxic Shock diagnosis. That night the Toxic-Shock girl, as she was starting to be called, started dropping her oxygen saturations. Jamison and the resident both agreed she would need to be intubated. Jamison ordered them to start with a Bird ventilator because that's all they had in the unit for immediate use, but he knew it would have been better to treat a patient like this with pulmonary failure with the big box ventilator. Of the four box ventilators the hospital had, three were in use here in the ICU, and the fourth was in use down the hall in the cardiac unit. Jamison had no choice but to start the Toxic Shock girl with the Bird ventilator.

The Toxic Shock girl hung in there on the Bird ventilator for two days, but her oxygen started to fall. Sam watched as they calculated her numbers several times a day. On the third day of her ICU stay, Jamison attempted to wean the smallest of the big men with pneumonia off the box ventilator. After about two hours on a T-piece he felt comfortable enough to extubate him. First, he sent the box ventilator down to respiratory care for cleaning so he could use it for the Toxic Shock girl. When it came back up Jamison had the respiratory tech hooked her up and added PEEP, or positive-end expiratory pressure, something they could not do with the Bird ventilator, and immediately her numbers came up. Meanwhile, the smallest big man with pneumonia was holding on with a high-flow oxygen mask. The third day passed without any problems. Sam's team admitted a diabetic in ketoacidosis, but he did not require any ventilators.

In the wee hours of the morning on the fourth day, both the Toxic Shock girl and the pneumonia man took a turn for the worst. Sam stayed up all night in the unit when he was on call, which was every third night. Even though there was a sleep room down the hall, Sam needed to be in the ICU room to monitor all the patients. It was 4:45 am and first, the big man's oxygen level desaturated so much that the high-flow oxygen mask was not helping. Sam knew he would need to be intubated again. He pre-oxygenated him as much as possible and then climbed up on the metal rail at the head of the bed, and with two hands on the laryngoscope pulling with all his might towards the ceiling, Drysdale assisting him slipped the endotracheal tube into his vocal cords.

The respiratory tech hooked up the Bird ventilator at 100% and hoped for the best. But Jamison knew it was not going to be enough, they needed to pull the box ventilator off the Toxic Shock girl and switch it to the man who just got intubated. The Toxic Shock girl would have to get by with the less efficient Bird ventilator. So, Barbara Warren's box ventilator went down to respiratory care for a STAT clean. Twenty minutes later as Sam's fingers were getting numb from squeezing the bag to ventilate the patient who needed the clean ventilator, it returned. They hooked the big box ventilator back up to the big man and his numbers held. He needed the extra PEEP setting that only the box ventilator had to maintain them.

Now Jamison had to send the Bird ventilator that the pneumonia man was using back down for a clean. Sam switched from bagging the man with pneumonia to bagging the Toxic Shock girl. Another twenty minutes of squeezing and letting go for Sam, but it was easier on the smaller girl. The Bird came back up cleaned, and she was hooked up too, a ventilator swap completed. She was able to keep her saturation at 80 % oxygen and she held steady. Sam called for early morning portable chest X-rays to see where things were at with both of them. His fingers were still cramping from bagging through the ventilator switch when a nurse came and called for him to get to the first room. The big man had just coded. This time Sam jumped up on the bed itself to get enough height above the patient's chest since doing effective compressions was going to be a chore. Sam straddled him and started pumping on his chest, while the resident took over the bagging duties. Sam had to jump down every time they placed the paddles on his chest to defibrillate him, so he would not get shocked when they yelled "all clear" then jump back up on the chest, straddling the big man to continue CPR. They went on for over an hour. The patient went in and out of a sustainable rhythm, then back into ventricular tachycardia. Sam ran the code and he ran through several doses of lidocaine and bretylium, and dozens of doses of epinephrine every five minutes, but after 70 minutes the patient was flat-line and there was no getting him back.

After the code Sam was drenched in sweat, his arms were aching, and he was having trouble breathing. His fingers were still numb from all the mechanical bagging to breathe for the patients. The coding patient was incontinent of stool and the room reeked. There was no place to shower, but Sam threw some water on his face and hair in the sink. When he looked up in the mirror above the sink and he saw quite a sight. His hair was matted, something was smeared on his chin, he thought maybe sputum. No sleep in 20 hours, and he just had a major workout from the code. Sam's scrubs were soaked in sweat down his neck and armpits. More running on adrenaline than exhaustion, he was dizzy. But inside he felt as though he was making a difference. Someone had to be up in the ICU in the middle of the night and Sam wasn't tired, he was jazzed up.

He had but a second to consider his reflection in the mirror when the nurse called him back to the third room of the ICU. The Toxic Shock girl had dropped her oxygen saturation to the 70 % range and her heart rate shot up to 150. *What the hell is going on now?* Sam probably needed to get her back on a big box vent. He asked the nurse to have someone run the box vent from the now-deceased big man so it could be STAT cleaned. But Sam also worried about something else, patients who are stuck in bed for several days often had a pulmonary embolism, and maybe that was the reason for the sudden deterioration. *Do I have enough suspicion to start her on blood thinners without a scan? No!* Sam picked up the phone to call nuclear medicine. The only way to diagnose a pulmonary embolism was with a nuclear medicine VQ scan. (The CT of the chest to make the diagnosis would not come into use for another decade) The phone to nuclear med rang and rang and rang. Sam hung up and redialed, again lots of ringing without anyone picking up. *What is wrong down there, it's already 8 they should be in house already.* He told his resident, "I am heading down to nuclear med, have them bring the big box vent down there when it is clean and we can hook her back up to PEEP while they are scanning her." Sam grabbed a D-cylinder of oxygen, the size of a scuba tank, and clicked the brakes off the wheel locks on the bed and started to roll to the elevator with the bed, and the little green Mark-7 Bird hanging from its U support on wheels.

CHAPTER 21

FIVE FLOORS DOWN IN THE characteristically calm nuclear medicine department, everyone was just getting into work. They all had coffee cups and some were reading the newspaper. The secretary had not come in yet, so no one thought much about the phone that kept ringing, then stopping, then ringing again. Ding, the elevator door opened and Sam rolled in, an oxygen D-cylinder over his shoulder, bagging the Toxic Shock girl and rolled past the empty chairs of the waiting area through the double-wide swinging doors into the main hallway of the nuclear medicine department. "Is anybody down here? I need a VQ scan and I need it now."

"Who the hell do you think you are?" The nuclear medicine doc jumped in front of him with her palm out defiantly, "This department runs on a schedule. You can't just barge in here with a patient and demand a scan. We need to prepare the radionucleotides in advance for something like this. This is way more sophisticated than just taking a chest X-ray. Did you even order this yet? I don't see any urgent cases in the computer."

The nuclear med resident who just finished yelling at him, now was glaring at Sam and the Toxic Shock girl, daggers of anger in her eyes. Luckily Benny, the rotating radiology resident, who knew Sam from his month in the ER was there, apparently on a rotation. He said he would work it out and showed Sam where to move the patient to. Ding. The elevator door opened again and the big box vent, now cleaned and ready to use, rolled out the door with a respiratory tech. They hooked up the Toxic Shock girl. Meanwhile, at Benny's suggestion the nuclear med team bumped another patient out of line and used that case's two radionucleotides for the Toxic Shock girl's VQ scan. Sure enough as Sam had suspected, there was a right-sided pulmonary embolism. He was beginning to feel more confident about these critical cases. Sam turned to the now less angry nuclear medicine resident and said "Thanks, ... and sorry for the intrusion, but as you see this patient was critical." He grabbed the oxygen D-cylinder, popped the brakes off the bed, and rolled back to the elevator, big box vent in tow. Ding. The elevator doors opened, then closed behind them. Within a second nuclear medicine department was silent again. Sam was headed back to the ICU to start a heparin drip, a blood thinner, to treat the embolism.

As Benny and the nuclear med resident were cleaning up the remains of the morning's tornado, she looked at Benny and asked, "Who the hell was that guy?"

Benny sensing something more in the question than a mere query for a name of a resident to blame said, "I know what you're thinking. No, he is not attached, but no, you definitely do not want to go out with him. He literally lives in the hospital, and from what I have seen in just a month, he always will."

She sighed and went back to the desk. "You know he was kind of like the Lone Ranger, sweeping in here to save the day."

"No, he is kind of like a workaholic from the ICU. Remember why we went into radiology? For the ability to go home and sleep at night. Besides he kind of smelled quite badly, or didn't you notice?"

Once back in the ICU they were getting ready for rounds. Sam wrote orders for the Toxic-Shock girl to get heparin to thin her blood so she would not have another embolism, and to check her labs every 4 hours. Sam wrote some notes in the chart about the code for the big man, so he could do his death charting later after rounds. The nurses had already called his family, so at least he did not need to do that as well. Now the main ICU room had the two big pneumonia patients and the Toxic Shock girl all on big box vents, after playing musical chairs with the vents all night. Sam was beginning to learn, as Fish had put it that night Sam had come for his interview, how to juggle.

CHAPTER 22

SAM GOT UP EARLY THE next day. He could not sleep much thinking about the Toxic-Shock case. Part of his sleeplessness was how hot it stayed all night, and his apartment never cooled off. It was one of the hottest days so far, that August morning. It never got this hot in Buffalo, Sam was thinking as he walked along the open asphalt from the parking lot. The outside temperature was already in the upper 90s even though it was only six in the morning. The windless night had not blown the heat in the valley away like it usually did. Sam was not sure if that was a good change or not from Buffalo. Maybe he should call home later and see how his mom was doing, it had been a while since they spoke. But pre-rounds started, and he got busy. As he stood at the Toxic-Shock girl's bedside for rounds he felt queasy. *Was it the lack of sleep?* He had just told the team her ventilator requirements for the last 24 hours from memory when it hit him. Sam noticed his balance seemed off. He touched the bedside rail to steady himself, but things got worse. The floor seemed to be rolling. The glass IV bottles swayed back and forth, clanging against the upright metal poles. The venetian blinds covering the windows started banging against the glass. Alarms on monitors started going off. Sam grasped the bedside rail tighter to keep his balance, his eyes darting back and forth at the others to see if they felt it too.

Jamison just said, "Everyone stay put. It's just an earthquake."

Sam's mind raced, *just an earthquake!* There were no earthquakes in Buffalo. *What should he do? Dive under the bed for cover? Save the patients first? And which ones first? His Toxic Shock girl probably. What if the oxygen lines were damaged? When would they evacuate the building?* Just then one of the plastic covers of the overhead fluorescent light fixture swung open and the light flickered.

"It figures," Mike, the charge nurse at the bedside with them, said, "I got up this morning and I said to my kids its earthquake weather. Take an extra water bottle with you to camp." Mike was a tough looking navy veteran with anchor tattoos on both upper arms.

"What the hell is earthquake weather?" Sam asked. As far as he knew he did not think there was way to predict these things.

"You know. Those still hot days with no wind. They used to call it earthquake weather when I lived in LA." Mike replied.

"So, that's it? Nothing more than take an extra water bottle? How about hide under a strong support structure. Or just stay outdoors far away from light poles and trees? Is that all you tell your kids?" Sam was speaking anxiously with a high pitch in his voice. He was more than a little worked up about the nonchalant way Mike was about an earthquake.

"It's not an exact science. If you scare your kids too much, they'll never listen to you. Damn they already never listen to me."

The shaking stopped. Jamison asked if everyone was OK, seeing nods, he had all the residents and nurses check their patients. Someone turned on the TV behind the nurse's desk and the news was already covering the event. The epicenter was near Hollister somewhere in the Central Valley. No reports of casualties or damage just yet.

Kip Drysdale said sarcastically, "That's all bunk about earthquake weather. They happen all year round. I lived in California my whole life. They happen in the winter, the summer, rain or shine. The Sylmar quake was in February in the middle of winter. Everyone thought that was the so-called Big One, too. No such thing as earthquake weather."

Sam was beginning to think they were all nuts, but he got his balance back and rounds started again. He only got to say a few more words when the floor began rolling one more time, not as much as the first shock, but the IV bottles shook and clanged. This time he grabbed the side of the bed tightly with both hands. He looked anxiously at Jamison for some clue as what to do, then over at Mike the Navy nurse.

"Just aftershocks," Mike, chimed in, noticing Sam's puzzled look.

"What does that mean? Your kids get an extra cup of water for camp?" Sam shot back sarcastically, not hiding his fear this time.

"No, the extra water bottle is for if they can't get home cause the road is damaged. That's the easy truth I could tell them if I had time. A little deeper truth is if I have to stay here in the hospital taking care of casualties. Or worst-case scenario, the building crumbles to the ground, I die and they are left on their own.

Any of those three scenarios and you only have three seconds to say something to your kids as the run out the door, and you know what, take extra water works for all of those." Mike paused then shaking his head added, "They say you are always on your own for the first three or four days after a disaster anyway."

"Not very reassuring," Sam looked shocked. The floor rolling stopped, and Sam loosened his grip on the bed rails.

"You know this wing of the old county hospital never passed earthquake code when it was built ages ago. They keep passing the buck on when they will do something about. My kids are safer than I am. It's part of the hazards of working here. Sometimes I think my time in the Navy living on a sub was safer," Mike replied.

Jamison wanted to move the conversation back to the business of taking care of patients and rounds proceeded. The aftershocks continued all day. Each time the nurses had to reset the bedside alarms, especially after the stronger after-shocks, once they went off. They pulled the Venetian blinds all the way up so they wouldn't make so much noise when then bashed against the windows. It was hot and the sun blazed in like under a magnifying glass; there still was no wind. The nurses put cold wet towels on the patient's foreheads. Sam was generally ill at ease over the whole thing; it was his first earthquake. He skipped lunch, still feeling queasy. By late afternoon when it was time to go home, Drysdale told Sam it was probably smart to not use the elevator, just take the stairs. One more mental note, one more rule to follow, Sam added it to his growing list of dos and don'ts. What to do in an earthquake was definitely not in the intern's manual.

CHAPTER 23

SINCE THE EARTHQUAKE DAY WAS Jamison and Drysdale's last day, Sam got a new faculty attending and resident the following morning. Fish came on his new resident. The new attending was Corbin Michelangelo, one of the most respected pulmonologists at the hospital, possibly in line to become chair of medicine once the current chair retired. Corbin Michelangelo was practically a legend. He had done medical school, residency, pulmonary and critical care fellowships all at the County. He was well versed in every aspect of medicine, having a reputation as extensively well read. He also had published some key papers on lung disease and a new tool to diagnosis it, the bronchoscope.

He was also the nicest guy anyone would want to meet, modest, smiling, and everyone's role model of the perfect attending. And he loved to teach, especially in what he felt was his personal fishbowl, the ICU. As expected, ICU rounds that first day with him lasted much longer than usual, but the teaching Sam got was incredible.

By the time all the team wrote all their medical notes and checked all the labs, it was 6 pm, and Sam finally went home after being in the hospital since 6 am. He would have less than 12 hours off essentially to sleep and take a shower before he was due to be back the next day at 6 am for another shift on call. He was still on a 90-hour week. Benny, whose comment Sam did not hear, was right, Sam lived in the hospital.

Sam's apartment was empty. There was only one box of cereal on the counter, and if he remembered, milk in the fridge. He had one bowl and there was no kitchen table. He ate leaning over the countertop. He had bought a mattress and a second-hand couch, that was all the furniture he could afford when he arrived in California. At night he would cut a line in the faux leather couch and practice suturing it back up again with left over suture material from work. He sat for hours in a room with only a couch, cutting a line with a steak knife, then suturing it back up, trying different suture ties to master the skill. His pile of dirty surgical scrubs in the corner, the only clothes he actually ever wore, he even slept in a clean set. Sam sometimes asked himself why he even had an apartment anymore, as he spent almost no waking time there. It was just a sleep room, and a place for his laundry to wait for the one day he had off each month to wash it.

The next morning both Fish and Sam hit the elevator to the fourth floor ICU at the same time—5:45 am. "Learning fast my boy, always show up 15 minutes early and stay 15 minutes late." Fish said smugly. One more of his many tips for survival. "We don't punch a clock like working at the supermarket. Being ready to go on-time means getting in early to scope out the potential problems before they happen." This cycle of 36 hours on in the ICU—12 hours off to sleep continued all month. Barbara, the Toxic Shock girl survived, as did the two big men with pneumonia. The ICU month taught Sam a lot about decision-making and critical care. It taxed his endurance with the day-on and day-off cycle, and the five to six hours of rounds, but in the end felt like it was one of the best teaching experiences of his life, especially the last week working with Fish as the resident and Michelangelo as the attending.

Michelangelo taught Sam all about reading chest X-rays, and how to finesse all the dials on the big box ventilator to help the patient breathe. Sam got to talk on the overnight shifts with Fish and his dream of critical care from the 911 call to the ER to the ICU, and starting a teaching program to train docs for this. Sam was now convinced that routine internal medicine was not for him, this new notion of critical care and emergency medicine suited him better. He was, despite the fatigue, having a great time. He meant to call home, but was too tired by the time he got back to his apartment each night besides it would be after midnight in Buffalo.

On the last day of Sam's ICU rotation, just as morning rounds where finishing, a secretary from the internal medicine residency office came up and handed him a note that he had an urgent call in the internal medicine staff office. Sam hurried down the hall to pick it up. It was his father in Buffalo, Sam's mother had just died.

CHAPTER 24

SAM, DAZED BY THE NEWS, somehow managed to buy a plane ticket, take a cab and just make the red-eye overnight flight from San Francisco to NY. His eyes were actually red as he tried to resist the urge to cry in the darkened plane. His father and brother met him at the airport. They all cried together.

Somehow back in County, they got Harry to cover Sam's last ICU shift. The chief of medicine and the program director expressed their condolences, as Sam had to tell them that morning about the phone call, but there was also a tone of *hurry back because someone is covering for you after all* when Sam left the office that morning. Sam in a slow-motion reflex was able to drive to his apartment, pack a bag, and get to the airport in time for his flight. He thought his mom would make it, he was still in disbelief, bargaining with the unknown that it all wasn't really true.

The next week remained a blur. Sam was the one who dreamed of leaving NY, and had wanted to go to California, but then he thought about changing his mind when his mom was diagnosed cancer late in his final year of medical school. She was the one who insisted Sam follow his dream to go west and be a doctor. She had said "we keep our commitments" so many times, he could not argue. She got better, she seemed stronger, like his usual feisty mom. He believed he would see her again. He thought about all the phone calls he made from the road driving out, how something was off in her voice. Now Sam anguished over whether he made the best choice. *Could I have just stayed in Buffalo?* The thought encroached on him constantly.

The push to achieve, and ultimately his decision to go to California, was driven by his mother. Although they generally had a comfortable life when times were hard Sam's parents made sacrifices to get by. No one in Sam's family had finished college before. Every parent wants more for their children. Sam's generation growing up in the 1960's middle class, was keenly aware of the expectation that you go to college. His dad once took a few courses at the city college on the GI bill after coming back from World War II but never finished college. Sam's dad joined his own father in their small store. His brother, Sam's uncle, joined them after his service in Korea. Two sons returned from two wars with their options wide open, but they chose the family business over all else. There they were, two generations with two sets of brothers in the furniture and appliance business. Sam spent many afternoons doing his schoolwork in the back office of the drafty warehouse. Sometimes his dad talked about whether Sam and his brother would also work in the family store, but Sam said he wanted to go to college, even if it was just in town in Buffalo. There was enough money saved for the state school. While in college Sam realized that he needed to do something more with his life than be the third generation running the Wyatt Brother's store.

His mother was even more vocal about it. She too worked in the store when Sam and his brother were in high school. She got to see first-hand what that life did to her husband, worn down slowly but the same daily routine. To her, Sam needed to go beyond college to graduate school and have all the advantages Sam's father passed up. His mother's vision of a doctor at the time was to see Sam in an office with a large wood desk, counseling patients, at least that was her 1960's idea of medicine. On his trip home after the funeral, Sam told his dad about what emergency medicine was, and that he was thinking of doing this new specialty instead of sitting in an office behind a big wood desk. Sam's father did not know what to say. He had no basis on how to advise him, it was all too complex to him. His only encounter with emergency rooms was remembering taking Sam's mother to the emergency room the first night she had belly pain, and leaving without an answer. That part did not seem right to him. The emergency room did not get to the bottom of people's problems in his mind. Sam's father also had a lot going on with Sam's mother dying, and business at the store falling off since he had taken so much time to take his wife back and forth to a myriad of doctors. He couldn't remember what each type of doctor did and what each specialty was about. He wanted to caution Sam not to take a big risk at doing something untested and new. He had grown cautious with age and regret, but said nothing.

Later that evening Sam and his brother were digging through his mother's old record collection. The three B's of her generation—

Belafonte, Broadway tunes, an old Blue Eyes. She loved Frank Sinatra. They put his album on the old phonograph in the living room, and Sam slowly dropped the needle at one of her favorite songs that Sam remembered she always sang to him as a boy.

> *Just what makes that little old ant*
> *think he'll move that rubber tree plant*
> *Anyone knows an ant can't move a*
> *rubber tree plant.*

Sam and his brother joined in on the chorus:

> *But he's got high hopes, He's got*
> *high hopes.*
> *He's got high, apple pie, in the sky*
> *hopes.*
> *So, any time you're getting low*
> *'Stead of letting go*
> *Just remember that ant.*
> *Oops, there goes another rubber tree*
> *plant*
> *Oops, there goes another rubber tree*
> *plant*
> *Oops, there goes another rubber tree*
> *plant*

Sam had wanted to stay home longer, it was sad, and nostalgic both, but the time had come. Two days after the simple funeral he took the red-eye back in the other direction to California. By 4:00 pm Sam was back inside the County picking up a new ward service from another intern that had covered for him. In all he was only gone five days; more time off was not allowed. Now however, he had rubber tree plants to move.

CHAPTER 25

For Sam, the next month on the ward turned out to be a slower pace than the ER and the ICU. Rounds were spent in long queries from the attending to the four residents about what the differential diagnosis could be, essentially an extremely long list of possibilities for every case. Instead of snap judgment decision-making, Sam needed to be able to verbalize all the causes of low potassium levels or the meaning of the color of sputum. Sam was less familiar in these areas. He was still not thinking clearly when his thoughts drifted to his last days with his mom, often becoming aware that he was being asked a question when he appeared to the attending that he was off day dreaming.

Dr. Ruisseau, the attending, a nephrologist, pulled Sam aside one morning after rounds to tell him what in his opinion Sam needed to do. In his polite French-Canadian accent he advised, "Doctor Wyatt, I think you need to hit ze books a lot more. See how the others know the answers on rounds? You need to get up to speed, and fast. Internal medicine is about the broad differential diagnosis, not a snap judgement." He snapped his fingers in the air for emphasis. It was clear from his tone that he thought Sam was less prepared than other interns at his level, unfocused perhaps, and that Sam must know every electrolyte disorder inside and out. He suggested a large volume on kidney disease on reserve in the library that Sam should study. Sam felt criticized as a dunce, but in retrospect, his attending was just trying to kick him into gear and get Sam to be more of an internal medicine doctor.

Sam spent the next few nights that he was not on call in the library taking copious notes into a pocket-sized notebook that would become as he called it, "my peripheral brain", and making lists of differential diagnoses on potassium, sodium, calcium, magnesium, phosphorus, and anything else of importance in the kidney textbook. Now more than when he first got to California, he felt he did not want to let his mother down. Sam had sacrificed spending the last few months of her life with her to be the good doctor she insisted he become, and now he was not going to disappoint her and be an unprepared one. Sam was driven by his guilt that he had missed being there for her, being so busy he barely kept in touch for the last two months. Now he wanted to make sure it wasn't a wasted choice. *Keep your commitments,* kept repeating in his memory of the day he said goodbye. Both the peripheral brain and his real one slowly grew fatter with facts.

The ward was less intense in its on-call rotation as well. Where the ER was working 24 hours and off 24 hours, and the ICU was every third night, the ward was only every fourth night, with a short admit day on the second day in between. Short admit days were often spent admitting only elective patients of clinic doctors. They had a particular need to be admitted to the hospital and much of the groundwork for why they were being admitted was already done in clinic. An intern could only admit up to three patients on short admit days. However, on long admit days they could start admitting once the short team was full with their three patients, up to change of shift at 7 am the next morning. It was not unusual to get that 6:45 am admission from the ER that had been sitting there all night. One very early morning Sam got such a case, one that was to be his albatross.

Vern considered himself a drifter. He had worked for the Central Valley railroads before heading off to serve in Europe in World War II. He drank and smoked, as most veterans of that era did, whenever he could. He fought in a war where it was smoke 'em if you got 'em, and one last round for the road. Cigarettes and liquor were considered good manly things. During his time in Europe, they were practically a form of currency unto themselves. It would be another generation before anyone thought otherwise, and by then Vern would not be convinced of it. Even Reagan, the recent Governor of California, once appeared in ads for Chesterfields. Work for the railroad was good when Vern returned but eventually it started to dry up. Railways needed fewer hands. Now life was two packs of smokes a day, and a daily six pack of cheap beer after dinner. He often lived in single-room occupancy rooming houses, or in railroad camps. The long warm days of the Central Valley were suited for sleeping outside much of the year. Sometimes he slept by the river or railway lines during the summer months. He knew the railroad routines and could get around by freight train easily. He might have been a mythical hobo of the Woody Guthrie stereotype, but more recently he was what the docs and nurses started calling a regular ER visitor. Later, once airlines started point programs, people like Vern were called frequent flyers, co-opting the airline promotion program's name, but having a very negative connotation. But the moniker frequent flyer replaced an even more repulsive name for people like him, based on the abbreviation "Get Out of My ER", they were derisively called Gomer, a word that was known not to be said outside the confines of a cluster of interns.

After a night in the ER Vern almost got the Gomer treatment. He had been kicked off the Greyhound bus at the station in midtown when it was discovered he overstayed his fare destination and had an open can of beer with him. The police were called to take him to jail. He was probably headed for Southern California now that the weather was starting to turn, having learned over the years just when to move on from his hobo camp near the switching yard. He complained to the police twice that he could not breathe, but since he was talking just fine that seemed not to impress them. He was prepared to up the stakes to not go back to jail. He stuck a finger inside the beer can opening as he was tossing it, and purposefully cut the side of his finger so it would bleed. He then went into a coughing spasm, dripping some blood into his spit and showing the cops the bloody globby mess he now had on his palm, with a trickle from his lips down his unkempt gray beard. That did the trick and the police backed up a step to keep their distance and radioed for an ambulance, soon to be rid of this infectious vagrant. The bus station wasn't far from the County and Vern figured it was good enough for a night in the ER. This stalling tactic was a good way to avoid getting arrested for cheating his bus fare, or drinking in public, or both, and a good transition to figuring out what to do next, not to mention an easy way to get a meal, or two, and a bed—two hots and a cot. By morning typically someone would have told him it was time to 'get out of my ER' and discharged him.

This time a new internal medicine intern took a pretty long history. Vern liked to ramble probably as much as Fish, and told a disjointed story including the part where he had been in the local jail for a week. During this time a TB outbreak had occurred, and there was a notice about that on a bulletin board in the charting room in the ER. That room was more a cubby hole than a full-sized room. Any larger space was needed for patients. While the intern was writing up his notes his eyes drifted to the public health bulletin about six cases of tuberculosis in the county jail in the last three months and decided to get a chest X-ray. Sure enough, Vern had a right upper lobe scarring, likely pneumonia the intern presumed. On further questioning, Vern admitted to coughing up blood-tinged sputum from time to time, including a great example for all to see right there in the ER. The appropriate cultures were sent, and although Vern did not look any worse than his usual description in the medical chart, he was admitted. Pending an isolation bed, he was held in the ER until 6 am when his in-patient bed came open, and Sam was called about his last admit for his long call night.

Unlike the intern in the ER, who did not think to wear a mask and would need to get TB skin tested now, again in a month, and again in six months, Sam put on a surgical mask when he entered the isolation room to interview Vern. Vern was pretty tired and just wanted to sleep, that was his motivation from the start. Vern did not want to repeat his story for the third time to some youngster doc. He rolled over, pulled the first blanket he had had in weeks over his head and told Sam to "piss off." Sam's motivation however was to get his medical history, write up an admission note, and be done before rounds started in an hour. Sam persisted in trying to ask Vern some basic questions, which Vern ignored until he had had enough and finally said, "You don't look old enough to be in Kindy Garten. Come back when you grow up." And with that Vern rolled over, his back to Sam, and refused to respond. Their two individual paths were different and now had crossed. Vern refused to play the hospital game. Vern won that round. Sam kept pestering him for more, but Vern just grunted in answer to all Sam's questions. Sam had to reconstruct the history from the ER notes and Vern's medical record, but that was quite doable. Sam wondered if this was how it was going to be, with patients he was trying to help telling him to piss off and refusing to cooperate? He finished his admission note and entered all his orders. He checked his peripheral brain for hemoptysis to make sure he did not miss something. It all seemed complete to him so he hurried off to grab some coffee before rounds.

CHAPTER 26

AFTER ADMITTING VERN, SAM RAN into Harry getting coffee and both a donut and a slice of pie in the cafeteria, and Harry looked unwell. Sam tried to avoid the ever-present hospital donuts, but coffee was essential now that he was starting his 25th hour awake. After subbing for Sam one day in the ICU Harry started his own ICU rotation of every third night admitting and staying up to care for the patients in the ICU. Harry could not have been crankier that morning. As they were drinking their coffee and comparing stories about the ICU, Sam noticed that Harry looked a light shade of yellow around the whites of his eyes. There were extra rolls of skin below his eyes and they appeared to sag like that of an old man. Harry had not shaved in at least a day or two and had a black stubble with one small patch of gray under his chin. Despite this, he looked like he had gained some weight, mostly in his mid-section. Harry stifled a yawn and drank the last of his coffee.

"Harry, you look like shit, what's going on?"

"I look like this after I've been up all night on call."

"No, you look a bit, if I had to say, jaundiced in the eyes. Do you have some liver thing going on?"

"I have something called Gilbert's disease. It's benign. You got a good eye to notice it; most people don't, or I am just a deeper color yellow this morning after no sleep at all last night. But stress causes my liver to not handle bilirubin well and it backs up after a sleepless night, so here I am jaundiced. I just need to go home and get a good night's sleep and a hot shower. But we still have ICU mega-rounds for the next six hours going over every organ system of every patient, both old and new. Each day on call is a 36-hours of total hell shift. I should not have to be treated to all this, and really neither should anybody else, including you, Sam. So yeah, not only do I look like shit, I feel like shit."

"There's a rumor they might limit call to 26 hours and send us home after a night shift and just two hours of rounds."

"I heard that, but the surgeons and the ICU faculty pushed back hard and even if it happens for you on the ward, it will never happen in the ICU, and never, ever, ever, for any surgeon. That's why I'll be none of the above, just 9 to 5 in an office somewhere someday, if I can just get past these rotations."

"Wouldn't that be a self-destroying tactic? Just like you choosing to not do that, why would anyone want to put up with a surgery residency if they're the only ones ignoring the call requirements? They are on every third day for six years. After all that they don't even make that much more than anyone else anymore, unless they do ortho or neurosurgery. Other specialties will be a better draw for medical students desiring residencies. And Fish told us about this new specialty up and coming, emergency medicine, that may draw all the types who love hands-on procedures right out of their specialty. No matter what, when you're done for the day, you go home."

"Good luck with that. Emergency Medicine, a real specialty? That'll be the dumping ground for rejects and oddballs. Who would specialize in something that is really specializing in nothing?"

"Or everything?"

Harry looked down at his empty coffee cup craving another sip, "Well I am still heading for rheumatology, if I can survive the ICU. These hours are killing me. No one wants to see a yellow doctor. I need to sleep in my own bed every night." Turning to Sam and getting angry, "don't go trying to be the jack of all trades and master of none. Me, I know my limits. I just want to go home at the end of each day and not live in the hospital." Harry stood, dumped his empty coffee cup on Sam's tray, and added, "you might as well get used to taking out the trash now if that's what you're going to do with your life." Along with the jaundice in his eyes, it seems Harry himself had become jaundiced. Sam felt bad for him as Harry walked away heading for the elevator, but Harry's claim wasn't enough to talk Sam out of wanting to work in the ER.

CHAPTER 27

SAM FINISHED ROUNDS ON THE ward that day by 3:30 in the afternoon. Sam knew all Dr. Ruisseau's gotcha questions on renal diseases that he asked to stump the new interns. Sam spent what little time off he had for the last few evenings reviewing the kidney disease articles in the library and making notes in his peripheral brain. When they got to Vern on rounds, Dr. Ruisseau asked which of the TB meds might cause kidney problems. "Rifampin was most likely," Sam said with greater assurance. Sam was unfortunately familiar with rifampin through personal experience. Once as a medical student, enthusiastic to get as many procedures as he could, Sam did a lumbar puncture on a teenager he suspected had meningitis and who ended up having meningococcus. She died a day later. Everybody was completely panicked and they handed out rifampin to anyone who was in the room with her to prevent them from dying from meningitis. What they failed to tell Sam was that rifampin would turn his urine, his tears, his sweat, and all his body fluids orange. The bright orange urine was the biggest surprise, but that's why Sam remembered it was excreted by the kidneys, and too much or too long and it could cause kidney damage itself.

Truthfully far more of the TB meds caused liver problems, which made Sam think about Harry. *He looked terrible this morning, something worse than just Gilbert's disease.* But since Sam had never seen a case of Gilbert's disease, and Harry had lived with it all his life, Sam figured Harry would know if it was normal to be that yellow. After he signed out at the end of the day, Sam went to the library to pull some articles on it. He was not sure why, after all, Harry had just told him he was making a career mistake and choosing to know nothing and do everything. Perhaps something inside Sam wanted to prove him wrong.

There were several disorders of bilirubin, but the only one that allowed you to live to adulthood was Gilbert's disease. For the most part, it was completely benign, just like Harry said, except for being jaundiced when under stress. In a way, it was the perfect disease that defined Harry. He was nice and thoughtful when he could work at his own pace, but the ER with patients coming in way too fast, and nights in the ICU running from one patient's crisis to another just made Harry hate what he was doing. With that hate building up inside his comments turned towards gallows humor and insulting his colleagues. ***He became jaundiced.*** By morning he was yellow. After a good meal, or even a donut or two, and a whole day's sleep, he was back to being clear-eyed Harry. The yellow bile within him had washed away. For Harry, the worst world he could imagine for himself was being an emergency room doctor, where he would become more jaundiced each day. Seeing one little old lady with arthritis one at a time was his speed. *He probably would have loved my rotation in Pasadena*, thought Sam. Harry's plan was to never be a yellow rheumatologist. Sam could not follow that path.

CHAPTER 28

BRENT PLUMBER WAS PERFECTLY SUITED to the ER. He had come to the County after a mixed residency—first for two years in surgery, but not making the pyramid cut in the crucial third year he jumped to anesthesia. He had done both in the rough and tumble town of Chicago, in the roughest hospital, Cook County. He carried himself as a Chicagoan and did not take any crap from anyone. It was not much of a transition from one county hospital in Chicago when he graduated to a junior attending job here at the County in California.

Sam just got out of his car in the far back lot one morning and saw Brent a few spots over. Sam noticed Brent was locking, then unlocking, then locking his car door. In between each turn of the key, he wiped the lock with his finger. After a series of four turns, Brent went around the passenger side and repeated his ritual. Sam thought this was odd, but as he walked closer, he struck up a simple conversation, "Why do they make us park all the way out here in the far lot?"

"They tell us its so the patients can park close to hospital, since the assumption is we can walk further than they can."

"Yeah, but when we leave at midnight, or two in the morning. We are the last ones walking out to the last cars left in the lot. It's pretty dark out here. I am worried about it getting stolen or mugged."

"That's why I double check every time I lock it. And take a look at this, I devised it myself," Brent pointed through the windshield of his Karmann Ghia to the heavy-duty chain around his steering wheel, with a solid metal bar though it. "Locks the steering wheel."

"Isn't that a bit much?" asked Sam

"Not really considering. I had three cars stolen from me while I was in Chicago. The first one very likely could have been on me. I was in a hurry and I still to this day don't remember if I locked the doors. It was the car I drove all through college. Ever since I always double check. After that I used to tie my bicycle chain around the wheel, but one day they just cut through that like it was spaghetti."

"Oh my. What did you do then?"

"I was driving by a construction site one-day and saw how they were closing it up for the night with a heavy chain, so I thought why not, and bought one. That worked for a few years, but one day poof, that car was gone too. I think the insurance companies put me on some sorta black list by then. So, I started experimenting with different contraptions and came up with this bar and chain combo, with a heavy-duty key lock. So far, so good."

"I didn't think Central City is as bad as Chicago. Are there a lot of car thefts here?" Sam asked.

"You got to be aware all the time, especially after you worked a 12 or 24-hour shift. The city has been changing. Poverty, drugs, gangs, murders—they are the death cycle of most cities, and here it looks like it's heading that way. I wouldn't go too far south of the hospital, especially at night. And I'd be looking around when walking out here alone, too."

"I still don't see why we can't park in the garage closer to the main building. All these rules are nonsensical. Why can't we move our cars closer to the hospital after five o'clock?"

"No one has a good answer other than its easier to just make one rule that says we can't park in the parking garage, period. Rules around here are made as a result of one person who caused a problem. Then everybody else gets to suffer under the ridiculous burden the rule places on them. The art of survival is knowing exactly where the rule ends, and to just walk up to that line and stop."

"Hey look at this for example," Brent said as they approached the ER entrance circle and saw an old El Camino truck with a camper shell on back parked in the no parking zone in front of the ambulance bay. "No parking, right. There's a sign here, here, and over there, but hey this guy's right in front of the ambulance entrance. Why? Well, probably has someone sick in back, no sign telling you where to go if that's the case, and no one is out here to help him, or…." Brent had a sudden recognition as the man behind the car stood up that something was not right and tried to hold out an arm to stop Sam from walking right up to the back of the truck, but Sam had stepped in too close, too fast.

"Do you need a hand getting someone out of the car?" Sam asked the man now standing behind the back of his truck, reaching in right next to him. The big man swept his arm high in the air looming tall over Sam holding a crowbar.

Both Brent and Sam had white coats on and looked obviously like doctors.

"You two docs? Save my girlfriend!" He pointed at the back of the truck and raised the crowbar menacingly. Brent looked around the back of the car, his arms raised in the air. In the back was a young girl obviously pregnant, in labor, knees drawn up to her chest, and red in the face. She did not say a word. Fear was in her eyes. Sam was standing right in front of the big man, a bad position to be in. Brent looked back at the man and took a slow breath.

"Fast, go get a gurney,.... and Doctor Armstrong", Brent said to Sam. Then to the man, "I am just sending my young friend here for a stretcher and some helping hands." He looked back at Sam with a sideways jerk of his eyes towards the ER door, indicating he need to get out of where he was. Sam raised his hands too and stepped back two steps.

As soon as Sam was inside the ER he asked the clerk, "Who is Dr. Armstrong?"

"It's the code word for security," she said, "Why?"

"Brent just asked me to get him and a gurney for a woman in labor"

Sally pushed a button under her desk and pointed Sam to an empty gurney near the door. "They're on the way."

Sam wasn't sure he should go back out with the gurney and put himself at risk of being hit by the man with the crowbar, but he couldn't leave Brent out there alone. He had to go back outside, so grabbed the gurney and rolled it back out to the ER circle where Brent was trying to shimmy the girl out of the back of the camper shell.

"I am not sure we can get her out alone Sam, is Armstrong coming to help?"

Sam hesitated a little, since he relied on Sally for that, "Yeah, real soon."

Brent turned to the man still unmoved with the crowbar held high and said, "Hey man if you put the crowbar down and just help us, we can save your wife here. All you had to do is ask and we are here to take care of everybody."

"She ain't my wife, she's soon going to be my ex-girlfriend." He said not moving a muscle with the crowbar still raised. "As soon as you deliver my son, I am going to beat her fucking brains in."

"You know I kinda thought something like that," Brent said widening his stance slightly, "but if you want me to save your son, I still need to pull her out of the car, so hey, just give us a hand."

The big man lowered the crowbar, and Brent with a lightning-fast maneuver gave him a karate punch with his knuckles directly to his throat. The big man fell to the ground gagging and gasping for air holding his neck. Brent kicked the crowbar under the car.

Just then three security guards ran out the ER door guns drawn. One rolled the still gasping big man over face down and handcuffed him. Another put his foot with full force on his back to keep him down.

Brent lifted the girl right out of the camper shell and onto to gurney and turned to Sam, "Let's get inside. The Armstrongs can deal with this mess."

Once inside Sam was visibly shaken by the event. He hadn't even started his day and he was being threatened with a crowbar. He asked Brent, "how did you know something was wrong before I got close to that guy."

"You get a sixth sense after being in the pit long enough. The girl had nothing but fear in her eyes. When I looked at the dude, he had a tear tattoo on his face. That means he already killed someone, maybe gang-related, but who knows? Either way, he had a weapon and I was only going to give him one opportunity to put it down. I don't negotiate with people like that. They also never expect the men in white jackets to slug them."

"That was a pretty precision punch there. Where did you learn that?"

THE COUNTY

"Black belt in karate, I needed a hobby after they stole my first car. I pulled back and just winded him. The only part I wasn't sure about was whether you knew who Armstrong was, and would bring some help."

"I didn't. But Sally at the desk did and she called once I said it was you who asked."

"Yeah. Sally's been through some of my antics before. She knows the drill."

They whisked the girl up to Labor and Delivery, or L&D, where Dr. Corkerin delivered a healthy baby boy. After being checked for injuries, the crowbar man was arrested and taken to jail. His car was towed, and once they got a warrant to search it, they found heroin in bags in the back. But the most amazing thing was that Brent just went about his shift as if nothing had happened, as if he never sucker-punched a crowbar-wielding heroin dealer who just wanted to kill his girlfriend. Sam was dumbfounded that he seemed to not even break a sweat. *Was that what it took to be an ER doc?*

CHAPTER 29

IT DID NOT TAKE LONG for Jablonski to get wind of what happened in the ER. There was no formal reporting mechanism for such an event. Even the public safety officers who arrested the suspect, although sworn police officers, did not need to report their activity immediately to anyone in the hospital. But that did not stop the whispering pipeline, "Did you hear what happened this morning in the ER?" and then various versions of the encounter spread. Jablonski had a daily lunch check-in meeting with the heads of the five major departments—surgery, medicine, OB/GYN, pediatrics, and ortho. The head of OB was taking his seat when he mentioned that the police were questioning "a

THE COUNTY

girl in L & D as we speak," but did not have more information. He shrugged it off and said, "It was probably about drugs. It's always about drugs. Isn't it?"

Jablonski slipped his secretary a note and told her to find out what was going on. By the time the standing meeting was breaking up a half-hour later Jablonski had his answer. The version he heard was that Brent Plumber punched a patient. Jablonski's plump pale face turned red and he yelled at his secretary, "Get him up here NOW!"

When Brent Plumber got paged, he was just about to do a procedure, suturing up a dog bite to a kid's face. He had just numbed up half the field and needed to get started to not waste anesthetic time. He told Sally at the desk to see what the "boss wanted" and to tell him "I'm busy." Brent went back to carefully suturing up the kid's face as an orderly held the boy's head from squirming side to side.

Fifteen minutes later he was done, pulled off the sterile drape, and said "good as new" with a nod to the orderly, who knew what to do from there as far as bandaging him up. No sooner had Brent stepped out in the hall when he met Jablonski arms crossed and grim-faced, "We need to talk and I mean now!"

"We can talk here," Brent said calmly.

"Do you have somewhere more private that the hall?" Jablonski motioned with his arms outstretched.

"OK how about the Ortho room, no broken bones going on right now." They walked over to Room Four and shut the door.

"I heard you punched a patient in the face," Jablonski started right in.

"No, I did not!"

"Well then what did you do?"

"First, he was not a patient. He was a menacing threat in the parking lot. He was not even in the building. Second, he was threatening me, Sam, and an actual patient, his girlfriend. In her case with death. And third, I did not hit him in the face. I nailed him right in the windpipe and left him breathless for a moment so the police could arrest him. They checked him out medically, nothing broken, off to jail, end of story."

"Well, you cannot do that!"

"Which part?"

"You can never strike a patient here at County, ever! Can you imagine the headlines?"

"Again, he was not a patient until after I struck him. When I hit him, I was in fear for our collective lives, that's why I called a code Armstrong."

Jablonski leaned in close to Brent's face, "Somehow Brent, I don't think you are the type of person who is ever in fear for his life. I heard you have several martial art belts."

"While that is true, but he was definitely going to kill his pregnant girlfriend, so let me ask you which looks worse for the hospital?" He moved his hand across the front of Jablonski's face as if revealing a banner headline. "Pregnant teenager with her head bashed in in the parking lot, or hospital staff saves patient from assailant? Which headline do you prefer?"

"OK. I am going to check out this story. But, you have to promise me right here and now,… and forever, that you will never under any circumstances strike another patient."

"I never punched a patient in the first place, so there is no another. But before you blow a gasket. Yes, I will not punch, or strike as you call it, any patient of the County." Brent knew exactly how far to walk this rule up to the line.

Jablonski walked off to talk with the security team, and for the second time that day, Brent went back to work as if nothing had happened. Although when he opened the door and stepped out of Room Four there were several staff members hovering nearby to see what was up. Jablonski was red-faced, and Brent was, well just Brent, "Nothing to see ladies and gents, let's all get back to work, we have lives to save. The boss just wanted to know if we had enough plaster."

CHAPTER 30

WILSON WAS HAVING A HARD time with the ward service until there was a change of attendings. Wilson loved discussing unusual diagnoses, even if his patients never ended up having them. It was the process of thinking about those diagnoses that he loved. He wondered how he ended up doing an internship in a place like County, instead of a big-name university or a place like the Mayo Clinic. In the back of his mind, he was sure racial prejudice probably played a role. Every residency program it seemed wanted one black doctor, not more than that, on their new intern roster. Wilson was always the second on their lists. Plus, he was from Duke, a respectable school but not an elite northeast school like Harvard, Yale, Princeton, or even Penn. He always considered it the Harvard of the South, but Harvard considered it just another school in the South. When he went on interviews, invariably he would be asked if he played basketball. Only one time he said no, and had the guts to ask the interviewer if he asks his white applicants the same question. Without missing a beat, the chief at some elite residency replied, "No, rugby." He gave up pushing the issue as he understood challenging the status quo was not going to be productive. He would have to become someone first then he could work on changing the system. Nevertheless, he never fumed over it. He was going to be the best doctor he could be and work hard. The County wasn't Harvard, but a great education was there for the taking if he was doing his job right.

The ward was the essence of medical practice for an internal medicine intern. The ward patients had the usual diseases of neglect that amassed in the County—obesity, diabetes, and with those heart failure, kidney failure, and out-of-control infections for which they often waited too long to see a doctor. It was not always their fault; they usually had no insurance so they waited to get seen at the city's free clinic down the street from the County hospital where it often took months to get an appointment. By the time they got into the clinic that weird blackened spot on their foot had turned into gangrene, or their trouble sleeping at night that led from one pillow to two pillows to sleeping upright in the easy chair was advanced heart failure. Wilson wanted to help them all.

The problem was his attending was Dr. Waldenstrom, an old but well-respected hematologist. All the patients had problem lists of a dozen or more active medical problems, but all Waldenstrom seemed to key in on was that they were anemic. Seeming to forget he had just spoken at length about the workup for anemia he started anew at each patient's bedside asking the interns how they would work it up. After going through microcytic and macrocytic, and even normocytic anemia Wilson was losing it.

One day when another intern was asked to give a list of possible diagnoses, and mentioned sickle-cell anemia as being on the list, Waldenstrom looked over at Wilson and said, "I would have thought you would have come up with that diagnosis first?" Wilson stifled his gnawing anger. It seemed more than Waldenstrom thinking Wilson would know that diagnosis, and more like Wilson, should have thought of the disease first since it mostly affected black people. After five days of this with ten patients per intern, every day on rounds Wilson had heard about every aspect of anemia at least 100 times. He wanted to talk about how the kidneys responded to heart failure, or hyperglycemic states in diabetics, or which antibiotics worked in the bacteria's cell wall, or anything but anemia.

The only part of this rotation that provided some comfort was that Gina was one of his co-interns. Gina had her own issues and she spoke to Wilson after rounds one day, "You ever notice that Waldestrom calls you Dr. Harrison at rounds and the other guys doctor, but when he gets to me to present a case he calls me Gina?"

"I didn't notice, but I'll look for it? Do you want me to say something to him?"

"No, no it's my issue. Plus, there's a risk it could get him upset and he would give me a bad evaluation for the rotation. He's about as an old school doc as you can get. It's a hard place for me to not say something yet restore some balance."

"We could try this. Every time he turns to you and says Gina tell us about your patient, the three of us could chime in—Yes Dr. Bautista what is up with your patient? Maybe he would get the hint on how to address you?"

"He does this in from of the patients too, you are all doctor, and me just Gina. Then the patient thinks I'm the nurse. On rounds today Mrs. Donnelley in room 45 told him she had just told all that to the nurse, and glared at me, when he asked her a question. How do I get past this?"

"Well, it's clear from your name tag that it says MD after your name."

"I am not sure everyone knows what that means or bothers to read it. I introduce myself each time I walk in the room as Dr. Bautista, I do all the usual doctor things like an exam, and then she asks me to get breakfast or turn on the TV like I am the room nurse or something. One patient asked if I was from housekeeping and that she needed more paper towels in the bathroom. Does housekeeping wear a white coat? She then spoke extra loud as if she thought I did not understand English, as if somehow speaking louder made English understandable. I am getting so frustrated by having to repeat myself to these patients, but it starts with Waldestrom not addressing me correctly."

"I get that from the patients too. I walk into the room and they say Oh no I don't want to go to X-ray this morning, like I am the orderly who is going to take them there."

"Oh. I am sorry Wilson. Not you too. What can we do?"

"I'll talk with the others, Let's just plan on calling each other doctor this and doctor that in front of the patients and the staff, maybe go overboard a little until it starts to rub off."

Finally on the seventh day of Wilson's rotation, Waldenstrom's time on the ward was over. Waldenstrom went back to the blood bank where he felt most at home. Waldenstrom would have droned on and on and on during rounds about low red blood cell counts. He never picked up on the intern's plot to call each other doctor all the time, calling Dr. Bautista Gina until the last day. As he was leaving on the last day he finally said to her, "Make sure you keep checking the coags on Donnelly, Dr. B." She felt it was a small victory, and this year was going to be one of a few small victories, so she would take them when they occurred.

Michelangelo, the pulmonologist, no pun intended, was a breath of fresh air when he arrived the next morning for rounds. Corbin Michelangelo was knowledgeable about every medical problem, not just the lungs. After all, he also was one of the three attendings who covered the ICU, where he needed to know about every disease. He called all his interns doctor. This made Gina happy. Michelangelo stood at the bedside of those same patients they had rounded on with Waldenstrom and discussed all those things Wilson had long wanted to hear about. This not only made

Wilson happy but somehow was the jolt that reinvigorated him from his growing depression. These comprehensive teaching rounds encouraged him. He loved the give and take of the discussion they had about his cases, and he thrived once someone showed him the respect he craved. Consequently he began to read as much as possible to be ready for rounds since he knew Michelangelo could ask anything, and he wanted to be prepared. During the first week by the third day with Waldenstrom, Wilson had more or less begun to slack off and read a whole lot less about anything even hematology. But now the climate had changed and Wilson thought the world of Michelangelo.

They eventually got to Vern, the tuberculous patient whom Sam had admitted three months earlier. He had refused every attempt to discharge him. He would not willingly take his meds so was never deemed to be safe for discharge to a SNF, or skilled nursing facility. Social workers tried but no nursing home wanted an outbreak of TB on their hands. The SNF administrators insisted that any patient sent to them have a negative PPD, the skin test for TB, and of course Vern's was positive. The County public health officers tried too, but all the old TB sanatoria had closed, and neither The County, nor any other hospital, still had a TB ward just for patients like Vern. Finally there was a group committee meeting about where to place Vern, but in the end, they all decided he needed at least six months of direct observation therapy, meaning someone had to watch him take his medications each day. That someone turned out to be six sequential interns, starting with Sam, and now it was Wilson's turn. Like every fresh intern who thought he could solve a problem that everyone else could not, Wilson tried. He wanted to show the world he had Mayo Clinic skills. Who better to pair up with than the best pulmonologist in the County—Corbin Michelangelo.

Wilson started where everyone else had with an insolvable problem, the library. Wilson thought he was more compulsive that the others, so he and he alone would find the answer. He pulled every article, new and old, about TB meds and treatment options. He even explored a few protocols used for shortened therapy in third-world nations where resources were limited. There seemed to be no easy answer. After that first deep dive into the literature, he had a long discussion with Dr. Michelangelo one evening.

"I can't believe we have the same drug to treat TB as we did twenty years ago. Why haven't we discovered new ones?"

"Mostly because there is no profit margin in them," replied Michelangelo, "For kids with ear infections there is a new antibiotic every year or so, none is a breakthrough, and at the end of the day we are just treating viral infections with worthless antibiotics anyway. When you look at global health there are only a few entities doing something about it, the World Health Organization, for one."

"What about those countries where there are millions of TB patients, some of them have money for at least government-sponsored research?"

"True but even if they discovered a breakthrough drug or even a new version of an old drug, the FDA would make the drug company jump through all sorts of hoops to get it to market. The drug companies don't do that unless they think they will sell millions of doses. And who is going to buy those meds? Nearly all TB patients in America are poor, have no insurance, or are in jail. Not a pathway to marketability and a 4-color ad spread in the New England Journal."

"You know what we need? Do you ever read Thomas Mann's *The Magic Mountain*? I read it in a literature course at Duke."

Michelangelo shook his head, "Sorry didn't do many English courses, just the sciences."

"It's about life in a Swiss TB sanitorium before the war. Back then there was a theory that low oxygen levels at altitude starved the TB bacillus."

"That does make sense. TB often affects the upper lobes of the lungs because there is better oxygen there, as opposed to the lower lobes where it would be harder to multiply due to lower oxygen levels."

"The whole book was a parable about pre-war Germany, set in a high-altitude TB sanitorium that Mann once visited with his wife."

"Well, you know there is a famous pulmonary hospital called National Jewish in Denver, also at altitude and initially it was used the same way. I think that's where Doc Holliday, of the gunfight at the OK Corral, went afterward when he had advanced TB. But they did not have any antibiotics back then and he died somewhere near there. In fact, and no one knows this yet, Jamison just got accepted into an advanced pulmonary research fellowship there."

"So, are there any TB sanitariums up in the mountains around here where we can send Vern to recover?"

"Good question, I remember there used to be one, but let me ask around."

CHAPTER 31

WILSON HAD ONE OF THOSE days, one out of four, where he wasn't on call for new admissions. With some extra time on his hands, he thought he would delve deeper into Vern's case, maybe he could discover something, some missed clue that would help. So he masked up and went into Vern's room. Vern was facing the window with his gown open in back, and Wilson noticed a scar on his right upper chest. It looked to him like an old surgery scar, it was linear with the tell-tale puncture wounds of a poorly done suturing job.

"I am Dr. Harrison, your new doctor. I know you probably went over all this with everyone but I was hoping if you could answer a few questions, we could maybe find a way to get you home."

"Home? I don't have no home. This room works just fine for me."

"Where did you live before you got to the hospital?"

"Mostly the big railyard in Roseville. All the trains from east to west and north to south come through there. We have a bunch of little camps scattered around the fields there."

"Had you just come off a train?"

"You might say that. I hop the freights from time to time. The Central Valley is great in the summer, but not so much in the winter. I was trying to go south when we all got chased by the bulls. When the city cops caught me on the bus, I pretended to be sick with a cough knowing they just as soon take me to a hospital than jail. Less paperwork for them."

"So, what do you mean you pretended to be sick?"

"I know my lungs are all scarred up from the ping-pong balls and TB, so all I have to do is show up at the hospital, mention I coughed up some blood from time to time when they get around to asking that. Don't want to lead with that, make them think they discovered something, and poof here I am until I cough up a negative specimen."

"Wait. Go back. What's with the ping-pong balls?"

"Well, I did have TB once. I was up in the Weirdo institute and after a year of their poison meds, I was still coughing up blood. Then this one old doctor said if the antibiotics are not working, they could put ping-pong balls in my lungs and collapse it until they healed. After pestering me about it a dozen times I finally agreed. And the crazy doctor was right. They took me off the institute to a hospital and inserted about a dozen ping-pong balls into my chest. After about two months they said I was cured, and let me go."

"Wow. Are you sure it was ping-pong balls? I never heard of anything like that?"

"Well neither did I. But one of the other inmates at the Weirdo institute said his brother got it after the war and it was like a miracle. I wanted to go home to Utah and get out of there so I agreed."

"Then what happened?"

"I was working in a mine in Draper, too much dust and I got sick again. They got another chest X-ray and those docs thought they should take out the ping-pong balls and wash the insides of my lung with antibiotics. They did that and I got better. I worked the mine for another few years, then they fired me so they would not have to pay anymore sick days. I ended up on the rails again."

"What do you mean by the 'weirdo institute' were you in a psychiatric hospital?"

"No way! I am as sane as you doc. There was one of these old-time sanitariums up in the Sierras. We all called it the Weirdo institute, but it had another name. Something with a W, run by a bunch of Huns."

"Nuns?"

"No Huns, Nazis! I was in the war you know. I can spot their accent a mile away."

Wilson needed some time to unpack all this. Ping-pong balls, Nazis. Weirdo Institute. He looked through Vern's chart. None of this was in there. All his sputum samples from admission were inconclusive. Vern on purpose just never gave it a good deep cough that was needed for a decent culture sample. The original ward team just assumed with his lung scarring, blood in his sputum, and his week in jail during the TB outbreak, that he had TB. That meant six-months on the ward, and Vern just went along with it as the best option. It would be great to get a sputum sample to prove it, but either way, he needed a year of therapy. One nurse's note said patient stated he had been through this all before but that fact never made it back to the chart.

Wilson ordered all his old records, a pile of paper charts hauled up in a cart from medical records, and started looking through there. Finally, he found an old note from many years ago—Surgical history: failed plombage. It was signed by Dr. Westman when he was a resident 25 years ago. *What the hell is plombage?* Wilson thought he go right to the source.

Wilson waited patiently outside the OR for over an hour. Finally, the surgical team came out, with Dr. Westman.

"Dr. Westman, sir, if I could ask a non-urgent question?"

Westman looked Wilson up and down, noticing he had a County name badge on, and nodded.

"I have a patient you saw two decades ago and you wrote he had a failed plombage surgery. I am unfamiliar with that. So, I was wondering if you could explain it?"

Westman smiled. The two things he liked were operating and teaching. Here was a moment to dispense a bit of medical wisdom. "Long time ago we used to insert inert sterile bodies into the pleural cavity to collapse the lung. The thought was without oxygen if they had TB it would stop multiplying and the infection would end. It was only done for rare cases for a few years. Once there were better antibiotics, they stopped doing it. I never did one of those personally but I have seen a case or two, way back in training."

"No, I don't think you did the procedure. It was just one line in a note you wrote from the 1950s. It is on a current TB patient of mine, and the only notation that he had a surgical procedure was your note that said failed plombage. Were ping-pong balls ever used as the sterile objects?"

"Well, son, as crazy as it sounds, yes that was what was used." Westman smiled at the remembrance of the archaic way medicine was practiced back then, when everyone, including him, just accepted it as dogma, "They were easy to sterilize and lightweight. But you can usually see them on X-ray. I know I always took a thorough history, but someone should have figured that out just by looking at his chest film."

"Well, I finally got a history from him and he claims they were taken out somewhere in Utah. Now every time he comes to the hospital, we all assume he still has TB, but it may be just scars on his lung."

"Interesting case. What was your name again son?"

"Wilson Harrison, sir. Thank you for that, it was helpful."

"Good luck to you."

Wilson couldn't wait to find Corbin Michelangelo and tell him the information.

"Wait, you are telling me this guy had ping-pong balls put in his chest and then removed a few years later for his TB?"

"That's right Dr. Michelangelo. I was looking through his chart and during this admission we never confirmed his diagnosis. He won't or can't cough up a specimen. I was thinking maybe we could do a bronchoscopy, wash out some alveolar fluid for cultures, and definitively prove he does not have TB. Then we can discharge him home, or to wherever he wants to go." Wilson paused and thought about what that would mean for Vern, "He really does not have a true home. But we should not have him on a ward in isolation under the premise that he still has TB."

"That could be complicated, bronchs are invasive, we would have to consent him. You think he'd go for it? We would have to use isolation precautions for the whole OR suite so we don't get exposed to TB in case he really does have it. It's a little risky, but I like your thinking on this."

"There was just one other thing he kept saying that I never figured out. He was at something he called the Weirdo institute, although that is what he called it. It might have been another word that started with a W. up in the mountains somewhere."

"When you were talking about the sanitorium and Magic Mountain and all that I went to ask Jamison who knows the local geography. There was a TB sanitorium up in the Sierras for many years called the Weimar institute. Not like the German Republic, but it was in the town of Weimar. They had a lot of cottages and the state paid for the care of a lot of TB patients up there back then. Jamison said he last remembers discharging a patient there about three years ago. I checked the phone book and found a number, but no one picked up. I asked around and it seems like it closed just recently and sent its last patients to regular hospitals."

"You sure it had nothing to do with the Weimar Republic? Vern told me he thought the doctor who convinced him to put the ping-pong balls in his chest was a Nazi with an accent."

"Nazis no, but a fair number of European doctors worked there, they had a better understanding of tuberculosis than we did. They got into exercise, some hydrotherapy, and other healthy life choices. The whole US TB sanitorium model was based on Saranac Lake. It was a high mountain enclave in the Adirondacks with a bunch of cabins, away from society, and the clean air. The low atmospheric pressure up in the mountains helped about as much as the INH did, the antibiotic we put everyone on. Well, Wilson between your literature class and Jamison's knowledge of the area we may have cracked the case."

"And your skills as a pulmonologist. We aren't done until we get him bronched."

CHAPTER 32

QUIET MORNINGS IN THE ER meant that Brent could do his routine of karate stances in Room Four. He started posed with one arm outstretch and the other flexed behind him, then pivoted silently on the balls of his feet as his arms switched position. Every so often he let out an exhalation as he swept his arms into the next position. The nurses kept out of the way as they always thought he was an odd duck. But he was the doc they needed to call when things heated up, and soon enough they did. "Dr. Plumber, incoming ambulance, do we want to use Room One?" On the radio, the ambulance said they found an old man in the bathroom near the museum downtown bleeding from the head. They were not sure if it was a gunshot wound or something else. Because it could have been a gunshot wound the crew wanted to bypass the closer Brannan General Hospital to bring him to County. What they did not say over the radio, but did after bringing him in, was that he "looked like a County patient anyway."

Brent took one look at him, head bandage wrapped and bloody, and when Jenni came in the room asked her, "Do you think we should page the surgeons for this? Certainly looks like head trauma?"

"No just another drunk who spent the night in the bathroom to keep warm." Jenni said dismissively. She thought she smelled some alcohol about him. Brent remotely remembered Fish's rule about Jenni being a negative barometer, but waited until he had a good look at the patient.

Brent shined a penlight into each eye and noticed the man's pupils were not quite the same size. "You know what, let's give the trauma surgeons a call anyway Jenni."

Jenni had just gotten an IV and drew bloods, and did not look pleased that yet again the doctor ignored her opinion. She just did not know they all considered her wrong most of the time, and whatever she said they just did the opposite.

Brent put the man in a rigid cervical neck collar to keep him from moving his neck in case it was fractured. The ambulance crew had not bothered to do so, but Brent knew head and neck trauma went together. He cut off the man's wet clothes and looked him over from head to toe. No other marks were on his body. He did not smell so good. *That is why the ambulance drove past private Brannan Hospital.* Not more than two minutes went by and a surgery resident walked in. Brent said, "I am sending for a CT scan of his head, looks like he hit it pretty hard. I think his pupils are a little unequal do you want us to call N-surg too?"

The surgery resident did not seem too impressed. "No chest or abdomen injury? You don't need me. Sure, call the brainiacs." And he left without seeing the patient.

As they rolled past the front desk, he asked Sally to page whoever was on for neurosurgery. As his routine, he would not call until after they had the CT in hand, but Brent had a feeling it was going to be positive. He did do two years of surgery so knew what to look for in a trauma patient. Sure enough the head CT showed blood between the brain and the epidural membrane, the thick lining outside the brain. By the time they got back to Room One, Snider was there.

"What happened to this guy?" Snider asked.

"We don't know much. Someone found him in the bathroom at the Gold Rush museum this morning, no idea what happened. There was blood from the right side of his scalp and his right pupil was a millimeter larger and slower to react than the left. I think he needs a tube and a trip to the OR."

"Give me 10 seconds to do a neuro exam and you can get ready to tube him, but wait til I am done," Snider said. Brent was one of the ER docs Snider grew to respect, otherwise, he would have told him that he was the surgeon and he will decide who does or does not need an OR. "OK he's got some lateralizing signs, the pupil is bigger, his arms a little weaker on that side. Go ahead and tube him and I'll call the OR."

"Just so we agree, I can tube him and paralyze him, you don't need the anesthesia team to do this? Jablonski yelled about the policy last time I did that."

"Didn't you do some anesthesia?"

"Yeah. A whole residency!"

"Good enough for me. Time is brain. I am not going to wait for them to come down and explain what's going on. Just tube him, and I should be ready to go as soon as you're done."

Brent smiled; this is what he was most trained to do. He got his equipment together, and within five minutes he had the endotracheal tube in, secured, and verified that he heard breath sounds on both sides. They called for a portable chest X-ray to confirm, but Brent was sure he was in his lungs, he had done this hundreds of times. Snider was too, and kicked the brakes off the gurney as soon as the X-ray was shot. "Just call the OR if I need to change the tube location, we are officially out of here." And he pushed the gurney out the door. Brent looked at his watch, *58 minutes, not a record but pretty darn good. We got him to the OR in the golden hour.*

Jenni looked at Brent and frowned.

"Hey sorry Jenni, I was up at the head and his exam was changing." Brent said anticipating some snide comment she would make in her defense. "I knew he needed Snider and surgery once I got a good look at his pupils. I did not mean to ignore you." But he did mean it. Omygod.

The tube position on the X-ray was perfect, but he called it up to the OR anyway, just to let Snider know.

Three hours later Snider came down to the ER and found Brent. "Good call this morning on the head trauma, it was an expanding epidural, we just got him in time. He's in the ICU now, but something does not make sense. That is not the type of injury I'd expect from slipping on a wet bathroom floor. Too well localized. There was a rounded depressed skull fracture at the back of his head at the site of impact, like, I don't know, someone hit him from behind?"

"Could he have fallen against the sink?"

"Not likely. Most people who are using the sink are facing it. Plus, the distance from their head standing up to the edge of the sink is not very far. It would be hard to fall, hit the back side of your head, and have enough force for a depressed skull fracture that way. Did the police come around to ask questions?"

"No. No one came to ask about him, police, family, no one."

"Well, let me just check in with the Armstrong crew to see if they know something we don't." Snider walked down the hall to the security office.

CHAPTER 33

LUNCH IN THE CAFETERIA AND Sam, Harry, and Wilson sat at the same table. Wilson was going on about the TB guy's case, and Sam who remembered admitting him asked, "How did you get him to talk? He literally told me to piss off when I tried."

"Well after three months of just sitting in an isolation room and sometimes you remember something you want to say. He told me this long story about being up in the mountains at a TB sanitorium, then some doc up there putting ping-pong balls in his chest to collapse his lung. Then when he got out, he goes to Utah and someone else takes them out because they got infected. Then he rides the rails back to Roseville railyard where he just about gets arrested for trespassing."

"Wow you got his whole life story, didn't you?"

"Yeah, when I dictate his discharge note I'll be sure to put in all the details this time," Wilson said, "We think maybe he doesn't actually have TB after all."

"Utah?" asked Harry, "One side of my family's from there. Part Navajo. We used to go up in the summer to ride horses and such. Where in Utah?"

"It started with a D, something like Daper or Drainer or Don't know exactly, he worked in some mine."

"Well, that's easy, the Delta mine near Draper is well known. I think it closed a while back."

"Was it a gold mine?" Sam asked.

"Hardly. The gold rush missed Utah." Harry went on, finally knowing a lot about something unusual, "In Utah they have three types of mines, all unique. They are well known for copper mining. You know that line from the song about Joe Hill, how the copper bosses killed him? Then we had the uranium rush in the southern four corners region. Mostly Navajo worked those mines until one by one they were shut down too as the Cold War ended. Plenty of lung cancer from those. One of my aunts sued the government after my uncle died from working there his whole life. Never got a penny. The last region to have mines was even more unique, near Delta on the west side, they had the only beryllium mine in the U.S. Not many folks know about it. It was used for the aerospace industry."

"Yeah, I think he did say Draper." Wilson admitted. "Beryllium, Hmmm why does that sound familiar?"

"Maybe because it rhymes with Bretylium the new cardiac drug?" Sam quipped.

"Maybe, but something else."

Sam looked over at Harry and asked, "Are you doing okay? You look more yellow today than I've seen you before?"

"Who knows? Internship is not compatible with Gilbert's. Now I am starting to itch all over. I am probably allergic to it too."

Sam looked concerned, but before he could say anything more, Fish sat down with them. "Sam, I have been looking for you. I was starting to write up the Toxic Shock patient for a journal, do you want in?"

"Sure, what do you want me to do?"

"I can write the discussion stuff, not much there as far as prior cases, but if you can write the case summary, I can do a table about the labs, and another about the Swan findings, and we can put the whole thing together. What do you say?"

"Okay. When do you need it by?"

"Yesterday would be nice, but how about next week?

Sam nodded, "I could do that, I think" The thought of publishing an article intrigued him. Wilson looked over at them, and Sam had the sense that he was getting jealous. Wilson wanted to be an academic, and publishing a paper in a journal was a critical part of an academic career, something that might get him noticed. Sam had yet to figure out what career path he wanted, but a paper sounded like a new challenge and he agreed.

That evening both Sam and Wilson were looking up different questions that had gnawed at each of them since lunch. Wilson went to his closet where he kept binders with his medical school class notes. He had dozens of them. They were heavily highlighted in several colors, that he used to study for his exams. He leafed through the cover titles until he found his pulmonary notebook and started to read. That's where he found it, the single reference to beryllium, that he was trying to remember. Duke had given him a great education and Wilson had written every word they told him in lecture hall down in these notebooks. Every bit of obscure medical science was in there. That is probably why he scored so high on his national exams, but it did not help get him into a named university residency. But he found a table where he wrote on the differential diagnosis of granulomatous disease, of which TB was the most common disorder. At the bottom of the table was berylliosis.

Sam was not so meticulous in medical school. He did not have a closet full of color-coded notebooks. Now he had his small "peripheral brain" as he called it, with key facts he needed to know to get through his internship. When he needed to look something up, he went back to the library. He found the journal volume he had seen before when he looked up Gilbert's disease for the first time. He went to the library to search more about Toxic Shock for the case report Fish wanted to publish, but something lingered with him after seeing Harry look uncomfortable at lunch. So before searching the journals for the Toxic Shock cases he thought he take one more look at the review of bilirubin disorders. His nagging suspicion was answered. While elevated bilirubin is the one and only sign of Gilbert's disease, it never gets high enough to cause generalized itching, or pruritis, as the medical journal stated. Harry was scratching his arms and shoulders all during lunch. Jaundice and itching were more likely signs of acute hepatitis. *Damn.* Sam went to the pay phone in the library lobby and called Harry's home number.

CHAPTER 34

LATER THE NEXT DAY IT seemed Brent was having a do-over. Once again, his morning exercise routine in Room Four was interrupted by a gurney being wheeled past in the hall.

"Brent, we need you! Room One."

Brent poked his head out just in time to see a bunch of white coats from behind push a gurney around the corner.

"What's going on here?" he asked seconds later as he stepped into Room One.

"This is Todd our med student we found him in the bathroom just now with his head bleeding." A neurology attending, who Brent did not recognize, told him.

Todd was still awake.

"What happened?" Brent asked.

"I don't remember. I went in to take a leak and I think I was at the sink and everything went black from there. And now my head is killing me."

"You were facing the sink washing your hands?" Brent was now sensitized by what Snider had said about falling in the bathroom the other day.

"Yeah, as far as I know. I think there was someone else there too."

The nurse cut in with her orientation questions, " What day is it? What month? And who's the president?"

"Tuesday, December, Carter," Todd replied quickly.

"How about governor?"

"Governor Moonbeam, you mean? Jerry Brown?"

"Yeah, he's completely oriented," The nurse said.

Brent went through his exam and ordered a head CT. This time the pupils were equal, so were his grip strengths, and he was talking, so he waited in the CT scanner looking at the images as they came out before calling Snider. He just skipped the surgeon this time; he was so useless the day before. Todd, the medical student, had a depressed skull fracture.

THE COUNTY

Snider came down to see the patient. He was completely intact neurologically. His CT told a different story, "See this here, that is a depressed skull fracture. It is rounded but not as deep or depressed as our guy from the museum. But I don't believe in coincidences. Someone is smacking people on the back of the head in the bathrooms. I'll admit this guy, but have the campus security boys come see me, and have them check that bathroom out too."

The Armstrongs interviewed Todd, Brent, Snider, and the neurology attending and wrote up an incident report. They took a look at the lobby bathroom where it had happened, but housekeeping had already been called when another visitor found blood on the floor. By the time one of the Armstrongs got there the little yellow sign that cautioned visitors about a wet floor was up and a housekeeper was inside with a mop. She had not seen anything suspicious. The lead Armstrong came back to tell Snider and he got into a heated argument with him telling him there must be somebody lurking in bathrooms. The lead security guy said there was not enough to go on, two different bathrooms, two different places, two unrelated victims, if they were victims at all. While they did not say the case was closed, it was clear that they were not going to do much more that day.

CHAPTER 35

UPSTAIRS IN THE OR, IT had been set up for negative airflow for the bronchoscopy; maximum airborne pathogen control protocol. Everyone wore masks, goggles, gloves, and splash-proof gowns. The anesthesiologist looked particularly nervous. He was first in, passing a tube with his face right up close to Vern's face. He wore a tight fitted mask to prevent him from contracting TB. Once the patient was intubated, he could isolate the airway and not ventilate any possible tuberculous bacilli into the room. Similarly, the fluid meant for the lung washout would be contained. The broncho-alveolar lavage would determine whether Vern still had TB. Wilson had a last-minute request for Dr. Michelangelo; he wanted to add a test of the lavage fluid for berylliosis. He told him about the mine and what he had found in his old med school notes, Dr. Michelangelo, said, "sure why not, let's be thorough."

The bronchoscopy was fascinating to Wilson. Michelangelo showed him how to manipulate the instrument, and orient himself as to what was up and down. He let Wilson do one of the wash-outs by pressing the button on the scope to introduce saline into Vern's lungs, then suction it all into a container with a loud slurping sound. Everything went as planned. Afterward, Michelangelo said that while he had seen a lot of TB patients' lungs this did not look at all like that, so he thanked Wilson for suggesting the beryllium test. They met Jamison outside the OR waiting for them anxious to see what they found, "So, how did it go?"

"Great, I don't think it's going to be TB in the end, but we will need at least a week to see if the cultures are all negative. Meanwhile, continue the same course."

"Yeah, I consulted on him a few months back when I was on pulmonology consults," Jamison said, "It all sounded like TB, but sometimes when you hear hoofbeats it's not horses, but zebras."

"You guys want to grab some lunch?" Michelangelo asked. Wilson now felt like one of the guys. The pulmonology clique.

CHAPTER 36

WESTMAN WAS DOWN IN THE ER waiting, and Jablonski was with him. They both cornered Brent Plumber who had just walked in the door at 6 am.

Westman spoke first, very politely asking, "You are aware we have new trauma triage rules, Mr. Plumber?"

"Yes, and by the way, it is Dr. Plumber."

Westman looked perplexed for a second. In his mind, he did not call anyone who did not finish a surgery residency doctor. Yet everyone who graduates from medical school is called doctor. He continued, "Yesterday there was a patient, one of our medical students precisely, who met trauma rules to call the surgeon. He had visible signs of trauma to his head."

Brent composed himself, "Well let's get the binder down and see, I am sure we both can learn from the policy." He walked behind the desk grabbed a large red three-ring binder from the shelf and started flipping through the pages. "I was fully oriented on this when I was hired, but let's see if anything has changed. Ah, here it is; All patients arriving by ambulance who meet the following criteria must have the trauma surgeon paged on arrival, and there is a long list of injuries, and yes there it is, trauma to the head."

"So, I am correct. You should have called us on this case."

"Well not to be picky. He did not arrive by ambulance. He was wheeled here from the front lobby."

"I think that is a minor interpretation error. All patients who come to the ER who meet these criteria need to have us, surgery, involved. Not everyone in the ER has the skills to evaluate a trauma victim. That's why we write these policies."

"So noted," Turning from Westman to Jablonski Brent went on, "Dr. Jablonski, I presume you are here then to collect this binder and re-write the policy so all patients, whether they arrive by ambulance or not are included?"

Jablonski got angry, "Listen, use some common-sense man, this is for patient care not to stand up in a court of law. This was one of our medical students. We have a responsibility to them to keep them safe and provide a solid education."

"No argument, sir," Brent said knowing now was not the time to walk up to one of those artificial lines in the sand over this case. "Is he doing well? Was there anything about my care that needs critical review?"

"He is getting better, He avoided needing surgery."

"Okay, well now I know better, I will, as we have spoken in the past, Dr. J, always follow the rules."

Westman was satisfied, and he had other things to do, He understood there is always a judgment call in medicine. He just wanted to give some constructive feedback to Plumber. Jablonski was not so mollified. He was always out for blood, especially the doctors in the ER, whom he always regarded as a motley crew of misfits. This was his second run-in with Plumber this week, but still, his number one target was Fish. He never forgot the night in the ICU, with Fish bagging the intubated patients without ventilators, and the humiliation of being yelled at and being insulted by Fish. At least Brent knew when to demure and be polite. Jablonski and Westman walked off in different directions. Brent put his backpack away and checked all the rooms in the ER for new cases. It was empty at this hour so he went to Room Four to do his warm-up exercises, again as if nothing unusual had happened.

CHAPTER 37

HARRY WAS CONCERNED ENOUGH AFTER Sam's call from the library. He thought he knew all the aspects of his disease. He looked at himself in the mirror, pulled his eyelids open as wide as he could tolerate, and tried it in varying degrees of light. His eyes were bright yellow. *I really do look bad.* Despite all his maneuverings, he could not convince himself that his jaundice was as it always was. *Was this hepatitis or something worse?* For one thing, his urine looked more and more like cola, especially in the morning. This was new. He was worried a bit about his drinking, a glass of gin and soda before dinner had become his usual when he got off call. No more than he saw his parents drink growing up. He did not see any spider angiomata lesions, typical of alcohol liver disease, as he had noticed on his father the last time he saw him.

He thought about the years in medical school in Mexico. *Could I have picked up some parasite down there?* He was especially careful after several other medical students got sick and had to go home without completing the program. He never drank the tap water, and never went swimming in the river that was heavily polluted. Besides he thought, it has been at least six months since I have been there. He racked his brain to see if there were any liver diseases that would show up that late after an exposure, and could not think of any off-hand. Wilson would know he thought, he knew everything obscure. Despite a night of worrying and reaching no easily explainable causes, he went into employee health the next morning to have his blood drawn.

To Harry's surprise, the staff in the employee health unit were not particularly concerned. They offered up that they had seen a few cases of hepatitis A in the last few weeks, but no common source. Most of the employees who got it did not know each other. Harry wanted to ask who they were, but he knew with confidentiality rules they would never say. Just as secure as if the next person came in and asked about him. Unfortunately, with this rule there was no way to connect the dots if the patients chose to compare notes.

A few days later Harry got a page. At first, he did not recognize the number but knew it was a hospital extension. He went to the desk and dialed it.

"Dr. Martin?"

"Yes, speaking."

"This is Mary the infection control nurse from employee health. Do you have a minute?" That did not sound like a conversation that Harry was looking forward to having but said that he did.

"We got your serology back, and the good news is you don't have Hepatitis B, but you do have the more common type A. You are now the 15th employee here this month with it, so we have launched an investigation. First, let me reassure you that you should recover completely, BUT…" Harry held his breath; he did not like what usually followed a BUT when delivering medical news. He had been on the delivery end of that BUT before. Mary continued, "You can't have any patient contact until this is over. A few other don'ts as well—no sex, no sharing of shaving utensils, or toothbrushes,…" *Who shares toothbrushes* Harry wanted to say? Mary went on with a variety of other steps to avoid spreading his infection. She also suggested no alcohol. Harry had been acknowledging each with an "uh-huh" affirmative grunt.

Finally, when she was done covering the rules, Harry had a question, "So where did I get this from?"

"Hard to say, we are zeroing in on the cafeteria right now. It's likely we will close it but we need an okay from the administration."

"You mean like Jablonski?"

"Well him, and the country health officer, both need to sign off on it."

"What about everyone who might eat there today or until whenever this decision is made?"

"We are trying to process this as fast as we can. We can't shut it down until we get final approval. For yourself, I would suggest bringing your lunch."

"You just said I can't have patient contact, so I assume lunch at the hospital whether I bring it or buy it is over. Am I being ordered to stay home?"

"It depends on your specialty. Some fields like radiology, you might be able to continue work to some degree. Others, likely your program director or chief of service will follow hospital infection control policy and mandate you stay home."

Harry went to the internal medicine office and they acknowledged that he needed to sign out his ward service immediately and go home. He called Sam to let him know.

Sam was standing with Fish at the moment he heard and looked upset on the phone. When he got off, Fish asked, "What's up? Is everything Okay?"

Sam shook his head.

Fish looked at him, "Is it your dad?"

"No, it's poor Harry who can't seem to get a break." And Sam told Fish how he prodded Harry to get tested for his worsening jaundiced.

Fish was silent for over a minute then turned to Sam and said, "Look at this from the positive perspective. You made the diagnosis correctly. You saved the patient, in this case, your friend, and you did not rely on the obvious explanation of his Gilbert's disease. You had a sixth sense that something more was wrong and you followed through on it. Those are the makings of a good doctor. Don't freeze focus on the common most obvious diagnosis. In medicine, we need to throw out the theory of Occam's razor, that the easiest explanation is most likely right. Most often it isn't."

"What do we replace that with?"

"Well, my uncle used to say that sometimes a dog has ticks and fleas."

Sam smiled at the thought, and he wrote it down on the back inside cover of his peripheral brain, along with Fish's other rules.

CHAPTER 38

WILSON COULDN'T WAIT TO SPRING the news on Michelangelo. He had gotten in early, as he was now doing regularly, and got the bronchial washing results back on Vern. All the samples were free of TB, but the beryllium test was positive. They had "found a zebra" as Jamison suggested they might. Michelangelo was proud of his new intern's enthusiasm, and they both worked on a presentation for the Grand Rounds the following week. Michelangelo would do the presentation, but Wilson tracked down as many helpful pieces as he could. He organized the timeline of events, got a photo from the library of the Delta beryllium mine, got the chest X-rays, CT scans, pathology specimens, and every article written on beryllium lung disease.

On the following Monday, the day of Grand Rounds, at noon, the chief of staff introduced Corbin Michelangelo as "the new local expert who will tell us about a fascinating case with a lesson for us all." Wilson clapped. At the podium as Michelangelo stood up to a packed auditorium of students, residents, and staff. He was tall and confident, Wilson hoped he could do what Michelangelo was doing someday. Michelangelo thanked the chief for his gracious introduction but announced that he wanted to express a special appreciation to Wilson Harrison of internal medicine who was essential in tracking down the answer to this puzzling case. He then dove into a lecture on the case and how the ultimately correct diagnosis was made. He showed all of Wilson's slides that he had made for the presentation.

He finished with these concluding remarks, "The patient is now on the right medication, high-dose steroids. This is something that no one in their right mind would dream of giving to a tuberculous patient. But as we have seen beryllium is a great masquerader, and steroids are what was needed." After a rousing round of applause, he once again acknowledged Wilson

THE COUNTY

whom he waved a hand upward for him to stand at that point. Wilson smiled. He felt like he should bow or something, but this was a Grand Rounds lecture not a school play, so he just nodded. It felt good to be acknowledged.

There was a brief question-and-answer session and then at 1:00 everyone started to get up to leave. Sam was sitting next to Wilson and was really proud for his friend, and congratulated him, but said he had to run back to the ward, and left quickly. Wilson was still on cloud nine about how well the presentation went, he really wanted to talk to Michelangelo about how he felt. Maybe they could write it up as a paper for a journal like Sam was doing with his Toxic Shock case. Wilson grabbed Michelangelo's slide carousel from the slide projector and started to walk out with it under his arm along with Michelangelo, Jamison, and the other pulmonology staff and fellows. He felt part of the team.

Just outside the auditorium, Wilson got paged. He motioned to Michelangelo by holding up the pager and motioning with his chin towards the bank of phones that were just outside the doorway to the auditorium. Michelangelo nodded and said, "Okay, I am just going to stop here before we go back upstairs." He tilted his head sideways to the public bathroom, then turned back and said, "take your time, you did a good job today."

Wilson did not notice anyone around him in the mass exodus from the auditorium, but there was one person there who did not fit. Wilson was waiting for an open phone when he heard a low moan, not a scream but a distinct "OW" followed by a thud. A few seconds later came the scream. Someone had just entered the men's room in time to see the person who did not belong, in a dirty overcoat, with a hammer in his right hand raised and prepared to strike. Michelangelo was already on the floor. The assailant turned and took two broad swipes with the hammer at the screamer, who stepped backwards and ran. The assailant then saw his opportunity to escape. He stepped out into the hall, looked right, then left, and saw a crowd in both directions all now recoiling in shock. Straight ahead was the hall through the back of the ER, empty, and he ran down it.

Brent Plumber had just finished applying a double sugar-tong splint on a man who fell and fractured his wrist, in Room Four. The classic fall on an outstretched hand, or FOOSH mechanism, gave the man a Colle's fracture of his forearm. He needed both the wrist and elbow immobilized for proper healing to occur. Brent had taken off his white coat and was just in his blue scrubs. Putting on such a splint by himself required him to place the palms of his hands on either side near the wrist to stabilize the fracture, then with some body English with his elbows pressing against the patient's elbows holding the back side of the plaster in place until it hardened. Brent had bits of plaster stuck to his skin from his fingers to his own elbows. He had just finished and heard a commotion in the hall and stepped out into the main ER hall that led from the auditorium straight towards the ambulance doors. Running straight at him was a man in a dirty overcoat, with a hammer in one hand. Brent thought he saw some blood on it.

"Stop him! Stop that man!" someone yelled from down the hall, pointing at Brent and the assailant.

Brent stepped out into the middle of the hall, wide stance up on the balls of his feet. "HEY, this area is for patients only! Are you a patient here?"

"No, get the fuck out of my way," growled the man.

"That's all I wanted to know." Brent reached one arm back, and one forward, curled his knuckles into a striking stance, and struck the assailant in the throat, hard. The assailant dropped the hammer and began choking and brought both his hands up to his throat as he gasped for air. Brent struck him again with his other hand open palm upward thrusting midchest. The assailant rose a few inches off the ground hit the wall behind him and crumpled into a gasping ball face down on the floor.

"Armstrong! Sally, I need Armstrong," then something Brent hardly ever said, "Now, on the double."

CHAPTER 39

FOUR ARMSTRONG OFFICERS CAME RUNNING down the hall, and Brent stepped back. The real struggle was going on in the bathroom at the end of the hall. No sooner had the man screamed than Wilson ran up to the door, just as the assailant pushed past him. Wilson stepped in and saw Michelangelo on the floor moaning, blood coming from the back of his head, onto his white jacket. Wilson immediately pulled a few paper towels from the dispenser and pressed them to Michelangelo's head to stop the bleeding. "Are you Okay? Are you Okay?" he cried. He did not want to move him afraid he would cause some irreversible injury.

"Head,... head hurts," was all Michelangelo could say before he went limp in Wilson's arms.

"HELP! I Need some HELP in here! Oh God, please help him!"

Brent had been relieved of his need to stop the assailant by the four Armstrongs. He heard the call for help from the end of the hall. He ran that way and when he got inside he knew he needed to get the man on the floor to the ER. He did not recognize him at first. Brent gave Wilson an order, "Grab his feet and we are going to lift on 3; 1,2,3." Brent stabilized Michelangelo's head with his own elbows tucked in tightly, similar to how he put on the forearm splint and held Michelangelo's neck immobilized with his hands. He knew that head and neck injuries come together.

They stepped out the door and luckily there was a gurney just a few feet away, and they placed Michelangelo's limp body on it, face up. Brent kicked off the brakes and rolled it down the hall. He yelled down to hall hoping someone at the desk would hear, "Trauma, call the trauma team, and find Snider no matter where he is, get him down here right now."

Wilson had jumped on the rolling gurney, looking at Michelangelo turning blue he started frantically to do mouth-to-mouth breathing on him. Michelangelo's blood smeared Wilson's face. Brent felt the side of his neck and said, "We still got a pulse." Then loudly to the air behind him once again hoping someone at the desk would hear he yelled, "And I need the airway equipment in Room One, and RT, and a vent." They rolled past the Armstrongs who had the assailant pushed face up against the side wall outside Room Four, past Rooms Three and Two, and made the sharp turn into the resuscitation Room One.

What happened next was a blur, but a perfectly coordinated trauma code. Once the gurney stopped Brent grabbed the bag-valve mask and started to breathe for Michelangelo. Wilson was pushed away. Several nurses descended on each extremity, clothes were cut off, IVs were started, blood was drawn. Snider and the trauma team arrived simultaneously, within three minutes, they completed the head-to-toe exam and Snider nodded to Brent to go ahead and intubate him. The paralytic sedative cocktail was pushed and flawlessly the endotracheal tube was passed. RT was there and began bagging him, Brent heard good breath sounds on both sides, Snider listened too and agreed. Snider said, "CT then OR, we are not coming back here, have them set up a craniotomy room in the OR." And off they went; time in resus was eight minutes.

Wilson just stood staring from the foot of the bed the whole time, numb all over. He disappeared into a soundless tunnel, all the noise in the room blotted out, just wordless sounds bouncing in his ears, broken by occasional beeps from monitors. None of it registered in his brain. He did not move, he did not speak, he did not hear, he just disappeared inside a deep dark tunnel. Then the sounds disappeared too, as they wheeled Michelangelo past him, out of Room One, to the CT scanner. Wilson, his face still spotted with blood, was the only one left in the room. His world had just disappeared.

Unfortunately, the CT scan showed a severely depressed skull fracture and massive intracranial bleeding. Time in the CT scanner was also remarkably brief and the OR was ready for them. Westman and the chief of neurosurgery met Snider in the OR and reviewed the scan. Westman allowed the neurosurgery team first move, he broke his 'torso first' rule after hearing the circumstances. There were enough witnesses to say there never was a strike anywhere but to the back of the head. Westman knew judgment prevailed over rules, the brain would take precedence. In the end, everything was done right and incredibly fast, but where the blow landed with the short striking distance in the bathroom was critical. They all seemed to know after the procedure to evacuate the blood that things were bleak. Very bleak.

CHAPTER 40

THE POLICE WERE ALL OVER the hospital within an hour, regular cops, hospital security, and a set of detectives. The two detectives got copies of the Armstrong incident report from the medical student assault, and that led them to Mac Snider, who had reported the event. Detective Lowry flashed his badge in the neuro-ICU where Snider was on rounds and asked, "Is there somewhere we can talk?"

Snider shooed the medical students and interns out of the charting area and said, "This is about as private as we get here, sit down."

"We just read the campus security report about the first victim here and wanted to know what and why you thought this was not an accident?"

"You mean the guy from the museum?"

"No, the student. What museum? What guy?"

"There was a guy assaulted in the museum bathroom about a week ago. I did not report it but I thought his head wound looked suspicious for it not being an accidental slip and fall, but more like somebody cold-cocked him with a blunt object. It matched the injury to the med student here, which I did call our local cops about."

"We don't have any of this. And the part about the first victim is not in the security personnel report about your student. Just the fact you thought it was not consistent, in quotes, that his injury was an accident."

"So did they do anything about it? Did they talk to the city about the first guy? Did they even go to the scene where each of these assaults happened? Huh? Is everybody asleep at the wheel?" Snider pounded the desk with his fist.

"Just cool down a sec doc, we are looking at everything now, and yes, we are finally connecting the dots here, but we don't know about victim number one. Who is he?"

"He is a patient here. My hands are tied about giving you medical information, but I can do better. Come with me and I'll introduce him to you. No confidentiality violations in having visitors. He's on the rehab floor."

"Ok, happy to do that. But what about the injuries make you think they were all done the same way?"

"All three were to the back of the head, right side," he indicated with his hand and turned around to the detective. "All had a rounded depressed segment like a ball-peen hammer or something similar. And they all occurred in bathrooms, although only the last two were here at the hospital. Hey, who knows how many others there are that did not come here?"

Snider walked Lowry to the elevators still talking excitedly. There was an angry accusatory tone in his voice, like why haven't you idiots figured this out already? But Snider was trying to hold it together. He just did a craniotomy on his friend and one of the most respected doctors at County, and he felt the entire accident could have been avoided had someone done something when he reported the medical student attack. When they got to the physical medicine and rehabilitation floor, rehab for short, he went to the desk and asked about his patient. The nurse said he was transferred to a nursing home the day before.

"Ok, now we have a bit of a problem. If I tell you his name and where he is I have blown patient confidentiality, but if I don't you are behind on getting critical information from him."

"Well doc, don't do anything illegal. You know we already have the guy in custody. One of your docs nailed him in the act. But we want to put together as many pieces of the puzzle as we can. What can you tell us to help?"

"I am going to be writing a note here at the desk, you wouldn't happen to be peering over my shoulder when I do. I'll try to write a lot clearer and larger than my usual doctor's scrawl, how about that?"

"Did quite catch that," Lowry winked, "but finish your paperwork first, did not want to stop you caring for patients."

Back at the elevator Snider asked, "So who caught him, again."

Lowry flipped through his notepad, "Some doc named Plumber. Know him?"

The ER filled up again after the trauma code on Dr. Michelangelo. Brent ordinarily calm, if not completely unemotional and unfazed, seemed upset for most of the day.

However, he took care of everyone who came in in his usual efficient style. So it was out of character when he spoke first when he saw Jablonski coming down the hall. "Listen I called a trauma code on him, and I took down the asshole who nearly killed our doc. And I checked first. He was not a patient when I KO 'ed him. So save your rule-mongering for today I am not in any mood to hear them."

"Truthfully, Brent I just wanted to thank you this time. We caught a potential serial assailant and stopped him. Corbin is in very serious condition, though, in the neuro-ICU. We are going to have a debriefing for the five chiefs so that they can speak to their troops. I wanted to ask you to come at noon tomorrow and tell them all what happened."

Brent was disarmed but recovered to his usual just-the-facts mode, "Okay, I am sure I can do something like that. Where is this meeting?"

CHAPTER 41

IN THE NEURO-ICU, THE VISITORS started coming. Wilson stood out of the way of the traffic of people, out of sight, observing it all. First came Corbin's wife. She sat at the bedside trying to hold back tears, but she wasn't able to control them. She held his hand. His head was wrapped in white bandages and it was starting to show some blood stains from behind. His head was elevated at a 45-degree angle, a maneuver the doctors said may decrease swelling. The breathing tube was attached to a big box ventilator with its rhythmic inhalation and exhalation sounds. The neurosurgery team was at the desk pointing at a CT scan and not speaking. They had not discussed the results of the post-op CT scan with her yet. She was too torn up to receive information, and the information was not good. The neurosurgery team had asked the Armstrongs for two plain-clothes security guards outside the room, and they seemed to blend in invisibly just as Wilson did within the ICU. The bedside nurse came out and whispered to Snider, "Just a feeling, but I think she looks a tiny bit pregnant." No one would dare ask, of course, but she was.

Other relatives showed up. His brothers, his parents, her parents. They each hugged Michelangelo's wife. The pulmonology team, Jamison, Fish, the chiefs of staff of medicine and surgery all came in, put a comforting hand on her shoulder, and said a few words to Dr. Michelangelo's wife. Wilson wanted to go in, but he did not know her. He stood off to one side of the ICU desk, by himself, the same blank feeling he had in Room One remained. He had washed his face. Somehow he was able to walk upstairs to the ICU. He stood as far back as he could with tears dripping down his cheeks that he kept wiping away. He was feeling that he was just an intern, an inconsequential person in the grand scheme of the hospital hierarchy. Yet he had just worked so intensely with Dr. Michelangelo on the beryllium case, the slides, the presentation, learning how to do the bronch with him in the

OR, making the correct diagnosis. But most of all he had found a new mentor, perhaps the first one who ever spent time with him and made him excited again about why he wanted to be a doctor. He was not able to bring himself to say any of that to Michelangelo's wife. It would sound like something you say after someone has died. In his heart, he knew that was invariably the outcome, based on the looks on everyone's face, especially Snider's. After staring through the glass door at Michelangelo, his wife, and all the comings and goings for what seemed like an excessively long time to be standing at the desk in the neuro-ICU with nothing to do, he left. He was alone in the elevator ride down and tears welled up in his eyes. He never got to say what he wanted to say; that was the last time he saw Michelangelo.

CHAPTER 42

THE NEWS OF THE ASSAULT spread through the hospital, it was shocking and scary that such a thing happened. But the news of Corbin Michelangelo's death two days later was like someone punched the wind out of every last person who worked there. How does an institution grieve so deeply yet continue to function? Michelangelo's family took it extremely hard. The staff of medicine and pulmonology canceled all their clinics, still, someone needed to be there for the ICU and Jamison volunteered. In the ER the clerks to the nurses and doctors were barely functional, they could not walk down the hall where it happened and took the long way around to X-ray as a result. The bathroom was police-taped off; although later when the tapes were removed no one dared use it.

Wilson asked for some time off and reluctantly the medicine office granted him five days. Sam, Harry, Gina, and all the interns were in a state of shock, but none were allowed time off, even to go to the funeral that was set for that weekend. Someone had to run the hospital, the ER had to stay open, the wards had to have admissions and discharges. But the entire staff walked around like zombies silent, sometimes acknowledging to each other with a nod or a pat on the shoulder, that something terrible had ripped their hearts out.

The night after Michelangelo passed, Sam went back to his apartment, and his phone rang. It was his father in Buffalo, who had heard about it on the national news, "Sammy are you okay, were you around this nut who killed that doctor?"

"I was working that day. I knew the doctor, I had just heard him give a great lecture, he was such a great guy."

"Is it safe to continue to work there?"

"I guess so, there seem to be more police than ever hanging around now."

"Do you want to come home for a few days? Will they let you do that? Certainly, they would understand. I do miss you. Especially since … well you know how proud mom was the day you graduated. She would not want anything bad to happen to you. Of course I don't either. You know she would have worried about you, and I promised her I would too."

"I can ask. Maybe. I don't think I am working at my best right now. I am just slow-motion walking through taking care of my patients. I am afraid I will miss something." He didn't want to alarm his father too much so he added, "But hey, so is everyone else who works here. They can't give us all off. They only allowed a select group to be off for the funeral. I miss you too, dad. Let me see if there is some kind of leave I can take. I just don't feel like being a doctor right now. The world does not seem fair."

"If you can't come here, I could fly out to you."

"No, no, let me ask. It may be a few days. But I will call you. I miss you."

When Sam went to the internal medicine house staff office the next day, they flatly told him no. They were giving Wilson off since he had just worked so closely with Dr. Michelangelo, and he seemed completely broken up. Plus Harry was on sick leave with hepatitis. They had called everyone in from electives outside the hospital, and they were going to switch call from every fourth night this week to every third, just to cover the wards.

THE COUNTY

"Didn't you already use up your week of leave time?" the secretary asked Sam.

"Yes, but my mother died. Besides, it was only five days I think."

"Well, five days is a work week."

"No, the hospital is open seven days a week. I am just asking for maybe two days off then if that is all I have left."

"Five days, Monday through Friday, that's all you can take. The weekends are off anyway."

"Well maybe for you in this office. I am in the hospital seven days a week, both days and nights. I quite frankly I am not so sure right now I am capable of working."

"Well that's different. We have a bereavement leave limited to one week a year, or five working days, but if you don't feel capable or working, you'll need a medical leave."

"It's not really medical, maybe psychological, but definitely stressful."

"Still you need a doctor to sign off on a medical leave. You could go to the clinic if you want."

"But they are all closed for the funeral for a few days"

"We are not the only doctors in town. You can get a private doctor's note. We do have a form for you if that is what you want. Let me find it."

"No. I don't know any doctors outside the County. I doubt I could get an appointment even if I did. And no doc is going to accept a new patient to see whose chief complaint is a work excuse. So, No I don't think any of that will work. I am just asking for a few days' rest to recover from this."

"Are you a direct relative?"

"No"

"Sorry then, that's not allowed. We are so short-staffed right now. We need everyone who can work to work, no exceptions, Sorry Dr. Wyatt. You need to stay and work."

So no, Sam could not go home, he would have to stay, and work every other day in the emergency room. He wanted to say "I quit" and run as far away from this place as he could, but inside he knew if he said that then he would never work in medicine again. The repercussions of quitting were enormous and life-long in medicine. The death was so unfair, and this was just as unfair.

Something else was happening with Sam. After the attack in the bathroom at the hospital he could no longer bring himself to use the public restrooms, not just the one where the murder occurred. As it was, he had pretty much trained himself to go almost a full 12 hours anyway without going to the bathroom.

THE COUNTY

He drank his usual one cup of black coffee in the morning and little else all day. He rarely ate in the cafeteria; he just brought a box of Fig-Newtons to snack on each day. Now if he had to use the bathroom, he sought out the single-use locking patient bathrooms, and not the bathrooms still open to the public.

Sam finally worked out a solution in his mind. After calculating some trades on the schedule he came up with a massive multi-day trade that would let him fly home mid-week for two days. He worked the details with Gina and another intern and bought a round-trip ticket to Buffalo. He felt he needed to clear his head.

He was getting to the point where he was fearful of coming to work. On top of all that he was beginning to ask himself did he want to be an internal medicine doc anymore. This month he was back in the emergency room but every time he walked into Room One or down the hall past Room Four he had flashbacks to the assault. The first day after it happened, he broke into a cold sweat and felt his heart racing. In his mind, the question he was asking himself over and over was, *"so why should I continue to do this residency?"* What he did not know was that he was not alone in that thought, none of the interns talked about it, but all were thinking about it. Maybe, he just needed to start over closer to home. This dream of coming to California was not what he thought it would be. Central City and the County were dangerous places. He had friends here but felt alone, pressured to continue to work. Wilson was having the same thoughts, too.

Winter in Buffalo changed his life once more. He was waiting at the gate in the airport to fly home when he found out, after two flight delays, that there was a massive snowstorm in Buffalo making travel impossible. The gate agent made the announcement apologetically and collected everyone's colored plastic boarding number. Sam watched the TV screen with no sound on as the weatherman stretched his arms out from Chicago across the Great Lakes, then they cut to a picture of snow falling in a near whiteout. He thought he recognized the street they were filming from home. He could not go home to Buffalo, even though he had traded away three days for three nights in a row when he got back. Sam walked to an isolated back corner of the airport. The sun had just set, through the large glass pane it was dark outside and he could sense the cold. He stared out the large glass window for a while, then sat down alone in a row of chairs. Head in his hands, he started to cry, feeling lost. He felt like he could not go on, *there must be a way out.* No one

THE COUNTY

came near him. A sound out of his backpack brought him around. His pager went off. *Why was he getting paged?* He had no patient care responsibilities for three days; he was sure the trades all would work. Gina was going to cover his ER shifts. The phone number on the pager was the internal medicine office. *Maybe they had second thoughts about granting him time off?* He went to a pay phone and called the number displayed on his pager. Another intern was out with hepatitis and they needed him back, even with the trades he made, he was always at jeopardy to be called in.

"*Oh, why the hell not,*" thought Sam, "*I can't go home I might as well work and keep busy.*" He told the house staff office he could be in an hour.

They said, "Thank you for helping out, and by the way, bring your dinner tonight, they just closed the cafeteria for health reasons."

CHAPTER 43

SAM WAS FINISHING HIS NIGHT of the shift he got called in for the day the funeral was scheduled. He had been up since the day before. First waiting at the airport, then coming to the hospital at 6 at night to cover for the intern who went home with hepatitis. The Saturday night shift was about as crazy as it gets in the ER. Stabbings, a drug overdose, a heart attack, lots of lacerations, and fractures. He was just signing out to the next day intern who asked if he was going to the funeral. Sam felt that he needed to, but was too tired to drive. Fish overheard them and said he was going and he could drive Sam.

Sam went looking for a bathroom that locked and found one he knew on the ICU floor. He had taken his backpack with him, which still had some clean clothes he was going to wear in Buffalo. He threw water on his face, peeled off his scrubs, and tried to clean up the best he could. He swished some water around his mouth to try to rid himself of the stale been up all night taste he had. He put on his clean shirt and pants, but all he had was his sneakers to wear. He hoped no one would be looking at his feet. He found Fish in the ER and they walked to his van which was at his house. Fish lived in a square one-story cottage home across from the street leading to the ER entrance. The home was small but well kept. One side was a small kitchen that opened to a living room with a fire place and a couch. There was no TV. On a large coffee table, and the two side tables, were hundreds of medical journals, some with bookmarks, others with notes on them. A yellow writing pad was on the coffee table with lots of notes as well. Fish went to the other side of his home into the bedroom, and came out wearing a faded herringbone sport coat, and held up two ties.

"I did not know you lived this close," Sam said trying to knot his tie in the visor mirror as they drove. He noticed Fish had given him a nicer tie than he was wearing. Fish had one of those old straight black ties, skinny and dull, and with a few food stains on it. For the most part Fish's long beard covered it up.

"Yeah if I ever had to get paged in, I can run and be there in less than 30 seconds. Sometimes when I am in the ICU, I just step out to grab food, or refill my thermos with coffee, or find a journal or something I need over here. Truth is, I spend practically no time at all here. Maybe one night out of four, the rest I am in the hospital." Sam thought that sounded too familiar, and if that's the life that lay ahead for him.

Fish drove his beat-up VW van to the church where the funeral was scheduled to start. The van was a throwback to the '60s. There was a mattress in the back and several boxes, some with camping gear, some with books, and an old tent. None of it was tied down and it rattled whenever they went over a bump. The shock absorbers in the van were shot so even a little bump in the pavement set the van rocking up and down and the mess in the back clattering.

"Do much camping?"

"Once upon a time. Since I got here for the last two years I more or less live in the hospital, but that's okay with me. I don't need much other than work to be happy. That is the life of an ICU doc. Don't know if you heard, but I'm going to stay here and do a critical care fellowship after next year and it will only get worse."

"Don't you want to ever spend time outside the hospital? I mean life is short. Don't you have a hankering to go to a restaurant or see a movie?" Sam asked. "Look what happened to Dr. Michelangelo. What if you worked for all those years and something like that happens to you? What if you never got to live a normal life?"

"I gave up on what you would call normal when I came here to do this. It was my choice and I can't have any regrets about it."

"I don't know if I can live like that," Sam shook his head. "Shit, today I don't know if I can even go back into the hospital, the ER especially, anymore."

"I get it Sam. But the reasons things like this happen are not due to either of us working too hard or not working at all. They just happen. Corbin was the best man I have ever known, and the best doctor this hospital ever had. If there was something someone did not know they went to him to ask, and either he knew it, or went about finding the answer himself. He worked hard and he went home, he balanced his life. He had a wife, started a family, and yet there it is. Tragedy. Why?"

"I don't know. There are too many crazy people out there. I really had no idea until I started working here. Just look at who we see in the ER every night."

"Mostly because we have never had a decent plan for how to take care of the mentally ill in this country. It certainly seems like his attacker was schizophrenic. The news said he was on a long-term psych hold in another county a year ago, but he got released at the end of it and disappeared from the system. No one was assigned to check on his whereabouts." Fish paused for a second while he negotiated a left turn, then went on, "Not too long ago, we had huge mental asylums. They got lots of bad press, inhumane conditions, frontal lobotomies, the whole one flew over the cuckoo's nest phenomena. So we closed them. But there was no actual backup plan. One of the last things JFK signed before he himself was assassinated, by yet another madman, was something called the Community Mental Health Act of 1963. Good intentions, he had a sister who was institutionalized and ultimately lobotomized after all, so it affected him dearly. But the politicians failed to anticipate the consequences. Not everyone had a close-knit family like JFK's to look after them, so it set the stage for whole-sale emptying the mental hospitals onto the streets and it never set up the community part with care programs. There was absolutely no back-up plan. They fell into an abyss of no longer having a mental health system. And the mentally ill took the brunt of it, no treatment, no housing, no options, and they were shunned. The cycle repeated itself and they got even less care, stopped their meds, and became more paranoid and fearful of society. They filled up the parks, camping behind the trees, and back-alley streets, highway medians, riverbanks. Then when Reagan was governor here, he closed several mental hospitals, cut their budgets, and created the law that let us only keep them for three days. When someone acts out in public, the police bring them to the ER to be cared for. But there is only so much you can do in the ER. Some get put on a 5150 psych hold, but 72 hours later it expires, they still can refuse the medications that might help, and we cut them loose again. Rinse and repeat."

"You think the bastard who did this will get off as insane?"

"To kill you must be insane, but no, I don't think he was so insane as to be spared a death sentence. Hate is not insanity, it is irrational, but wrong. He was filled with hate. Enough hate to want to hide and then hit people over the head. Maybe he was striking back at some inner demon, which maybe with treatment we could have dealt with, but sadly we just lost a good man, and we will sentence this man to death." Fish paused again, almost tearing up, but suddenly composing himself, "And our mission, you and I, must be to go on, continue to care for everyone, to try our best to make the system better, to fix what we can."

"Or what? Die trying?"

"No, we will have to be satisfied with just one success each day of our lives, save one patient each day. Prevent another tragedy like this. Get someone the care they need. In the emergency room just admitting someone is the first step to get them off the street. And yes, sometimes we will have to fight the bureaucracy, the Jablonski's of the world, to make that happen. At least I will. That too takes its toll, I burned some bridges there." After a final pause, he added, "It is going to be really hard to go back inside the County, but we will."

Sam was quiet. He did not know what to say. Here he was thinking about quitting and Fish was all in, doubling down on the rage, he had to do better for patients. Maybe Sam had it wrong. Maybe Sam needed to stay. They arrived at the church and circled the block twice unable to find any open parking spots. Fish pulled his van onto someone's lawn and parked it. Fish said, "My luck, this would be Jablonski's lawn, and", imitating Jablonski bluster, "no improvision or violation of the parking rules will be tolerated." They both laughed at that and got out of the van.

THE COUNTY

The service was an emotional affair. Fish and Sam barely could get into the packed church, and stood against the back wall. Sam saw Wilson dressed in a suit sitting two rows ahead of them. Many others who came later tried to cram in but were forced to listen from the hallway outside. There was a huge photo of Corbin Michelangelo on an easel near the podium. There were flowers everywhere. Somber orchestral music played. Michelangelo's family were in the front, each one hugged his wife as they arrived. His parents remained seated by her side. In front of her was a small child in a stroller. Sam thought back to his mother's funeral just a few months earlier. Maybe twenty people were there then. He had uncles and an aunt, a few neighbors, his father, and his brother with him in the front row. A single wreath of flowers. A few words were spoken, people were thanked for coming, and it was over in less than an hour.

Now there were hundreds of people coming to mourn Dr. Michelangelo. Colleagues from the hospital spoke about what a wonderful doctor he was, and how the world was robbed of his caring. His brother spoke. His brother looked just like him—tall, bespeckled, kind, and spoke warmly about the family growing up. A native son, athlete, husband, and father. Wilson sat head down, biting his lip, and crying. Wilson desperately wanted to go up and say something to Michelangelo's brother, things he wanted to say to Michelangelo a few days earlier. Wilson was too choked up, he could barely speak, or think, and he did not want to embarrass himself so he stayed sitting near the back without getting that chance to say how much Michelangelo had influenced his life in just a short time. For four hours people spoke emotionally from their hearts about how wonderful the man they all collectively lost was. A college friend read a poem; he could barely get through it he choked up several times. The priest read a passage from the Bible. The grief in the church was palpable.

Sam somehow stayed awake despite having not slept in over 24 hours; it helped that he had to stand through the service. If he was sitting, he might have dozed off. Every time something wonderful or inspiring was said he, like so many others at the church, teared up. He gazed around the room and saw the family, the medical staff, lots of strangers all wiping their eyes with every speaker's eulogy. Sam thought *"I barely knew him, but this hurts me more inside than my mother's death. With her, we knew for months it was coming, even though the very end was a surprise. With this, it was the shock out of nowhere. A lightning bolt out of a clear sky. How do you go on after that?"*

CHAPTER 44

FISH DROVE SAM HOME AFTER the funeral. They both rode back in painful silence. Sam fell asleep despite the ruckus the van made going over the bumps in the road. He climbed up the stairs into his apartment, just fell onto his bed in exhaustion, and fell asleep immediately. He had been up for nearly 34 hours.

Sam woke hours later. He was not sure what time it was. He took a shower and dumped his knapsack of travel clothes out on the floor. That reminded him he had better call his father again since his flight home was canceled and he had to come in to work instead.

"How you doing, dad? Is the snow still coming down hard?"

"Yup, snowed all night, and it's still coming down. We may get four feet before it stops. Good thing you didn't try to fly, airport's closed. You'd probably be diverted to Boston or something."

"Well, the plane was canceled at this end, so it was not going to even take off from here. Anyway, I got called in to work the ER. Someone got sick. At least I got to go to Dr. Michelangelo's funeral. Everyone had great things to say about him." He was going to say more but caught himself, he did not want to compare it to his mother's simple funeral on the phone to his father.

"Listen, I was thinking maybe in the Spring I could come out and we can spend some time together." His father said, then asked, "Are you going to be okay there for a few months?"

"Sure. It's still damn painful to think about, but what can I do but work at this point?"

"I don't want to tell you what to do, but I want you to know I support you. You have a wonderful opportunity, one that I never had. Once you and your brother came along, and there was never a way to go back and decide for me that a college education was the right choice. But I always wanted it for you two. As painful as the death of someone close is, and I should know with your mom and all, you have to follow your dream. And it was her dream too, you know. So, I don't want to make a decision for you, and as much as I miss you even more so now, don't make the same mistake I did halfway through by quitting." That was the first time Sam had heard his father talk about his mother since she died. It was a subject they just avoided.

"Thanks dad. I am going to stay. I talked with Fish, one of my friends, someone a few years ahead who has some perspective, and he said the same thing. I am going to finish this. And I will be safe. This murder was horrible but it is a random accident and it won't happen again. I can wait until Spring, and you can fly out then."

"Okay, Sam. I just want you to be safe, and happy, but for the short term I am okay with safe."

"Yes, dad, please pay one of the neighborhood kids to shovel the snow. You shouldn't have to do that anymore." Sam hung up. He stared at his clothes on the floor for a very long time. He was trying to remember when he needed to be back at the hospital and lost track of what day it was, and whether it was day or night. Fish had told him this would happen. Then he remembered his car was still at the hospital. Fish was right about losing track of that, too.

CHAPTER 45

THE GREAT DANE WAS JABLONSKI'S brainchild. With not enough money in the budget to hire more police or security, one of the things he could accomplish in short order and with high visibility, was to immediately add a canine officer to the security detail. The woman who worked the dog was fresh out of the academy, but she managed the gigantic animal with ease. The dog stood on all fours over three feet high, and when it stood its massive head came as high as her midsection. Their job was to walk through the ER once an hour, then circle the outside area, swing past the main entrance where the lobby was, and come back around to the ER again. She was good at her rounds.

The officer made friends with everyone, but whenever someone tried to pat the dog on the head, the massive animal growled, and people withdrew their hand sharply and gave a weak smile. Soon the dog knew everyone on the staff by smell. Jablonski was pleased he came up with the idea. He did not want a police state but he wanted the appearance of beefed-up security, and the large Great Dane was perfect for the job. So was officer Ryder, her handler.

An institution the size of the County could not afford even a half day off, even for the funeral of one of its own. The day after the funeral started slow. Brent was in Room Four at 6 am. The pace of the daily routine picked up. The Great Dane and officer Ryder walked through several times. One time when a patient was getting mouthy about not getting some pain meds, they happened past. Officer Ryder asked if everything was okay, and the Great Dane stared down the complaining patient, who got back on his gurney and pulled up the side rail. Maybe this was going to work out.

Just before lunchtime Dr. Corkerin appeared and found Jenni Omygod. "Oh, I just hate to do this," Corkerin smiled with his natural charm, "but we have a procedure running over in clinic and my nurse just left for lunch. She is the only one with the narcotics key and

I need some more Demerol just to finish up. I did not think we would run over, but we are short-staffed today, like everybody else, very sad about Dr. Michelangelo."

"Well Doctor Corkerin, you can come by anytime and borrow whatever you need," Jenni smiled back.

Officer Ryder and the Great Dane appeared. Corkerin patted the animal on his head, "Nice puppy." The dog did not growl and the three people around the desk were impressed.

"Dr. Corkerin you can charm any beast in the animal kingdom! One sec and I'll get your meds" Jenni unlocked the narcotics case and handed Corkerin a vial. "Will one be enough, dear?"

"Most certainly. I did not want to put you ladies out. Have a great day. See you around puppy." He winked at Jenni, at Officer Ryder, and at the Great Dane.

Brent just stepped out of Room Two with a clipboard in his hand, "What was that all about?"

"Just seeing how the other half lives. Clinics. Scheduled patients, no surprises," sighed Jenni, "Maybe it's time for me to move to a saner schedule. Somewhere close to Dr. Handsome, perhaps?"

THE COUNTY

"If you left, how would we know who to triage first and who is sickest?" Brent asked.

Jenni wasn't sure if he was serious or not; facetiousness escaped her.

CHAPTER 46

BRENT, LIKE CLOCKWORK, WAS DOING his exercise set first thing the next morning. He barely missed Dr. Corkerin's second appearance at the front desk. He was asking for some Demerol again, this time saying the GYN clinic just wasn't restocked the day before and they were out. He wanted to get started with his first procedure, but the charge nurse had not come in yet. Jenni Omygod was all too happy to assist and unquestioningly gave him two vials of Demerol this time. "Take both sweety. We don't want you running out of pain meds on the poor woman if she needs more."

Brent caught the end of the conversation and was suspicious. He too lived by the emergency physician's motto—Trust but verify. After five minutes he called the GYN clinic, "Is Dr. Corkerin there? This is the ER; he left his notepad and I thought he might need it since it has some patient info on it?"

"I'll check doctor, but he is not scheduled to be here today"

To Jenni, he asked, "Are you sure he said the clinic and not somewhere else?"

"You don't trust him? Why would he lie to us?"

"Why would anybody lie to us, Jenni? Do you think our patients don't lie to us every day?"

"Well maybe, but he is not a patient."

"Yeah, and I hoping that he won't be, so I am just following up, as they say."

Just then a nurse stepped out of Room Two, "We could use a little help here the patient is having trouble breathing. Dr. Drysdale thinks he may need a tube."

Brent pushed the hold button and handed the phone to Sally to wait for an answer from the clinic. Three minutes later the same nurse poked her head back out the door of Room Two and said, "We are going to need RT down here with a vent. Looks like Dr. Plumber is going to intubate our guy." Sally immediately hung up and called RT. And with that, the call to the GYN clinic was forgotten, as the day got busier and other things needed to be done. But Dr. Corkerin would not be coming back down for any more Demerol again.

CHAPTER 47

GINA WAS ON HER CARDIAC care unit, or CCU, rotation, and there was never a better time to be in cardiology. The standard treatment for a heart attack, an acute MI, up to that point in time was a week of enforced bedrest, nitroglycerin tablets for pain, and IV lidocaine drips to suppress extra beats called PVCs. That was about to change. Woody was a rising star as the new cardiology fellow, one of those cardiologists on the cusp of a seismic shift in heart disease. Young, curly-haired, in constant motion as he talked, he was thinking of creative ways to solve a common problem; what more to do for patients with a heart attack. He had a novel solution. He thought the thing to do was to insert a catheter, a very thin wire, into the diseased vessel as early in the process as possible and infuse some dye to see how severely blocked a coronary vessel was. For those with complete blockage, he thought of a few ways to unblock them and save the heart muscle downstream from the blockage. The problem was the status quo in cardiology was to never do such a risky procedure on a 'hot' MI. The prevailing thought was to wait until things cooled down, and how long that took was getting shorter and shorter thanks to Woody. He convinced some of his mentors that doing this procedure within a day was possible. With some of those, he was able to insert a catheter with an inflatable balloon past the blockage and drag the clot out of the vessel. But Woody felt that to coin a phrase, "Time is muscle" so he needed to do this as fast as possible. His new research was to take the heart attack patient straight from the ER to a specially designed unit called a cath lab and try to remove the clot with a Fogarty catheter, the one with a balloon on the tip.

Most of Woody's colleagues in the group of cardiologists at the County felt this was sheer madness and were just waiting for the first patient he killed by doing this to send him packing. But Woody's boss, the chairman of cardiology, believed in him and had hired him just for this reason—to quantum leap the field with cutting edge research. Of course the boss's name would go prominently on the paper that would get published if Woody was right. The rest of the old guard of cardiologists had other reasons to be skeptical. Perhaps they feared that if Woody was right, then cardiologists everywhere would need to live in the hospital to be ready at a moment's notice to do this invasive procedure. They certainly did not want to become just like those ICU docs, like Jamison and soon-to-be Fish, to spend all their time living inside the County.

Gina was starting her rotation as Woody's new intern and she was thrilled to be in on the ride. This was the reason she had applied to the County in the first place; she had heard lots of good things about their cardiology specialists while still in medical school in Boston. However, there was one aspect that irritated her. She had to wear the special-colored red scrubs with the heart logo of the cardiology team, and the doctors' locker room at that time was only for men. She was forced to ask someone to hand her out a medium size scrub, then go to the nurse's locker room in the OR to change. She asked that she be able to change once the men were done in the cardiology area, but that request went nowhere, probably because someone like Jablonski just ignored it. Women were well represented in pediatrics and OB/GYN, but the surgical specialties and the emerging procedural skill specialties of internal medicine were only sparsely populated with enthusiastic women ready to step into the conflict and suffer the hazing of the old guard. Woody, was glad to have anyone on board who believed in his mission, regardless of gender. In retrospect, he was a trailblazer on multiple fronts of medicine. As frustrating and time-consuming as it was, Gina put up with the routine of arriving earlier than the men just so she could go to another floor and change into scrubs. That morning she hustled out of the elevator wearing her red scrubs with the heart logo above the shirt pocket, as she was paged to see a new case in the ER.

"Look at this ECG. Classic tombstone changes of an MI. We upped the nitro and gave him morphine but I know they want us to page you as soon as we were sure it was an MI," Sam presented the case to Gina.

"Yeah, you are right. Get the usual enzymes and I'll call Woody to see if he wants to do his new procedure on him."

Within minutes Woody was at the patient's bedside consenting the heart attack patient for a new experimental procedure to retrieve the blood clot, "If you sign right here, we can get that out within the hour." He made one phone call and personally, with Gina's assistance, rolled the gurney up to the cath lab. "Go scrub up if you want to help on this one," he said to Gina as they arrived at the cath lab. She certainly did. This would be her first cardiac case. She had waited eight months for this.

As a technician washed the patient's groin with brown disinfectant and shaved away the hair nearby. Woody was scrubbing at the sink along with Gina and explained, "I might try something new I was reading about. Instead of the Fogarty technique, there is a drug called streptokinase which dissolves clots. I was thinking we could infuse a small amount of it right on top of a fresh clot and make it disappear."

They both stepped into the cath lab with hands elevated still wet from the scrub. The nurse opened two pairs of brown latex gloves for them to put on. Gina followed Woody's lead and stuck her hands into hers. She had never seen brown gloves, just the usual blue sterile ones that were at every bedside everywhere else in the hospital. As they were starting to insert the catheter into the man's groin Gina felt dizzy and noticed a slight itch in the back of her throat. It reminded her of the time she had peanut chicken in an Indonesian restaurant and suffered an allergic reaction. But there were no peanuts anywhere in the room as far as she knew. She tried to move her tongue to scratch the back of her throat but it just kept getting worse. Next, she felt increased difficulty breathing, like an asthma attack, and her knees began to buckle. She stepped back and tried to sit but there was nowhere to do that and she slumped down to the floor. Woody looked back at her, "Damnit, someone get her to the ER, I will do the procedure myself," thinking in his head *time is muscle*. It was not that he was not concerned about his intern, but he knew the system would find someone else to take care of her right this moment. His hands were full with a thin wire he was slinking into someone's heart. He was needed critically right here.

The technician pulled Gina up into a wheelchair and he headed for the elevators to get her down to the first floor, the ER was where all problems were solved.

CHAPTER 48

BY THE TIME GINA GOT to the ER, she had the noisy wheezy breathing and forward positioning of someone in a crisis from asthma. Fish was there with Sam who had just started his first day shift after a string of three nights. It took Fish all of one second to recognize Gina was in deep trouble; the "Aunt Millie Method" he would later explain to Sam. They hoisted Gina onto a gurney and put her in Room One. Fish gave her a shot of epinephrine in her arm, and the nurse (thankfully not Jenni today) started an IV. Steroids, antihistamines, and a loading dose of theophylline were all given in short order. Then Fish notice the brown gloves.

"Hmm, she probably has a latex allergy. Let's get these off and wash her hands clean," as he personally pulled off both brown gloves and took a wound irrigation bottle of saline to clean off her hands which were now both red. But Gina was not getting better, and Fish knew the next step was to intubate her. He explained to Gina what he was going to do. By this point, she was so out of breath that all she could do is nod her head rapidly. When Fish started to move away from the bedside to assemble the airway equipment, Gina squeezed his hand hard and had a plaintive look in her now bloodshot eyes. Fish knew it was the look of impending doom. Sam stepped in next to her to take over holding her hand while Fish prepared to intubate.

The intubation went smoothly. Fish gave her a big dose of IV Valium to knock her out so she would not remember all this later. He set the ventilator on slow breaths and small volumes, a trick he learned from Dr. Michelangelo, so the patient would not stack the inhaled oxygen and over-dilate her lungs to the point that they could pop. Three more doses of epinephrine and Gina looked a little better but still quite ill. He added magnesium to the mix, something they give to pregnant patients to suppress premature labor but also worked on the muscles of the lungs to relax them too. Nothing seemed to be working so Fish had a Hail-Mary idea. He called the OR and said he was bringing up a critical anaphylaxis patient with bronchospasm for helium anesthesia. He had read that helium could dilate refractory airways better than oxygen. Of course, you still needed oxygen to stay alive, so a balanced mix of both was needed. It was called Heliox, and for the rare severe asthma case, it sometimes worked. Helium was what was in toy balloons that when you inhaled them it let you talk in that funny high-pitched voice for a few seconds. It turned out that the same principle that gave you a change in voice also changed the properties of airflow enough to make the inflow and outflow of oxygen easier. It lightened the resistance of the movement of the gas mixture. Right now, Gina was not getting enough oxygen into her system. The arterial blood gas that Sam just drew for Fish showed her only 72 % oxygen, and that was not good.

Fish told the team "we are going to the OR", so naturally, they sent off the usual pre-operative labs. He took Sam along with him to watch the airway carefully, as Fish walked ahead of the gurney so he could explain once he got there what he wanted the anesthesiologist to do. Gina was placed in an open operating room suite and the OR nurse said, "I know this lady. She was up here this morning getting changed in our locker with the red cardiac scrubs. Doesn't she work here?"

"She does, so take extra good care of her. She is one of our interns. She had a latex allergy so absolutely no latex gloves by anyone working in this room!" Fish said. The anesthesiologist confirmed the breathing tube placement then dialed up the Heliox mixture, and sure enough over the next 30 minutes, Gina's breathing was more relaxed. She looked like she was going to pull through.

Fish stepped out of the OR to call the ICU to arrange the next stop for Gina. He now had time to explain what he said earlier to Sam, "The Aunt Millie Method is essentially a catch-phrase for pattern recognition. The original story goes, you walk into an old age home and there sitting all around are twenty or thirty little old ladies in the lunchroom waiting for lunch. To the uninitiated, they all look reasonably the same. But you are not uninitiated and you walk right over to your Aunt Mille and say hello. Why? It's because you have seen Aunt Millie hundreds of times, and know exactly what she looks like, what makes her different from everyone else's little old aunt. Hence, the Aunt Millie Method. I knew Gina was in the critical pre-arrest stages of an anaphylactic reaction because I have seen it a dozen times before. I don't need to ask her a dozen questions, which she was too dyspneic to answer, to figure it out. I just acted on my pattern recognition instinct. Once you develop your Aunt Millie Method into your experience, you'll be a great ER doc."

The the OR desk clerk tapped Fish on the elbow and held out a piece of paper. It was Gina's pre-op labs; her pregnancy test was positive. Pregnancy tests were routine for every emergency patient going to the OR, while Fish did not specifically order it, the ER nurses did their usual orders and it was on the list. "Hmmm," Fish thought, "Well this complicates things, but only a little." He paged Corkerin for an OB consult. Things got busy getting Gina out of the OR to the ICU, and Corkerin never called back to the OR desk. His pager was going off unanswered somewhere.

CHAPTER 49

UPSTAIRS IN THE CATH LAB, Woody had just done his first streptokinase clot buster procedure. The large artery to the heart, the left anterior descending, was completely blocked. He began infusing streptokinase right behind it. He had to guess a little at the dose. There were doses they had used to unclog a clotted peripheral IV line, but he incrementally increased those and after the third bolus suddenly the dye flowed past the blockage and he followed it on the fluoroscope X-ray. What happened next scared him but he remained calm. His patient started having all sorts of arrhythmias. First, a short burst of ventricular tachycardia, for which Woody ordered a bolus of lidocaine, then his heart rate slowed down dangerously to a rate of 25. Woody thought he would need to insert a pacemaker right then, but after a second, before Woody had time to react, it sped back up and everything was normal *First rule of code crisis management is to take your own pulse before the patient's pulse.* The patient's other vital signs were stable, Woody was anxiously filled with his own adrenaline, and his heart rate was up too. But both he and the patient's heart rates calmed down. Woody finished the procedure and moved the patient over to the CCU. He told the technician to save all the pictures from the fluoro. He couldn't wait to show it to somebody. The CCU nurse told him that Gina was going to be all right, in fact she was down the hall in the ICU. He took the fluoro pictures down to her first, maybe that would cheer her up.

When Woody got to Gina's room in the ICU he was shocked to see her intubated and sedated to the point of unconsciousness. "What the hell happened?" he asked the male nurse at her bedside. Mike, the nurse explained to Woody all about the anaphylaxis and the trip to the OR, and Woody felt less excited about his breakthrough case with the clot-buster. Due to his arrogance and indifference to his staff, he could have killed her. He just couldn't imagine that anything so serious could be so wrong with a young person. "You know I thought maybe she was pregnant or something," he told Mike. He left unable to show her his fluoro photos, to celebrate his first successful case, and unaware of how true his last thought was.

Fish was up in the ICU but needed to get back down to the ER. He paged Corkerin twice and still no answer. He signed out Gina's case to Jamison and let him know what he needed to tell Corkerin about. He told Jamison to just make sure she got some prenatal care once she got extubated and woke up.

Over on the OB floor an anxious father-to-be tried the handle on the single-occupant public use bathroom. Every time he anxiously jiggled it, he found the door locked. The three cups of vending machine coffee were finally catching up with him. He asked the nurse where he could find another bathroom and she directed him over to the next ward. It wasn't until later that day that the bathroom started to have an odd odor.

Woody found the group of cardiology attendings in the doctor's locker room and started to tell them all about his case, showing the before and after photos of the left anterior descending artery and how he unblocked the clot with streptokinase. They all were impressed and told him he needed to write it up for publication. Woody said he was going to wait until he had enough cases to make a statistical conclusion, and asked that they call him for all their acute MI patients so he can take them each to the cath lab. They were all too happy to do so, especially at night when they were unwilling to get up and drive into the hospital. For them, the old guard, it was great to have an over-eager hyperactive cardiac fellow on the case. The cardiologists lived up near the lake, out of town, in big nice houses. None of them lived close to the County in the old cottage homes, like the one across the street, as Fish did. They did not want to come in at all hours like him, but were concerned now their world would change.

CHAPTER 50

BY THE NEXT MORNING, GINA was extubated and ready to go home. Her breathing was much better and Jamison no longer heard wheezing when he listened to her lungs. As a pulmonologist, his job was done but Jamison waited until all the interns and the nurse had moved on to the next patient for rounds. "Listen Gina, they got a pregnancy test as a pre-op lab, and well, it was positive. I hope that's good news for you. But I would like someone from OB to come by and speak with you. I paged their chief Corkerin. I am sure they are going to want an ultrasound. So if you don't mind I'll order one."

A short time later Jamison got a call from radiology. The results of Gina's ultrasound showed a tubal pregnancy. That would not be good news, and she would not be able to go anywhere, except back to the OR to have it removed. A tubal, or ectopic pregnancy, could not survive without perforating the tube and killing the mother. He paged Corkerin again. He never called back. Jamison phoned the OB floor to see if he was there, but the nurse said "it was strange, he was supposed to be here yesterday and again today but I have not seen him at all."

The OB floor nurse called her charge nurse and relayed her concern about the missing Dr. Corkerin. Everyone was still anxious about the killings in the bathroom downstairs, even though it was well publicized that the murderer had been caught. The charge nurse called the hospital operator to ask to be put through to Corkerin's home number. She was surprised when someone answered who said she was his wife. His wife was also concerned as Lloyd Corkerin was due back after his procedures yesterday but did not come home. "Lloyd always has surprise cases, emergency deliveries, so I did not think that much about it, but no, he has not been in."

The charge nurse hung up and was just as surprised that Dr. Corkerin was married as she was concerned about his whereabouts. "He was always flirting with nurses, who have thought he had a wife?" But that did not deter her from calling Jablonski and relaying her concerns that a doctor was missing. Jablonski, of course, wanted to keep everything quiet, so he called campus security and asked them to check all around the building for anything unusual like a missing obstetrician. The Armstrongs were notified and made their rounds.

Jamison paged the second backup on-call OB, who came to the ICU to explain to Gina what needed to be done. He sympathetically asked, "Would you like to have your husband here for support or to help with the decision?"

"No, there is no such person."

"Well, then the prospective father?" He asked a little sheepishly.

"Now that would be a really bad idea. I understand what needs to be done. It's just me. Let's get on with it." She signed the consent for surgery, and just for good measure, the OB resident ordered two units of blood typed and crossed in case she needed any.

Gina went back to the OR, where to OR nurse commented, "Didn't we just see her yesterday?" Gina was intubated for the second day in a row, and surgery was started. All went as well as could be expected. The tubal had not ruptured, and Gina did not need the blood transfusion, but she had to have her right-side

THE COUNTY

fallopian tube removed. Her chance of getting pregnant again was now reduced, not exactly by half, but reduced. The OB team tried to page Corkerin again to assist since he was the chief resident, but again he did not answer his page so the OB team proceeded without him.

Officer Ryder and her Great Dane were making the rounds upstairs on the floors asking if anybody had seen Dr. Corkerin. When they got to the OB floor the Great Dane started barking outside the bathroom door. Even Officer Ryder could smell something was not right. "Easy girl," she restrained her dog. She jiggled the handle but it was locked, "Just checking if everything is Okay in there?" she said as she knocked loudly on the bathroom door, but got no response. She went to the desk and asked if anyone had a key to the bathroom. They didn't, but they called the custodian. A mid-aged Hispanic woman showed up with a set of keys and a rolling cart with a mop. She figured there was a toilet overflow again and came prepared. But no one was prepared for what they found when they pulled the door open. There on the commode, leaning towards the wall, with a dusky blue color, was Dr. Corkerin.

"Dios mi," screamed the custodian.

"Code blue," yelled Officer Ryder into her walkie-talkie. "Bathroom, 6th floor, OB wing."

ZANE HOROWITZ

Ten seconds later that exact language was being said over and over again by the hospital intercom system: "CODE BLUE, OB FLOOR!"

Jamison ran up two flights of stairs and was the first to arrive. He assessed the scene in seconds. Dr. Corkerin was blue, not breathing, and he had no pulse. What got his attention was that Corkerin's pants leg on the left was rolled up to his knee. In the large vein near his ankle was a plastic piece that was an IV hub with a U connector on it. In the end port of the U connector was a syringe, empty, but still in the IV in Corkerin's ankle. It was clear that Dr. Corkerin had used a saline lock IV to inject himself with an opioid medication and had stopped breathing. Jamison ran the code and transported Corkerin to the ER, where they continued to try to save him.

Brent was working in the ER, and when he saw the saline lock in the ankle vein, he knew exactly what had happened. After the code was called and he pronounced Corkerin dead, Brent brought Jenni over and lifted Corkerin's limp leg up, so it was nearly in her face, "This is why we don't share our drugs with anyone who comes down to ask for them! I should have verified the patient he said it was needed for the day he asked for it, and he would have been found out before he did this to himself. ***Trust,***

but verify! He would have been fired, but he would have gotten help. Now he's dead."

Later it would be confirmed Corkerin died from a lethal amount of Demerol.

CHAPTER 51

GINA WAS EXTUBATED IN THE recovery room and this time transported to the GYN ward which was on the same floor as the OB ward but in the opposite wing from the elevators. When she got there, she immediately sensed that everyone was in a somber mood. Even the food service person was all teary-eyed when she brought her first post-op tray of Jell-O. It made Gina think of a tall tale she had heard on her medical school OB rotation. There was a mother who couldn't decide what to name her newborn twins. This was back in Boston and the mother wanted to honor her Italian grandfather Angelo. After a long painful labor the two boys were born, one just before and one after midnight so they had different birthdays. The mom was too exhausted to think, but she wanted them both to have a bond together, and she could not decide on their names. The next day after a good night's sleep, when they brought the first meal menu to her there were only two items: orange Jello and lemon Jello, so she named her sons Lemangelo and Orangelo. Lemangelo was a day older than his kid brother, Orangelo. Gina always thought it was a tall tale until six months later on pediatrics rotation she saw Lemangelo for a fever.

When the food service worker came to collect the morning tray, Gina saw that she had been crying.

"What's wrong? Why is everyone so gloomy?" asked Gina in a deeper and huskier voice than usual. Having a tube for intubation dried out her throat and it still hurt a little.

"One of our doctors died today, sweet Dr. Corkerin."

Gina was shocked. She did not know him at all, only by reputation and name, but it chilled her to think that another doctor had died. This time no one was saying why or how. The whispering would have to fill in the details later.

Gina did have one visitor before she was discharged the next day. It was Woody who came to see how she was doing but mostly could not stop talking about the coronary case. It was the only thing he got excited about. He also wanted to say he was sorry for how he treated her having her carted off from the cath lab like that. He said that all the brown latex gloves were being removed from the cardiac unit, and replaced with blue nitrile gloves. He hoped she would come back soon to see more cardiac cases and finish her rotation.

Gina said, "Of course, I will. I'll be in tomorrow. I feel pretty good right now.'

"Don't go pushing it, come back when you are ready. Are you taking any pain meds?"

"I am ready now, but tomorrow will work. I don't do 'sick' very well. They gave me a new mild pain pill called Zomax. It's not a narcotic, supposed to be safe, like a super Motrin."

"There's already half a dozen Motrin-like meds. What's this one do any different?"

"I don't know. It starts with a Z and has a catchy name."

"You know what they say about new meds, don't be the first, or the last to use them."

"Alright. I'll only take it if Motrin doesn't cut it."

"Good choice, but I am also writing you a script for a syringe full of epinephrine to carry. I think you can handle self-injecting it if you need it again?"

"Yeah, Thanks." She looked at the paper the prescription was written on and had an interesting thought: *It'll be nice though if someone invented a device so you could just inject it without drawing it up while you're in anaphylaxis.*

CHAPTER 52

AS SHE PROMISED GINA WAS back the next morning, maybe walking a little slow but ready to go. She stopped Woody on his way into the locker to change and asked for a set of medium scrubs which he brought out. "I'll see you in CCU," he said, "Might have a case among the overnight admits."

Gina went down to the OR to change. As she was pulling her blouse off one of the nurses noticed her bandage on her lower abdomen. "Did you just deliver?" she asked.

"What? No. It's something else."

"I am an OR nurse, that looks like a Pfannenstiel C-section incision to me," she said pointing to Gina's lower abdomen.

Gina was not sure how much to share, but saw the nurse was pretty sharp so admitted, "It was GYN surgery, but it was an ectopic."

"Oh. Hey, I am so sorry. I didn't mean to get you upset. Was it a planned pregnancy?"

"No. I am an intern. There is no such thing as a planned pregnancy. They pretty much tell us to not get pregnant during residency. Some are a little more subtle than others."

"Wow, that's crazy," the OR nurse said, patting her own lower abdomen, "I am working on number three right now." The nurse immediately felt bad since she may have hurt the doc's feelings.

"Congrats. Boy or girl?" Gina asked, thinking how this nurse looked younger than her and was already working on number three.

"Don't know. How would I tell?"

"Sometimes you can see on an ultrasound. Sometimes if you get an amniocentesis then you would know for sure."

"Well the nurses have great insurance through our union, but no bells and whistles like an amnio, unless you had a prior high-risk pregnancy. I only had one ultrasound to confirm the pregnancy and it was too early to tell, I guess. Me, I have two happy, healthy kids. Got two weeks off for each. I am working overtime from now until this one's due to get some catch-up pay to try to take off longer."

"Two weeks. Is that all they let you off for?"

"Well, they ask we try not to give birth in December when the holidays are in high demand for RTO, requested time off. We all do some back counting so it's no sex in March. Sent my husband off fishing every weekend. That usually works."

"What about just using the pill?"

"I'm Irish Catholic. Not allowed. Besides I don't know if it's safe."

"Of course, it's safe!" Gina said sharply, *except when it doesn't work 'cause you were up three nights in a row and forgot to take it*, she thought.

"Well, our insurance doesn't pay for it anyway either."

"But they give you off for two weeks instead?" Gina asked, incredulous at the logic behind that.

"Hey, it's up to the union to negotiate. In a pinch, I could always quit. Finding a new job in nursing, especially with OR experience, is a snap. I could go cross town and with my two-year experience here they probably make me charge nurse. Just have to gamble on not having insurance during the break in jobs. Bit of a risk with three kids. But can do it if I need to."

Just then a woman appeared from around the corner and introduced herself as Alex Armenian. She was the first-year GI fellow, also changing in the nurses' locker room before going up to do some endoscopies. "Listen I know you said something about pregnancy and residency but wanted to give you a warning. Are you looking at fellowships?"

"Yeah, I really like cards, I am on that now."

"Well, let them know upfront you absolutely won't get pregnant."

"Why?"

"When I started doing interviews for my GI fellowship, they were saying stuff like, we have only two fellows a year so we don't have any wiggle room for unexpected time off. I did not know what they were driving at. Then they asked if I was married and when I said yes, they sort of frowned. Then it dawned on me they did not have a way to give me off for two weeks if I got pregnant. So, I chimed in that I had two kids already and had my tubes tied. You would have thought I just offered to work nights, weekends, and holidays or the rest of time. It was my guarantee that there would be no unexpected time off requests, which is what they were fishing for."

"I got a heads up on that when I started interviewing for residency. When I interviewed around the Boston area where I was in school, they just asked if I was married, and when I said no, I think they assumed no respectable Boston physician would have children before I got married, not that I was planning to. When I got to the Midwest, they frankly said they would revoke my contract if I had kids, one program even said that if I was not married now, they would not allow me to get married until I graduated, and had a form for me to sign. Here in California, they were more subtle, they told me that in their experience, this was old men speaking mind you, that having children and doing a residency were not compatible. They made it seem like they were concerned for my best interests but they were worried about how they would juggle the schedule."

"Yeah, happened to a classmate of mine. She lost a prestigious residency after the match when she called the chair and told him that she was expecting in October. He told her that was an act of unprofessionalism by not informing him before the match. He withdrew her offer, and they ended up hiring a Caribbean student in her place. She wanted to do surgery and ended up in pathology after taking a year off. Shameful."

Gina and Alex could have traded other horror stories all morning, but they both needed to get to their expected procedure areas. When Gina got to the cath lab Woody was there getting ready to scrub in and telling her the details of the case. "Are you sure you are ready to be

THE COUNTY

back? I heard there was something more than just an allergic reaction that went down."

Gina knew that news, especially private news, travels fast inside a hospital and said, "No. I had an ectopic. They took it out, Easier that an appendix since it was not ruptured." she then added, "I don't plan on getting pregnant again by the way. I am looking to do a cardiology fellowship, invasive cards probably." She paused for a second, cleared her throat still achy from her intubation, then drove home the crux, "Won't have kids screwing that up." Woody just nodded; he did not know what to say that wasn't awkward. The message, however, was delivered, as Alex had suggested.

CHAPTER 53

SAM WAS HAVING A HARD time digesting the most recent tragedy. He did not know Corkerin well, but Corkerin was diverting Demerol from the ER to go shoot up in the bathroom. That seemed so antithetical to all his values. He was still starry-eyed about doing good. While waiting for a trauma to come into Room One with Fish he started getting anxious for no apparent reason, and just blurted out, "I don't know if I'll ever feel safe in a bathroom here again. You can get beaten to death if it's open to the public, or die alone if you lock yourself in."

Fish knew now was not the time or place to talk about it, and said, "Let's just focus on this case coming in. What are your priorities?

If you need to intubate which meds would you choose? What are the indications for a peritoneal lavage?" Fish subtly was back in teaching mode, distracting Sam from his thoughts.

Later as Sam was alone in the charting cubby, Fish came in to talk. They were alone here and not in the fishbowl of a resuscitation room. "Are you doing Okay? When lots of bad things happen, we forget on checking on each other. You might have the early signs of survivor's guilt. What can I do to help you cope?"

"Not so well. I am trying, but failing to cope, I come to work but I can't stop thinking about the attacks, the overdose, even Gina's near-death experience. Then I see the violence we get in here, day-in and day-out, and wonder how safe is the world, really? I never had to face anything like this in college or medical school, they definitely over-protected us."

"I hear you Sam, and I get the worry. I don't want to diminish any of your pain. We see the suffering of those who were close to the dead, their wives, their families, but we don't always recognize the collateral damage on co-workers and casual acquaintances."

"So how do we, or me; how do I go on? I am in this internal medicine residency, and I like the ER, but I am horrified by the violence. People beating, shooting, stabbing each other, drunks in car crashes injuring the innocent. I went home last night and although I have only been on the ER again for one week I counted 13 people who died while I was their doctor or helping out to take care of them. Can I keep working like this where I see people die every day? I know we tell ourselves that some of them were victims of their own bad behavior and choices because it makes it more palatable to think about why bad things happen, but then you see a family of four just driving home and being hit by a truck. So where is the justice? Where is the justice for people like Dr. Michelangelo? I think about what would I be like if that were my brother. How do you go on?"

"I don't have the answers, Sam. Maybe there are no real answers except that life tends to be unfair."

"I feel like there is some evil god above throwing lightning bolts down and hitting everyone around me. Everyone but me. One day he will get me too."

"Well I am not a religious type, but except for Norse mythology and Thor, I don't think there is a god throwing lightning, or for that matter choosing who to punish and for what unknown sins. Bad things happen, but we can also be there to help salvage the injured from when bad things happen. I think if you want to be ER doc then you should go to one of these new residencies where they are training people to just do this specifically."

"And what, leave the medicine program in the middle? Leave my friends in the lurch picking up extra shifts next year because there's a hole in the schedule?"

"Well if you are that loyal to the other interns, and who knows if they would do the same for you, you can always finish medicine first, then switch to emergency. That may be the best tactic, give the specialty another year or two to mature and define itself. They don't have an independent board certification yet, and they are getting political resistance from the house of medicine, not to mention the pyramid of surgery. The last vote by the specialties board was 100 to 5 against making it a specialty."

"So what if it never becomes its own specialty?"

"Worst-case scenario then you'd be an internist. You could do pulmonary or critical care, or both like I am going to do. The thing you should remember is that you have lots of options at this point in your career. Don't throw it away by quitting."

Wilson walked in on the tail end of that conversation.

"Good to see you, Wilson," both Sam and Fish said in unison. Sam inside knew Wilson was suffering worse than him. Sam did not have the right to complain.

"Are you quitting?" Wilson asked, his voice in a whisper.

"No just pondering lots of different futures."

"I wouldn't blame you if you did with all that has happened this month, this year."

Sam was quick to reassure him, "No, I would not leave you guys stuck working overtime just because I thought I couldn't handle this. That would not be right to you."

"I hope you don't judge others harshly if they make the decision the other way," Wilson said, looking away to not make eye contact.

What Wilson could bring himself to say was that he had just come from the ICU where he had a long conversation with Jamison, which ended with him asking for a letter of recommendation. Jamison was pleased to do it. Jamison had several conversations with Michelangelo when he was working on the berylliosis lecture about how his new intern was such a go-getter and was going to put all of that in his letter. Wilson made a decision to go back into the internship match. He was closing in on the deadline in February to apply. He couldn't tell anyone, though. Wilson needed one of those other possible futures. He only applied to one program—the famous Mayo clinic.

CHAPTER 54

SAM WAS REFLECTING ON WHAT Fish had said about caring for the collateral people, so he thought he should check in on Harry. Harry had been off for the last month, and Sam did not know if he had heard all that had happened. On his way over to visit Harry he stopped at a deli he frequented. He thought it would be a nice gesture to pick up some sandwiches, and a slice of pie for Harry. The clerk at the counter, who had seen Sam in scrubs many times before, said "take care doc." It was then that the man behind Sam introduced himself.

"I am Stu Maynard, I could not help overhear you're a doctor, is that right?

"Yes," Sam was backing up as he was beginning to not like being recognized in public.

"Do you work at the County? Terrible thing that happened there. Horrible. I hate to think about his family." After a requisite second with a somber look, Stu continue, "I have that insurance office two doors down, and well it's my business to worry if other people have enough insurance. Do you know if that doctor's family was insured?"

"No, that's not the type of thing we talk about."

"How about yourself? Often when terrible events like this happen it's an opportunity to reevaluate your own insurance needs."

"No, I have not thought about it."

"Well, you could stop by my office. Here's my card. We can discuss your needs. You may be just starting out but before too long you'll need life insurance, maybe own profession insurance. What if you could not use one of your hands? Are you in surgery?"

Sam could not think of how to get away from this predator fast enough. "No, I am an ER doc." He realized as he was leaving the deli that he said it out loud to a stranger for the first time.

Sam arrived at Harry's apartment with his two sandwiches. In his rush to escape from the insurance salesman he left the slice of pie for

Harry on the deli-counter. Harry was glad to see someone again. Since living in his apartment Harry had picked up a coffee table, a second chair, and a brand-new state-of-the art 24-inch TV. Sam set the sandwiches on the coffee table. It was cluttered with unread medical journals and unopened mail. Harry asked, "want something to drink?"

"A soda will be fine, or just water if you don't have it."

"I am glad to see you, Sam, I have been going bonkers here at home. I haven't been anywhere. Everyone I know works at the hospital seven days a week so you are the first person to come by since I got put on the sick list."

"Oh, right. I'll get myself some clean glasses. I don't want to catch your hepatitis. Where do you keep them?" As Sam opened the first cabinet he saw three bottles of gin, one nearly empty. He closed the door, and tried another where he found the glasses. Sam did not know if he wanted to bring up the fact that Harry ought to be staying off alcohol while he recovers from hepatitis.

They talked for a while. Harry had already heard about the murder on the news. He had never met Michelangelo or Corkerin so it did not affect him as much as it did Sam. There was no massive funeral for Corkerin as there was for Michelangelo. His death was swept under the carpet.

Harry just wanted to get back when they released him to go to work. He didn't seem worried about murderers lurking in the bathrooms. "Most of our patients want a work excuse, so they don't have to go to work, but me, I am counting the days until I can go back to work. I am sick of being sick and staying at home."

After they finished eating Harry pulled out a box from under the TV stand, "Hey check this out I just bought something called Atari. It's got a ping-pong game you can play it on the TV." Harry and Sam played Pong for a few hours, like two normal college kids, just relaxing. Sam thought this was the opportunity to ask about the gin bottles, "Harry, what's with all the gin in the cabinet? Are you drinking while you have active hepatitis? You don't need any more damage to your poor liver, and I have no idea what that would do to your Gilbert's disease."

"No, no, no. I haven't touched the stuff. Those bottles are from when I moved in. Maybe I should just throw them out. But you never know when you're going to have guests. Not you, but you know, maybe a date. But who would want to go out with someone who only gets two days off a month and uses one of those to sleep and the other one to do his laundry?"

"I don't know Harry. You could always impress a girl with your turning yellow trick." They laughed for a while and played Pong. Sam told Harry about the insurance salesmen who just tried to capitalize on Michelangelo's death and sell him an insurance policy.

"Do we need all that insurance right now? Here I am stuck at home for six weeks and the County still pays me my salary. I would not dream of cheating on them and working while in quarantine. So why do I need more insurance? Those guys are just using fear and trying to sell you something you probably never use, but you get to pay them every month to manage your fear."

"Right." Sam's thoughts drifted to his father. His dad never was able to go back to work full-time at the store after his mother died. She had worked the store with him for all those years, no salary, while Sam was growing up. He had no idea if his mother was insured for her medical bills or if his father had enough money now to get by. When she needed an ambulance and she had no insurance did they bring her to the Buffalo version of the County?

His thoughts came back to Harry, "Yeah, I think I'll save my money for paying off my loans. Why waste it on more insurance?"

CHAPTER 55

DETECTIVE LOWRY FLASHED HIS BADGE again, but Snider already knew who he was.

"Dr. Snider I have some news, unfortunately, it's all bad."

"What did he escape?"

"Well, no, not quite that bad. Thanks for the tip on the man in the nursing home. First time we went out there he was too impaired to answer any questions. When we went back last week, they told us he had passed. He won't be any help. You also got us thinking about other incidents and we checked around the state. It turns out that three days before the museum attack there was a bizarre incident next county over at the college. A professor heard someone rustling around outside his office after hours and when he opened the door found a strange man checking door handles inside the building. The guy gave some lame excuse as to why he was there and asked for some room number, and the prof closed his door. Not much later he heard a loud sound and when they looked, they found another professor in the bathroom bleeding from his head. They took him to the hospital but he also died. So we went and tracked down the first professor and showed him a photo line-up and he picked out our guy. So, unfortunately, he is now a serial murderer having killed three people."

"I hope they fry that son of a bitch in the chair."

"Well, the DA is definitely working towards the death penalty. He is thinking of just trying the two murders here in this county first. Leave the third alone for now, in case we don't get a satisfactory jury outcome, we can then go back and try the third murder. But for the first trial, we are going to need you as a fact witness to the extent of the injuries sustained by the three people you operated on."

"Sure thing. And I want to be there in the chamber when they throw the switch and sparks fly out of his fucking head, too."

"Well let's not get ahead of ourselves. You seem a bit, worked up maybe? Do you think when we get to trial you can tone it down and be professional? Juries want to hear from respected individuals. I can't think of anything more respected than a brain surgeon. This very well could take years. So I wanted to make sure you were available for the long haul and not going to move somewhere across the country or something."

"No, I got five more years here, at least. I'll stay 'til hell freezes over to fry that prick though, so you just find me."

"OK, doc. I know you lost a colleague, and again my sincere condolences. We will be in touch. If you have records from surgery preserve them. But absolutely do not alter them in any way because of our conversation. The DA probably will subpoena all that soon."

Lowry patted Snider on the shoulder and said, "I am so sorry about all this."

"Do you think he'll cooperate?" Lowry's partner asked as they waited for the elevator outside the Neurosurgical ICU.

"Yeah. Trial could be years away, so hopefully time will cool him down. Last thing we need is a guy like that jumping over the witness box and strangling the bastard."

"I don't know, I'd love to be in the courtroom if something like that happens."

"Yeah, but we don't want the good doc going to jail. We want him to fix brains for a long time."

Lowry and his partner went to the ER and looked for Brent Plumber but he wasn't on that day. They left their card with Sally at the desk and left.

CHAPTER 56

IF SNIDER WAS GOING TO cool down it wasn't apparent to anyone who worked with him. Fish called him to the ER a week later to see a possible spinal cord injury. As the story went, an inmate at the maximum-security prison up by the dam fell out of his bunk in the middle of the day and now could not move his legs. He arrived shackled with chains around his mid-section and with both legs chained to the gurney. Six correction officers traveled with him. The two closest to the bed were unarmed, but the other four who stayed a step back were. Fish did a neurologic exam but could not get the inmate to move his legs or react to a pinch of his toes. He got a CT scan of his back but it was normal.

THE COUNTY

Fish wasn't sure if he was faking it or if he just had a spinal cord injury without a bone fracture. Getting an MRI would be tricky as the chief corrections man said there was no way they were going to unshackle him for that. The magnets of the MRI would not be able to handle metal shackles, so Fish was at an impasse as to what to do, except to call Snider to help.

Snider came down to the ER but was in one of his darker moods. He repeated the neurologic exam but the inmate did not budge even when he stuck an 18-gauge needle suddenly and without warning into the sole of each foot. "Well he is damn good at faking." Snider next grabbed his right little toe and twisted it so hard he heard it snap and saw that it was sticking out sideways. No reaction or movement from the inmate. Snider repeated the painful stimulation on the other side. Nothing.

"The only solution is to intubate him, put him under deep anesthesia so we can unshackle him for an MRI. He is either the best actor in the world or he has a complete lumbar cord injury. Either way, nothing to do, no bony fracture to stabilize."

Fish who had watched the whole encounter asked Snider to step out to talk.

"Do you think that was necessary to dislocate his toes?"

"If I was dealing with someone normal, no, but this guy has every reason to lie and fake an injury. Who falls off the bed in the middle of the day, huh? I am telling you it's my gut instinct that he is full of shit. So let's tube him, scan him, and send his ass back to the slammer."

"I think we'd have to consent him for that, don't you?"

"No, screw that. If you don't want to tube him, I saw Brent down the hall he'd go for it." And Snider walked away.

Brent listened to Snider explain his plan nodding his head. Fish caught up to them to join the conversation. Brent smirked and said, "Hey Jablonski's all over me because he thinks I am punching patients, which I am not, and this guy just broke both his toes. I am not sure I want to be a part of this."

"I did not hurt him, If I did, he would have reacted and we would not be having this conversation."

"Ok, maybe I have a better idea. When I was in anesthesia, we had a device called a train-of-four. It delivered a consistent electric impulse to someone under anesthesia to see when our paralytic agents were wearing off. If you use it on an awake person, I understand it is quite painful, but it is an approved medical

THE COUNTY

device for sorting out the degree of paralysis, which is the situation we now find ourselves in."

"I like the way you think. You are almost as twisted as me."

"Let me call up to the OR and see if I can borrow one. Fish, you okay with that plan, you are the guy's doc after all?"

Fish was not happy with it. But it seemed less involved than intubating him or breaking any more toes, so he went along.

Brent returned with a small device that looked like a tool from a low budget space movie. It was a small box with 4 buttons and two metal poles sticking out the top both of which ended in a rounded head. It looked like a miniature taser, but those would not be invented for several years. It worked essentially the same way. While distracting the patient by asking him a few questions Snider leaned his arm across the bed so the patient could not see what Brent was about to do. He turned the device to max and pushed the button as he pressed it against his upper inner thigh near the large nerve that ran down his leg. "OH SHIT. WHAT THE FUCK IS THAT?" yelled the inmate.

Snider smiled, "Proof of your guilt. Time to go back home."

"I don't have no home! I'm in jail."

"Yes, quite clear, but today's little drama is not your get-out-of-jail-free card."

Brent asked, "Would you like me to do the other side just to document our findings?"

"No, I can move it too, Keep that dude away from me." The inmate shook both his feet and bent his knees to show them.

Fish shaking his head started writing up his discharge orders. The corrections team was stoic, but you could tell the oldest guard was smiling like he had seen it all before.

"So glad you called me on this consult," Snider said sarcastically, as he left, and this event made him distrust criminals even more. Something turned very dark inside Snider and it would only get worse.

CHAPTER 57

WILSON CALLED IN SICK, BUT he wasn't. He felt bad about it, but he knew he had used up his one week of time off. He told the residency office that he had diarrhea, then started to go into some detail, to which they said "thanks but we don't need to know, just let us know when you are ready to return." He knew nobody wants to talk about diarrhea or ask more questions. If you said you had a fever, they may ask how high it was, but the office did not want to know how many times he had to run to the bathroom, what color it was, or how bad it smelled. It was a conversation ender. In reality, Wilson was quite well and had a secret two-day trip to Minnesota. He did not let on to his friends that he was reapplying for internship, but there was only one place he wanted to go, the Mayo Clinic in Rochester, Minnesota. He had had a long conversation with Dr. Jamison who agreed to write a letter of recommendation for him, and maybe that did the trick getting him this interview at this late date. Here it was the very end of the interview season on Groundhog's Day and he was flying to Minneapolis.

Wilson landed in Minneapolis just after a snowstorm, with another on the way. He had flown in his new three-piece suit figuring he may not have time to change before his interview. Everyone else on the plane was wearing flannel and wool hats. When Wilson got to the rent-a-car desk he felt he was being asked a few too many odd questions.

"Are you sure you don't want to add insurance?" the girl at the desk asked for the third time. "You're not from Milwaukee, are you? Why are you visiting Minneapolis? Are you staying long?" The tone and the questions felt more like a customs agent than a friendly rental center clerk. "Will you be needing a map?"

"Nope," said Wilson holding up a Triple-A Trip-Tix map he got before he left. He had planned out every aspect of the trip. He had to get to Rochester in the next two hours and do a series of interviews that afternoon. Maybe stay the night in Rochester to see what it was all about, and drive back first thing in the morning to fly home again. Just over 24 hours on the ground, just two days away from work.

The clerk then asked for his credit card and pulled out the roller imprinter to stamp a copy of it. It must have been freshly inked because when she handed him the receipt to sign, and to tear off his copy, Wilson got the ink from the credit card triplicate paper on his hands. With nowhere to wipe his hands he then got some ink on the sleeve of his new suit, but he did not have time to clean it off. Undeterred by ruining his interview suit, Wilson forced a smile. Satisfied that he had paid with a credit card, the desk agent still looked at him like he was going to steal the car, but handed him the keys and said, "spot A-27 out those doors." He stepped outside into a frigid wind and found his way to spot A-27. The car was outside not in a covered garage. It was buried in snow that had drifted onto the windows and hood. He had nothing to clear it off with and ended up sweeping it clear with his arms, getting the sleeves of his suit wet.

It took three tries for the cold engine to turn over, but it did. He turned on the heater, the defroster, and the radio. While waiting for the heater to warm the windshield to clear the thin layer of ice that was stuck tightly, he fiddled with the radio dial. On one station the weather reporter was warning everyone about the next incoming storm, then returned to country music. He looked at his map and memorized the roads he would need to travel, and he pulled out of the rental lot. He looked at his watch, he calculated he had plenty of time to get to Rochester. No sooner had he made the turn-off to Route 52 than it started to snow. Wilson had not driven in much snow growing up in Georgia, or in school in North Carolina, but he drove slowly and kept his windows clear. The snow just came down heavier as he drove south, and it became a white-out after an hours drive. Wilson figured he should pull over at the next exit and maybe call ahead to let them know he might be late. He got off the highway at Zumbrota and pulled into a diner.

He had a few quarters and found the phone booth just inside the front door, and called the number they had given him as a contact. In his most professional voice, he said, "This is Wilson Harrison and I have some interviews today for internal medicine. Listen, I am almost there but the snow is really coming down heavy so I pulled off the highway. I just wanted you to know I am here in Minnesota, and trying my best to get there, but I might be late depending on the road conditions. I hope that's okay?"

THE COUNTY

"Good thing you called doctor. The roads down here are terrible right now. You may want to stay put. They are trying to plow in front of the hospital but I can't say what the outer roads look like. Let me ask Dr. Hillenbrand something." The line went quiet and some symphonic music played while he was on hold. "Dr. Harrison, our chief of medicine suggests you reschedule due to the weather."

"No, no I can't do that I am almost there. It is really hard to get off work, I am in another internship right now. Is there any way I could interview today?"

"Let me ask." More symphonic music played.

"Dr. Harrison you are in luck. Dr. Hillenbrand rarely does this but apparently, your application is impressive with strong letters. He can do an interview over the phone. Please call this number at 1:00 and he will talk with you."

"Oh thank you so much, thank you. You have no idea what this means to me." Wilson hung up. He looked at his watch. It was 12:30. He looked at the snow and could barely see where he had parked his car just in front of the diner it was so thick. He looked around the diner. There were only three or four people in there and they were all staring at him, a black guy in a suit, not dressed warmly enough for a blizzrd. They were all dressed in flannel with the same wool hats he saw at the airport. One guy in the back may have had a duck-hunting gun propped against his booth. He needed that phone booth to himself for at least an hour, and he was clearly a fish out of water.

Wilson sat down and ordered lunch. Perceptive, as to his situation, he paid in advance with two twenty-dollar bills and told the waitress, "I could use about 10 dollars' worth of quarters for the phone booth. I have to make a very important call to the Mayo clinic here shortly. The chief of staff is waiting to hear from me."

"Are you one of those African doctors training over there? We see a lot of international types down there, but not too many this far north of Rochester."

Wilson was aghast, but composed himself and decided to go along the path of least resistance. "Umm, well yes I hope to do some advanced training there." He said truthfully, but not denying his origins. "If I could have some time in the phone booth at 1:00 that would be wonderful."

"Ok doctor. You are a doctor, isn't that what you said? What part of Africa are you from?

"Savannah, yes I am a doctor." He said truthfully.

"Oh, that sounds exotic. I think we have a Savannah somewhere in the south too you know. Small world." She went off to tell the cook about his order of meatloaf and mashed potatoes.

Less than a minute later the owner, a heavy man with a rim of red hair around his balding scalp, came back out from the kitchen in a stained apron, and Wilson thought that it was going to hit the fan, and he was going to be thrown out of the diner and miss his interview, but he was surprised.

"Young man. you don't need to use the phone booth for a medical call. Always more than happy to help the folks at the Mayo. They saved my mother's life when she had cancer, she is still with us today, praise God. You are welcome to use the phone in my office, sir."

Wilson was shocked, but pleased. He went into the cramped office. There were food catalogues open on the desk, food grease stains on the opened pages, a plate with a few remaining cheese fries on it with a dried blob of ketchup was right in the middle of the desk. An open and half eaten bag of fried pork rinds was next to it. On the wall were cork boards with all sorts of scraps of paper push-pinned on it, some old photos of the owner as a younger man ice fishing with an older man; Wilson assumed it was his father. There was a calendar with a date circled in red that read 'mom's doctor appt' for the end of the next week. A space heater was on in the corner on the floor, and its metal filaments glowed red and emitted a low humming sound. Wilson was glad for this as he was able to take off his overcoat that he would have had to wear if he called from the pay phone just inside the front door, where the wind blew in every time someone entered. He relaxed a bit, but touched nothing on the desk except the old phone. He picked up the heavy black receiver of the rotary phone and called the Mayo clinic's chief of medicine's number.

Wilson did his interview on the phone with the chief of medicine from the tiny office in a diner in the middle of Minnesota. They never got to see him face to face, nor his new three-piece suit which was stained and still damp at the sleeves. When the chief of medicine asked Wilson to tell him about a recent case of his, Wilson launched into Vern's story. He went over the details of the difficult to treat TB, the sanitarium, the ping-pong ball plombage, and their subsequent removal. He followed the tale through the mine in Western Utah and the beryllium exposure, the long-mistaken hospitalization for TB, and finally to the bronchoscopy that he and his knowledgeable attending finally did to make the diagnosis. He gave credit to Michelangelo, and tried very hard not to choke up at this point in his story. As he spoke with growing enthusiasm, he also evoked his empathy for Vern's plight as a returned veteran to a railway worker, then lost to homelessness over time. The chief said very little, and Wilson could not gauge if he was making an impression on him or not. The phone interview seemed awkward to him, but after an hour Dr. Hillenbrand thanked him for his time.

In the end Wilson never got to see Rochester. It was a double-blind interview, a color-blind interview, and maybe that's how they all should be. But he was overwhelmed by the kindness of the folks in the diner from Zumbrota. He over-tipped the waitress with a 10-dollar bill. She gave him a free refills of his coffee. After the snow let up, it was dusk and he drove back to the airport and slept in the terminal, and caught the morning flight back to California. He had to return the rental car after hours without a full tank of gas, and he had heartburn from the meatloaf. He would pay the price for both later.

CHAPTER 58

HARRY WAS BACK, LOOKING NO worse for wear. He had finished his mandatory eight weeks of no patient contact, and even though Sam stared carefully into his eyes he could not detect any jaundice. "Good to see you back." Sam and Gina said when he joined them for coffee during morning report.

"Yes, good to be back." To Gina, "I hope you are well, too?"

She did not know how much Harry knew, but privacy was a lost concept when you worked in a hospital. "Only slowed me down for a day. Hell, Wilson was out two days last week which was longer than me." There she was telling on Wilson for being sick when she did not want

THE COUNTY

anyone to know why she was. She hoped all they knew was the latex allergy part. "What rotation have they got you starting with Harry?"

"Well I need to talk with Sam to work that out, Sam if you can take a walk with me to the internal medicine residency office when report is over?"

Harry gave Sam a brief heads-up on his plan and when they arrived in the internal medicine office they were met by the chair, Jamison, and Fish.

"I don't know if you've heard but we were considering a split track for residency, based on a plan Dr. Fish put forward last year." The chairman started. "We will consider a mostly ICU and ER set of rotations for those who want to pursue critical care, and an all ward and clinic tract for those looking more at primary care. The thing is the doctors who we chose to do these have to balance each other out to make it work. Even numbers of each so both wards and ICU are covered. This match when we choose new interns, we can choose based on that. But Harry requested light duty on the wards when he returned, and the only way we could do that is to have someone cover his last ICU rotation and two months in the ER. I was willing to split it between two interns, but Harry tells me you just might be the person who would jump at the chance to do this?" The chairman said looking right at Sam.

"Yes. I'd be happy to do that." Sam said stoically suppressing a smile. Inside he was thrilled, but he was not letting on to the chairman how great that would be. "Does that mean my last ward rotations are going to Harry?"

"If that is okay? I don't want to overtax you with so many ICU rotations, the call is every third instead of every fourth so you will be working both harder and more often than your fellow interns."

"No. I am perfectly fine with that. Anything for my friend here," Sam replied glancing back over at Harry.

Fish jumped in, "This new track we are planning would continue for all three years. No other wards. About six months each in the ICU or the ER for the next two years, if you're game to be our first critical care tract guinea pig?"

"What about electives?"

"Sure, we have that built into the third year. You could even do anesthesia or surgery if you like to get some broad-based training. The hope would be that you follow it up with a three-year pulmonology critical care fellowship combined, like what I am doing."

"Yeah, I could go for that part, too. Do I have to decide on that today?"

"No. The fellowship component can wait, but do a good job the rest of the residency and we would guarantee you a spot here above any other candidates."

After the meeting broke up, Sam turned to Harry once it was only them outside the office, "You did me a great favor there. I hate the damn wards, and love the ER and ICU."

"I only threw you back into the briar patch you call home."

"True, everyone else may hate the ICU and the extra day on call, but I can handle it. And you got what you wanted too, no more super-stress rotations. Kind of a win-win for both of us."

"You can thank Fish. He was the one who thought of it."

CHAPTER 59

SAM WENT OFF TO ROUND on his new set of patients in the ICU. It wasn't as full as it was earlier in the year, but that was about to change. He got a call from the ER about a critical GI bleed, throwing up bright red blood. The ER had gotten two IV lines in him and ordered blood transfusions, but he needed to be in the unit so the GI consultants could maybe scope him emergently. When Sam got to the ER it did not take long to figure out what the possible cause of the bleeding was. The tell-tale smell of *fetor hepaticus*, as the patient smelled like a baby's diaper someone had forgotten to change for many hours. The patient's skin was also just shy of the color of an old school bus. Another

"Aunt Millie" case Sam quickly recognized with a different disease. Sam's new patient was a 32-year-old man who said everyone called him TJ, who worked as a bartender, and drank every day since he was a teenager. One look at his labs and it was clear he already had advanced cirrhosis. With cirrhosis, the pressure in the veins alongside the esophagus backs up and sometimes bleeds, and they bleed a lot. Sam got him up to the ICU as fast as he could with a unit of blood running in both IV lines. He needed Fish's help on this one.

Fish was waiting in the ICU and assessed the situation. The only way to stop the bleeding is to apply pressure. If you had a big cut somewhere just pressing on it would soon stop it from bleeding, but how do you apply pressure inside someone's esophagus? Fish had the answer; he always did. He sent the clerk down to central supply room in the basement to retrieve a Sengstaken-Blakemore tube. This interesting tube seemed to be an instrument of torture rather than treatment. The red rubber hose was passed through the patient's open mouth into his stomach, where a balloon on the very end was inflated to hold the tube taunt against the stomach where it joins the esophagus. Once that is done suction is applied to the end to empty the stomach of all the swallowed blood. Then a second sausage-shaped balloon in the middle of the tube is inflated so that it presses the length of the lower esophagus to halt the bleeding from the varices, the plump veins backed up by his failing liver. That's when the procedure got interesting. Fish said "There are two critical pieces we now need, a catcher's mask and a sharp set of scissors. Never ever forget the scissors. It could save his life."

Fish fit the catcher's mask around the patient's face pulling the end of the Sengstaken-Blakemore tube through the mouth opening. He then tied it so that it was pulling tightly. "This is how we press on the lower esophagus. We need maybe 25 pounds of traction, and the catcher's mask is the perfect way to do that."

"And the scissors? How does that fit in?"

"We need that at the bedside in case of emergency. If the patient starts choking on his own blood. We need to immediately cut the whole tube to deflate the balloons and pull it out. We may need to intubate him then to protect the airway. We may need to do that anyway if the GI docs want to scope him, which I am guessing they will."

Fish and Sam worked to adjust the device, apply traction, and suction down the central part to keep the stomach empty. When they were all done adjusting everything Sam turned

THE COUNTY

around to see Harry had been watching the whole thing. Harry was just as puzzled as Sam about this device which he had never seen before and asked what in the world it was for. Sam had Harry help him readjust the mask a little after they took a portable chest X-ray and had to move the patient to retrieve the X-ray plate. Harry's hands were trembling. He had no idea what he was doing. The whole apparatus looked like something from the Spanish Inquisition. So, Sam explained the case, the advanced alcohol liver disease, the bleeding varices, the need to keep the patient in a catcher's mask to maintain traction, and the critical scissors in case a life-saving cutting of the cord was needed. Harry recognized the dark yellow hue of jaundice and was intrigued but completely horrified, even more so when he saw that the patient was only two years older than he was, and looked like he was 30 years older. "Too stressful for me. But I did come over here to give you a transfer from the ward."

Harry presented his case to Sam. Andrew Stroh was college student with progressive weakness in his legs after a trip to Mexico. He had an extended bout of diarrhea down there he treated with some medication to slow it down that he got from a friend. The neurologist felt it was a classic case of Guillain-Barre syndrome.

His weakness would get worse and spread higher and higher up his body and maybe it could continue up so high he could no longer breathe on his own. That's why they wanted him in the ICU. Neurology rarely admitted their own patients to the ICU, so it fell to Sam and Fish and the ICU team to admit him.

After getting the Andrew, the Guillain-Barre patient, situated in his bed Harry motioned Sam aside. "Listen, I was not being completely honest with you the other day over at my place. Yes, those gin bottles were mine, old habits from college and the frat house. Now that I see that guy, practically my age, all yellow and bleeding out from his liver disease and that contraption you tied to his face, I realize I never want to get to that point. Sam, I am sorry, but I am promising you I am going to stop drinking, throw all the alcohol out tonight. I swear. Forgive me, you're one of my only friends here I can trust."

"Harry, I am always here for you if you need to talk. It's too easy to be completely isolated while doing internship. I can stop by a few times and make sure you are sticking with it too. Good excuse to play Pong."

The ICU rotation went by smoother. TJ, the GI bleeding patient was scoped by Alex Armenian and she made sure his varices coagulated so the patient would stop bleeding, The catcher's mask came off and Fish stored it in his "secret" corner knowing he would need to use it again someday. The Guillain-Barre patient's weakness progressed for another week but he never needed to be intubated. One day Sam was explaining to him what neurology had told him, that it would be a very long course of rehabilitation exercises to learn to walk again. Andrew asked Sam if he could get a beer with dinner. "I am looking at what? Living in the hospital for another few months? I just want some semblance of my old life back. I am no hard-core drinker, but hey, a beer with dinner or watching the ball game on TV would go a long way to recovery." Sam was unsure. He had just seen the ravages of uncontrolled drinking in his other patient, but this request for one beer now and again seemed reasonable to Sam. Once again, he would have to talk this quandary over with Fish.

Sam had a long discussion with Fish on their overnight call about Andrew Stroh's request. On one hand, there was a strict policy of no alcohol in the hospital. Who needed unruly patients getting drunk? On the other hand, why not? One of those rules that this exception was made for. They wanted to motivate this guy to get better. There was a precedent, too. Every once in a while, they allowed a bottle of champagne for a special occasion, sometimes for a mother after a difficult birth, and sometimes a cancer patient got married in the middle of chemo. But Fish knew this one was going to be above his head. Somehow, he knew it would have to be a direct decision by Jablonski, but Fish knew he wasn't the best messenger for this problem given his track record with Jablonski. He discussed it with Jamison, who agreed to talk with Jablonski.

It took a week, an official consult with ethics, the pharmacy committee, dietary services, and psychiatry just to make sure he did not have any unforeseen risks for alcoholism. In the end, Andrew was cleared to have one beer a day provided he did not get drunk and misbehave in any way. Sam had to write an order for one beer, 3.2 % alcohol by weight, q night with food. When he went to thank Fish he added, "So how many administrators does it take to order a beer?"

Fish took the bait, "I don't know."

"One, but it takes two sub-committees, six meetings, and an executive order."

CHAPTER 60

IT WAS THE IDES OF March; the day Caesar was murdered by his friends. It was also Match Day. At exactly the same time, noon on the east coast, in every medical school around the country every medical student was handed an envelope that determined the rest of their lives. For some, it was a decision as to what specialty they could practice. For some, it was what part of the country they would live in for the next three to six years. For some, it meant separation from their families or their spouses for an equal amount of time. And for a very few it meant a new beginning. Wilson was one of those. When he opened his envelope there were the words after Dr. Harrison, "Congratulations, the Mayo

Clinic is proud to offer you a position in the internal medicine residency."

That day the Country posted its new list of interns for each of its many specialties. There were fresh faces coming from around the country. There was also a note at the bottom of the page, they had hired the nuclear medicine doctor as a transfer in the middle of her internship to replace Wilson. Wilson was going to take an immediate leave of absence, and in reality, he was not coming back.

Wilson met one more time in the cafeteria with Sam, Harry, and Gina. They had re-opened the cafeteria after discovering it was the bakery that delivered the pies that was the source of the hepatitis outbreak. Sam, however made another rule for himself, vowing never to have anything other than a cup of coffee from the cafeteria, which is what he was drinking when Wilson came to say his goodbye. "I am really going to miss all of you. You guys have been my family this last painful year. But I was not holding it together after Michelangelo died. I could not bring myself to let you know I made a last-minute application to Mayo. I figured I'd never get in, and then no one would be the wiser. I would either just still be here or quit."

"We are all happy for you," Gina said.

THE COUNTY

"So you are doing a complete do-over on internship?" Harry asked.

"Yeah, but I can live with that. They sent me a packet about the 'Mayo Way' and it's pretty interesting. Their philosophy is that everyone responds to a request for help and does their best for the patient. You can ask a surgeon passing by to help clean up a mess that you spilled on the floor, or an orthopedist may yell out to you to help hold someone's leg as you walked past as he was working with it. Basically, if you are consulted, you respond with a smile and an eagerness to help. When in doubt you admit. You look for zebras when you hear hoofbeats because it's the Mayo. They encourage thinking of a wide differential and ruling out rare diseases. They want you to get consults to cover all the bases. To collaborate with multiple specialties and support services to deliver the best patient care possible. That's the 'Mayo Way'. And their pulmonology program is great, I could see staying there for that too."

"I heard you have to wear a suit every day to work?" Sam said.

"True. I have some shopping to do. My only suit was trashed in the trip up there. I actually gave the jacket to Vern before he was discharged. I'll have to ask my brother for a loan to buy at least five suits, and wow there will be a big dry-cleaning bill to go along with that."

"You better get some long underwear and earmuffs while you're at it. Isn't it freezing cold up there?" Gina added.

"Yeah, the day I interviewed, or almost interviewed. I was caught in a blizzard; I did not make it to the hospital, but they miraculously agreed to interview me over the phone. I never saw them and they never saw me. I never had to deal with snow in Carolina. But we all adapt somehow. You guys all adapted to the craziness that is the County. Me? Well, not so well, which is why I need to move on and put some distance between this year and the rest of my life. I will miss you three, but I won't miss this place. It would take an awful lot to bring me back here."

CHAPTER 61

SAM SPENT THE LAST TWO months of his internship in the ER, He finally worked out some time when his father could visit and he might have a day off. Sam needed a haircut before his father got there. He had not had one in months. No one at the hospital seemed to care how he looked; all the interns looked as beat as they felt all the time anyway. But one afternoon before his father showed up, he did manage a free hour to get one. He finished a night shift the day before and did not clear the ER until noon. Downing two cups of black coffee before he left, Sam stopped at a barber shop on the way home. After telling the barber how much to take off, he fell asleep in the barber's chair and had to be woken up when the barber was done. Later that night he drove out to the airport to pick up his father. They ate dinner together, but Sam had three more nights in a row to work after that.

Westman had started something new in the ER. He posed it as a teaching opportunity, but most of the ER docs saw it as looking over their shoulder. Every morning at 6 am he would round with his surgery residents and interns on all the patients still in the ER. Sam was one of the few who liked to join them as they went around and examined everybody. He figured teaching was teaching, so why not, plus it allowed him to check on all his patients before sign-out. Westman did like to teach and Sam learned a lot about abdominal pain. Westman demonstrated Kehr's sign in some patients with gall bladder inflammation, Grey-Turner's sign in an alcoholic with pancreatitis. He showed how to subtly elicit rebound at McBurney's point in appendicitis. On the third morning, they stopped at the bedside of a 60-ish woman with vague abdominal pain off and on for a few weeks. Why she came to the ER at midnight for this was a mystery, but that seems to be what people do. They are up at night worrying about something that had been going on for a while and finally work up enough nerve to get it checked. Westman talked to her in his usual subdued voice, then felt something, a small bulge around her navel. Gesturing to his team to feel the bump he asked "Does anyone know the importance of this finding?" as they exited the bedside to gather outside Rooms Five and Seven.

"An umbilical hernia?" suggested the surgical intern.

"Those are easily reducible, and this was not," Westman replied in his soft voice.

"A fatty tissue residue of the umbilicus?" A more senior surgical resident chimed in. Westman merely shook his head. Noticing that Sam had joined the group, asked him if he had some thoughts.

"It felt like a solid lymph node to me," Sam said assuredly.

"Very good. Do you know whose name we associated with that node and why it is an important clinical finding?"

"Um, not really. Is it Saint somebody?" answered Sam.

"Not a saint, but she should be. It was Sister Mary Joseph's node. Sister Mary Joseph was Dr. William Mayo's scrub nurse. Whenever she prepped an abdomen for surgery and noticed one of these lymph nodes, she alerted Dr. Mayo and it soon became associated with internal malignancy, metastatic from the gastrointestinal tract, as it was cancer in the node that made it palpable. She had just recently passed when I studied at the Mayo."

As they were about to leave Westman said to Sam "Glad to have you on rounds." Then as if remembering something added, "Is your colleague Dr. Harrison still here too? He might be interested in joining us."

Sam was a bit surprised that out of all the interns he would ask about Wilson, and he certainly did not want to tell Westman he had quit, so truthfully said, "No he is getting ready to move. He just got accepted to Mayo Clinic in Wisconsin."

"I believe it is in Rochester, Minnesota," said Westman, peering over the top of his glasses, giving Sam his look of disapproval.

"Of course, sir. I don't know why I always get those two states confused. Yes, Minnesota. Big move for him." Then Sam thought he saw the unflappable Westman smile just for a microsecond.

"Good for him. Medicine or Surgery?"

"Oh, Medicine." Sam almost said of course, but realized whom he was standing in front of.

Westman nodded and added, this time with his usual blank soft-spoken demeanor, "Well he made one out of two good decisions then. The

Mayo brothers were the foremost surgeons in the country. No better place to train."

"Sir," the senior surgery resident cut in "we have a cold leg on the wards I'd like you to see. Vascular refused to admit it last night, so we did. I am concerned about arterial insufficiency."

"Lead the way," Westman gestured with an outstretched arm, and with that Westman and the team turned and walked out of the ER.

Sam's father drove around town to see the local sights during the day while Sam slept after his night shifts. In the evening when Sam was awake and they had some dinner together. He told Sam that he went to the museum downtown. Sam got upset and told him to be careful when he wandered around town. He did not want to bring up the hammer murders that started in the museum bathroom.

"It seemed clean and safe. Lots of Gold Rush memorabilia. Not at all like downtown Buffalo."

Finally, after the last of his night shifts, Sam had time off. After a good night's sleep to change his night and day cycle around, they loaded up the rental car his father had and drove to Yosemite.

The views were magnificent. They walked around the valley, and had lunch at the lodge on the deck staring at the magnificent piece of granite that was Half Dome. The sky was crystal blue, and there was the peaceful sound of the late Spring water dripping over the waterfall nearby.

Sam's father asked, "Do you remember your mom once had a postcard of that mountain her uncle had sent? She put it on the fridge with a magnet."

"No, I don't remember that. When was it?"

"You must have been really young, maybe three or four. The postcard was from a famous photographer, I think. She talked about that mountain on the postcard all the time. Then one day she must have taken it down. Who knew, spring cleaning or something? After she died, I found it in a drawer. She never threw it away. I think she always dreamed about going to places like this," he motioned to the Yosemite Valley with his hand. "But we never did. Never left Buffalo. We had enough to live on. We saved, then there was enough to send you and your brother to college. I know you had to borrow after that for med school, but we both were so proud you might come out west and be a doctor someday. She would be so proud to be standing here with you now. It would have been great if we both came to visit."

"I know, dad. I know," Sam looked into the distance at Half-Dome and choked up, his throat too tight to say more. It was half a mountain, half a world away from his childhood. Someday maybe he would take the hike to the top, but probably not with his dad. On the drive back Sam did not have much to say. His dad was obviously happy to be here, to be with him, to be out of Buffalo, too. Sam at one point in his mind began to review the cases he had seen the night before. *Did their old family doctor in Buffalo ever check his mother for Sister Mary Joseph's node? Maybe she would still be here to see all this if he did.* Somehow, Sam fulfilled her hidden postcard dream, but now it most certainly was his own. How could you still have high hopes after such a year?

CHAPTER 62

DESPITE HAVING SURVIVED HIS INTERN year Sam was a wreck. He had created for himself a growing list of rules. He could not eat in the cafeteria without worrying about catching something. He always brought his lunch. He could not walk through the parking lot without picking up his pace afraid he might be accosted by a man with a tire-iron. He could not use any bathroom unless he could lock the door and make sure he was the only one there. Every time while working in the ER that he was called to go into Room One his heart started racing. This was not because a critically sick patient was coming, which he was growing comfortable treating, but the persistent wondering if a

THE COUNTY

gunman would come in and shoot the patient, or the staff, or everyone in sight. When he did ward admissions he could not be anything but compulsive about every matter with his patients for fear of missing something, or forgetting something. But he never missed an Aunt Millie case. On new admissions he read through all their old charts to find every detail of the past history, but other than Vern there were none who spent time in a sanitarium. If they need an x-ray, he wheeled them all to x-ray, and waited to get it read right away. He also brought them back for fear they would be left alone and forgotten in the hallway outside. He never room eighted anyone. Although there were no more earthquakes he did not take the elevator, always the stairs. Because there were no stairs directly there, he never went back down to nuclear medicine again. In stores he was suspicious he would be approached by some patient from the hospital who thought he knew him, or worse someone who wanted to sell him something.

He visited Harry when he could, but often could not find anything to talk to Harry about. When the conversation lagged he worried he would offend him over his drinking if he accidentally said the wrong word. Harry seemed fine one day, they cranky the next morning, especially if he was up all night admitting. But as long as he could trade all his critical care rotations with Sam, which Sam was happy to do, he did not complain. This was partly from guilt on Sam's part, somewhat from sympathy for Harry's condition, and to learn more about taking care of the sickest patients at the County. Sam rarely traded shifts with anyone else, and he would not bother Gina about switching call days, after the last triple trade to get off did not work out. Of course Wilson was gone, one last vestige of intelligence, yet no one had heard from him. But that was the way things were at the County, people came and then they left. Gone forever.

CHAPTER 63

SOMETIMES GONE FOREVER IS ONLY but a year. Jablonski held his usual noon briefing with the five chairs, and he had an announcement. "I had been in talks to hire another OB, one that many might remember. But now that Corkerin is gone I made her an offer to run the department. I hope you will all make her welcome when she starts on Monday. I am pleased to announce that Dr. Della Damone will be returning to the County after getting an MBA." There was a paucity of applause.

Fish had tried to befriend Della again after he found out she was back, but she did not seem to remember him. She was appointed Jablonski's key administrator for critical care areas. Della was not a people person, she was an ice-cold bureaucrat at heart. Her sphere of control now included the ICU and the ER, areas Fish cared about the most and wanted to integrate them into a care continuum. But that dream began to fade after a few meetings with Della. At one meeting he had to tell her his name again. "Fish. OK, I have this little memory jogger trick they taught me in the MBA program," She seemed to work in the fact that she did an MBA into too many of her conversations. This annoyed everyone. "Fish. Carp. I can remember that as Carp."

"What's wrong with just Fish? It's not that complicated of a name."

"It's a game they drilled us on to make associations to remember. You always seem to be carping about something. More doctors. More nurses. More supplies. All things we can't afford. I can remember Dr. Carp, Dr. Fish."

With that Fish gave up trying to be friendly, it was clear every meeting with her was a business meeting. One day when he had to consult Snider to the ER Snider retold his story about soaking some poor intern with feces during a proctoscopy in Room Six. That was Della. Of course, she had nothing but hate for the ER. She was baptized in shit there a long time ago, and just like her memory joggers that was what she would always associate with the place. One day when she announced more budget cuts, she told Fish that she planned to use internal medicine fellows as extra faculty in the ER. They could save money using a fellow as a moonlighter, rather than hiring a new full-time doctor. Fish explained that the old standard of twelve on and twelve off for a faculty member was not working when it was busy. Della agreed but her solution was to add a fellow from 6 pm to midnight when she thought it might be busy.

"I am not sure an endocrine or infectious disease fellow adds that much. They can't see trauma, or ortho, or kids. I am not even going to bring up the psych boarding problem."

"Let your regular guys see those. Just direct the medicine fellows to the medicine stuff. They all did some internal medicine at one time."

"It's just not equitable. Maybe our full-timers might want an occasional 6-hour evening shift. The way it splits out now they are on half days and half nights. That is seven nights per month."

"No one told them to be an ER doc their whole lives. Some day they may grow up and get a regular job." Della's last retort burned Fish to his core. It showed a complete lack of understanding of the unique job the ER did, and all he was trying to do. It was massive headwinds like this that put the brakes on his dream of an emergency residency. She added, "Aren't you doing an ICU fellowship? You certainly don't plan on wasting the rest of your life in the *pit*? Do you?"

CHAPTER 64

TWO YEARS WENT BY. SAM finished his internal medicine residency with the special track in critical care, and Fish finished his critical care fellowship. Fish was about to be made chief for the ER, so maybe he could influence who got hired in the future. Maybe he could start hiring Emergency trained doctors and not recycling internal medicine graduates who left after a year or two. With this in mind, he spent the last six months counseling Sam to apply elsewhere to do a full emergency medicine residency. He promised he would hire Sam back afterward and he could be the start of the new generation of ER docs at the County. Fish had written a letter of reference for him and called a few places to recommend him. Sam picked a new residency on the East coast to move closer to his father. But one day before he was set to fly back for an interview, his father called and told Sam he had sold the store. He was moving to California to be closer to him. Sam withdrew his application, cancelled the interview, never telling his dad he was thinking of moving in the other direction. He had enough training, life was all about experience, and he would just stay on at the County. There was a job open here, as there was every July, and Fish now had the power to hire him. Despite his hope Sam would go do an emergency residency elsewhere, Fish hired Sam to work in the pit.

One day that summer there was a surgical Grand Rounds. Westman gave a speech that Fish thought would doom the whole program. Westman was giving a lecture on the future of trauma care. He summarized all the advances that were being made. Lessons on the Golden Hour, as he called it, that were learned from the Vietnam war. Aggressive trauma triage taking patients from the scene of an accident past other emergency rooms and bringing them to the trauma center was a core principle he outlined. He then went on to call the other emergency rooms mere entrepreneurs more interested in how fast they treated their "customers" than the quality of care. They did not have the training a surgeon develops over years of experience, and they never will. All trauma patients need a surgeon waiting for him at the door when they arrive. He called for the establishment of the County as the one and only trauma center in the region. In his blueprint for the future, the emergency doctors could take care of the other folks "down there" but surgical disease needed to be cared for only by the surgeon. Jablonski and Damone went along with it. They made matters worse when they rewrote the policy in the red binder to state all critical trauma would have an anesthesiologist waiting for them too. This change even made Brent mad.

Della Damone took this as the signal she was waiting for to advance her cost-cutting plan for hiring of more fellows instead of full timers, now for the day shift too. The old group of ER docs were left with more and more nights only. Jablonski wouldn't hear any more pitches for an emergency residency. Fish grew frustrated but decided to hang in there. Fish had an option with his duo training, to spend more time working in the ICU, and started working less in the ER.

Fish still loved his shifts in the ER, despite it all. One night both he and Sam were back in the pit. It started drizzling when they came to work and stayed cold all day. It was that cold foggy night in December. Two 12-year-old boys were the victim of a gang fight at a drug deal gone bad. Who knows why they were there in the first place, but drugs and gangs had taken over the south end of the city. Sam and Fish tried to save them but couldn't. Snider was not on that day. A junior inexperienced surgical resident came down as part of the trauma response team to help, but in the chaos he just yelled at everyone making everyone tense. Everything went sideways and there were side by side codes with the two kids under CPR in Room One.

The police came in after the two kids were pronounced dead, and talked to everybody to get statements. All the young boy's friends knew nothing and saw nothing, at least that's all they would tell the cops. Ultimately, they sent an officer with a police chaplain to their homes and their distraught mothers came to the ER. Sam had to tell one mother the horrible news, and walk her into the room so she could view her child one last time. She fell to her knees and sobbed. Sam had to step out, he could no longer bear it. Sam had reached the end of his frustration. The grind of the violence had finally got to him. *He was officially burnt out*, but where could he go from here? He stepped outside near the ambulance side door, head down, hands on his knees, breathing heavily. He lifter his head and stared into the distance as the December fog rolled in. He fell back on the rickety old smoker's bench, bumping his head. He was numb. Fish came out to commiserate with him; they talked.

Fish secretly had already made his decision to leave, but only told Sam about a job back east he was considering, in an ICU. He would give up the ER and run the ICU, a step-up in most people's opinion. Fish told Sam there are two rules if he wanted to survive at the County: "Rebels are shot at dawn. And always pack a parachute."

"What does that mean?"

"If you complain too much and fight too much, too hard, and with the wrong person to try and make things better you will be branded a rebel. Maybe I did that to myself, but once they decided I was the rebellious doctor who couldn't abide by their rules, that gave them the chance to all-out ignore me. I burned all my bridges here. Jablonski and his hench-woman Della, both want me gone for good. It will only be a matter of time they find some way to fire me. Not the way I want to go out. But I knew something has to give so I polished off my CV, added all my teaching responsibilities and publications, like the one we wrote about the Toxic Shock girl. I packed my parachute. When the day comes that they kick me out of this plane I'll have somewhere to fall. Sorry if I have to leave you with the mess that this place has become."

"Those rules sound like they're for you for the day you're planning leave. What about me? I think no matter what, I have to stay. But I am barely hanging on."

"Did I ever tell you about the astronaut and the bus driver?" Fish asked. "It's an essay I read in a journal just recently. Basically, it's about training in a place like this with all of its intensity, the sickest of the sick, the gunshots, the stabbings, the critical medical cases, and yes, the violence. It trains you to handle everything, and maybe instills a dose of fear and anxiety as a side-effect. You become the astronauts of the medical world, prepared for any crisis should it occur. Most of the others, the ones who can't stand the ER or the ICU, those are the ones who leave. They find a job driving the bus. Regular schedule. Mundane even. But once you're an astronaut do you think you can go back and drive a bus? Ask yourself that after a day, or night, like this. Try to imagine what a day or a month of that would really be like."

Just then an ambulance siren broke up their conversation. By the ascending pitch they knew it was approaching fast. The smell of chimney smoke had gotten stronger as they sat outside in the cold. Water kept dripping from an overhead pipe. An orderly came out to hose off the two bloody backboards the two kids were brought in on. Fish and Sam met the fire department ambulance crew at the back door. Inside sitting on the ambulances rear bench seats was a mother, father, and two young children all on oxygen masks. The fire department paramedic told them, "Furnace busted, they tried to light a fire in the fireplace but it was probably blocked up. There was a sooty odor throughout the house. We think maybe carbon monoxide poisoning? The kids here were asleep when we got there, but mom and dad were throwing up, with headaches." Fish and Sam nodded to each other in agreement and helped take them all inside.

"Just like Apollo 13," Fish smiled at Sam. "Lovell had a problem with the ventilation, but he had the training to solve it. Turns out these are the two kids you get to save tonight."

CHAPTER 65

SAM SETTLED IN TO A state of complacency with it all after that night. The anger and the frustration backed down but rarely went completely away. He thought about the speech Fish had made the last night they worked together in the ER, about being the astronaut. As much as Sam wanted to leave too, he knew he couldn't. He could not think of working somewhere else without the surge of adrenaline that he got daily with the job. Perhaps he was addicted to the County. Just like addicts inside who know each day could be their last. But even so, every time he heard about another job somewhere else, he knew he could not move and leave his father.

Fish followed through on his plans to go to Iowa. He preempted any move that Della could take against him, and jumped with his parachute packed before it was too late. Their paths seldom crossed in those last days; Fish in the ICU and Sam in the ER. After one admission from the ER Sam had called the ICU and Fish came down to the ER to tell him goodbye. It was busy and they could not talk for long, but agreed to get together for lunch. But that never happened, Sam did not hear from him after that. Sam would have liked to say something more to his friend and mentor, thank him for saving him again and again, and maybe Fish would have had some final profound last words for him. But it was not to be. Like the way all things change at the County, one day Fish was gone.

Snider eventually finished too. Six years as a surgery resident and six years as a neurosurgery resident and one would think he would go into private practice, but Snider still lacked the social skills to be hired by anybody, except the Army. He tried private practice briefly but got kicked out of the group before his 90-day dismissal for no-cause deadline kicked in. He went from that directly to Europe to work in a military hospital in Germany. Every severely head-injured service member was airlifted from their assigned duty area there. Snider was never going to be in a place that was not institutionalized. Snider now had new battles to fight, but he held the record for the longest continuous resident in the County.

Gina was doing a cardiology fellowship at the County under Woody when he moved on, too. First, his boss, the old Chairman, retired. There ensued a power struggle between some staff and Della Damone, intent on cutting costs, and one day half the cardiology department quit. The young Turks, as they were branded, all were in the intervention section of cardiology. They wanted to cath all the hot MIs, while the older group was happy with the status quo. Much like Fish, they were rebels about to be shot at dawn, they too had packed their parachutes. The young Turks were recruited to start an emergency cardiology service with a 24 hour-a-day cath lab in a University Hospital back east. Gina went with them, and soon she got a faculty appointment as a cards attending in her new job.

Harry did a rheumatology fellowship after his residency and was working in town at the office complex across the street from the Sam Brannon Hospital. Sam Brannon was famous during the gold rush. He did not go into the hills to dig for gold that was soon tapped dry.

THE COUNTY

Instead, he made a fortune by selling the 49ers' picks and pans, and those new blue jeans Mr. Strauss had made in San Francisco. There would always be a demand for them even if there was no gold. Sam Brannon's heirs donated several plots of land to build a hospital. They named it for him. At first it was a single for-profit community hospital, and soon became a chain of hospitals throughout the valley. They would be the ones that Westman had the ambulances drive past with their trauma patients. Harry now worked in their office building, happy to be away from the stress that turned him yellow and jaundiced.

Sam stayed and worked in the ER and tried to make peace with himself. One day as he was writing a note, someone came into the doctor's charting area and thumbtacked a flyer to the wall. There was to be a guest lecture at Medicine Grand Rounds next week, Dr. Harrison from the Mayo Clinic would be speaking on Berylliosis: TB's great Imitator. Sam would not miss it for the world.

The auditorium was packed the following Monday at noon as the chief medicine resident rose to the podium, "We are honored to have the return of one of our star residents who has since gone on to greater things. Today is the inaugural lectureship honoring Dr. Corbin

Michelangelo, one of our pulmonary physicians who died several years ago and left a lasting legacy of scholarship. Please welcome Dr. Wilson Harrison of the renowned Mayo Clinic, professor of pulmonology to speak on a topic of great interest to us all: How to differentiate TB from one of its great imitators—berylliosis." Loud applause followed and Wilson, looking trim, and sporting a few gray hairs, stepped to the stage in a tailored three-piece gray suit. He gave a fabulous lecture to a packed house, finishing with an even louder and longer round of applause than when he was introduced. After a question-and-answer period and many personal words of thanks, and shaking of hands, Sam made his way forward to the stage.

"Wilson, you were great. And you look great. Are the Wisconsin winters treating you well?"

"It's Minnesota, my geography-challenged friend." And they hugged.

"Of course. I have been waiting all weekend to see you. This was just great."

Another person worked his way up to the stage from the back of the room, as the crowd was exiting. It was Harry. He had gained many pounds, never losing his love of doughnuts. He was starting to look round like Jablonski. He was dressed in an unbuttonable wool sport coat that did not hide his weight, paired with a flashy red tie. The whites of his eyes were clearer than they ever were. He shook Wilsons hand vigorously, "Wilson. Holy cow. You made the big time!"

The three old friends talked for a while as the crowd disappeared. Sam caught Wilson up on the people that they knew. Gina was a cardiologist, Fish an intensivist, others that they knew had left. Harry finally said, "I've got to get back to my office. Lots of old ladies with arthritis to see." He shook both Wilson's and Sam's hands and smiled, "You know that was the best year of my life. I never would have said it then, but it was."

Wilson stood alone in the auditorium with Sam, "Sam I have a flight to LA later, but would like to spend some more time. Can I ask you a favor? There is one place I need to go." He felt inside his pocket to make sure the item he brought all this way was still there.

Sam remembered the drive to the church. He had not come this way since the ride in Fish's old van. He passed the house where they parked on the lawn. Wilson and Sam spoke a little but grew more silent as they got closer. Sam let him out near the graveyard. Sam got out himself and strolled around the perimeter. He saw Wilson walk to Michelangelo's grave and he saw him talking but could not hear what he was saying. He left him alone for a long while. Wilson had a lot to say. He wanted to thank his lost mentor for everything, for stimulating him to read, for writing up the case, for just being there to talk while on call, and for making learning exciting. He choked up when he got to say "if it wasn't for you, I never would have got into Mayo," because he knew if Michelangelo had not died, the series of decisions to leave would never have occurred. He would have done anything now to change that all back if only Michelangelo was still here. He stopped, he had run out of things to say and stood there silently for a few more minutes. He finally reached into his pocket and pulled put a small rock he had been carrying with him. It was silvery and jagged, and very light-weight. He left it on the corner of Michelangelo's head stone. It was a piece of pure beryllium.

When Wilson got back to Sam's car it was clear he had been crying. "I think I finally got to tell him what I should have, what I wanted to, all those years ago." After a long pause he looked at Sam, "We can go now. I'm finally ready to leave the County this time."

Sam drove to the airport with Wilson in silence. A Spring thunderstorm was moving in, dry lightning flashed in the distance. It did not bother Sam; he knew the lightning bolts were no longer coming for him. Wilson was off to give the same lecture at another Grand Rounds in LA, some hospital in Pasadena. Mayo encouraged their doctors to take these speaking tours. It helped the doctors gain poise and national recognition, and for Mayo, it bolstered their reputation even further. People flew to Rochester, Minnesota from all over the country, and all over the world, to get seen by their experts. Experts like Wilson. Whenever some visiting scholar came and it was Wilson's task to take them out for dinner, he took them to a little diner to give them a taste of local cuisine, Minnesota style.

Before he got out curbside at the airport Wilson wanted to tell Sam one more thing, "I did not find this out until years after I got in, but I had asked Westman for a letter. He told me he only writes letters for surgery residents, and I thought well that was that. But one day I was talking with our chairman and he told me that the day before I interviewed, he got a phone call from Westman. Apparently, he told him what a good candidate I was, the next Dr. Arrowsmith, or something to that effect. It had a huge impact on my acceptance. I forgot to ask if he is still here because I wanted to thank him."

"Westman will be here forever. He is even softening his stance on emergency medicine. So, now you need to come back and talk about some other exotic pulmonary disease next year to see him. And I'd want to see you again too when you come. I really missed you my friend."

"Well come to Rochester sometime."

"To do what, go ice fishing?"

"No, just to experience the Mayo Way."

Wilson got out at the curb and they waved goodbye. He walked into the airport terminal to catch his next flight. He was the expert he wanted to be. He earned their respect.

Sam made it home about an hour later. He opened the door quietly thinking the baby may be sleeping. His wife holding a finger on her lips to signal ssshh. "Did you see your friend?" she whispered.

"Yeah, it was nice. Do you remember him from intern days?"

"No, the only one who ever barged into my unit was you."

"Wilson was too civilized to barge in."

"Do you miss it? Intern days? Camaraderie? Being on-call?"

"No, just the people."

"Do you ever think about what would have happened if you stayed in internal medicine like him?

"No, I think I had emergency medicine in my bones since the day I met Fish," Sam said then paused, "Do you regret leaving nuclear med?"

"Never, we would have been replaced by the CT scanner in a few years anyway."

"I am sure glad you became a medicine intern. Do you forgive me for barging into to nuc with an oxygen tank and my Toxic-Shock patient?"

"I may have married you, but I am not crazy," and then thought to herself, *"Someday you might eventually learn there is a world outside the ER."*

CHAPTER 66

UP UNTIL THEN, IT APPEARED that Sam would stay with the County. Few things changed over those years; the County was still the County. Sam was now clearly on his own, the last remaining member of his intern group, trying to teach the new interns how to survive the pit. Little progress was made to start a training program for emergency medicine, but Sam taught the internal medicine interns who came down to the ER. Every July a new set of interns arrived and although it once was Fish who used to welcome them with his speech on the first day, it fell to Sam after that to orient them to the ER. He repeated Fish's speech to them almost word for word. Over time he learned that some

THE COUNTY

of them would learn the skills well, and he told them they could be the medical astronauts, some would not and ultimately leave. As much as Sam thought no one would ever stay as long as Snider again, Sam inherited the title of the longest inhabitant in the County. He learned to adjust to its ways. No one could understand why he stayed inside its walls. He was often met with the salutation, "What are you still doing here? I always thought you were smart enough to get out?" He should have been a little bit insulted by that, but when he thought about the full meaning of what they said, in the end, they were just calling him smart.

The best thing that can happen to you is not to have to be brought into the County. Live well, avoid strange neighborhoods after dark, and watch where you park your car. Stop smoking (or never start), forget drugs and those who would entice you to use them, always wear a seat belt, and most of all, that insurance card you have, don't leave home without it, or the paramedics will assume you belong at the County. A full menu of rules; Sam's rules, but they're the best way to never experience a night in the pit. Not to say you won't get good medical care at the County, because you will. There will be no amenities. You'll be treated like a cross between a tray of entrails and a convicted felon. The sounds will drive you insane, the smells will make you want to vomit, the waiting will make you think you've entered some purgatory where you will need to atone for your sins before proceeding onward. If you complained too loudly a police officer with a Great Dane might come by to see what the matter is. But after all that, if you don't die, as that is the quickest way out of the County, ultimately you will be released, perhaps psychologically scarred from your experience. Before you call your lawyer or the city council think for a moment about those who are left behind. Think about those who worked there for years. Think about the Sam Wyatts, the Mac Sniders, the Fishs, and the constantly changing staff of residents. If they did not adapt to survive, your chances of surviving would be a whole lot worse. There are few places on earth where a nightmare, that was the County, serves a useful purpose.

Sam's own nightmare kept recurring in pieces, yet never seemed to go away. Perhaps it started one night after going to a revival showing of *Gone With The Wind*. In his dream, he is in the streets of Atlanta, and all around it is burning to the ground. The buildings, all

THE COUNTY

old dry timber, are going up in flames. The wounded lay moaning and dying, bleeding from the wounds of war. The war that tore our country apart by killing an entire generation.

From out of the smoke and dust, amidst falling burning beams, Fish calmly rides up on a white horse. As he dismounts, he pulls a saddle bag filled with bandages off the back of the white horse and flips a bandana over his face like a mask to keep out the smoke. The noise from the inferno is so deafening you can't hear him speak across the open plaza where the wounded lay moaning and screaming for help. One by one he examines them, attends to their wounds and administers a dose of laudanum to those in pain. Over the pandemonium it's possible to hear his voice saying, "Bring some more gauze, we've got to triage the wounded on Magnolia Street."

Then from behind him, Snider runs across the plaza with a surgical mask on and a carpetbag full of crude tools. His gloved arms are dripping with blood and caked with dried tissue. His pants are stained with gunpowder and blood. He starts saying something about operating in the basement of the train station. He's been up for two days but he wants to know where he needs to go to operate next. Fish points to a line of bodies laid out on horse blankets and Snider drops down to his knees beside the first one and begins sawing his leg off. The soldier screams in pain.

"Shit, don't we have any more laudanum for this poor bastard?" Snider curses.

Jablonski appears on a horse-drawn carriage, Della Damone by his side. Turning to the three docs working on patients in the open square he barks that they need to conserve the laudanum for the grieving widows' pain and sorrow. He jumps on the white horse telling Fish and Snider that there is a better use for this horse in the general's tent. Then before angrily turning to leave he yells at them, "Back to the front line the two of you. I want you up at the front lines defending our county." Before Sam can yell to them not to do it, Fish tosses his saddlebag to him and starts to walk off past the blazing fire to his new post. Snider picks up his tools and follows him.

"No, don't leave me here!" Sam screams, "I need help. People are dying all around me. Where am I going to find an experienced surgeon and ER doc in Atlanta in the middle of the night?"

"You're going to have to be the one to do it now." Fish tells him as he walks away, "We'll be back when this horrid war is over. We'll build a new hospital right here from the ashes." Sam has an empty feeling inside as they walk off. He knows the war will never bring them back. He tries to yell after them but they walk off into the smoke unable to hear his plea. As Sam looks down, a line of soldiers laying on horse blankets are looking up at him with pleading eyes. Some motion with desperate arms, or parts of arms, to come help them. One begins to seize and then just as suddenly lays motionless. More litter bearers arrive with more soldiers on horse blankets. A nurse appears, her white uniform covered in blood. She applies a compress to the man with the half-amputated leg.

"Who were those masked men," she asks calmly attending to the man with the mangled leg.

"They were the last of the Rangers. The three of us, the caregivers who stayed to work while everyone else was fleeing Atlanta, and who tried to save some lives."

"They're all leaving, doctor, why did you stay?"

"I guess, I guess, I am the last lone ranger now."

"Lone Ranger, why do they call you the Lone Ranger?" the man with the half-blown-off leg asks.

"Because now all the other Rangers are gone!" Sam tells him. He leans over his patient and braces himself to steady his hands. He grabs the saw that Snider had left still half buried in his thigh, "this won't hurt" Sam grimaces, knowing inside he has to lie to him, and continues to saw it off. Behind him four stores high a fiery blaze erupts, without any warning the winds whipping up the flames, a roaring sound of a building being consumed in the conflagration drowns out all other sounds, the screams and the tears, and left burning to the ground is the County.

ACKNOWLEDGMENTS

This book is a work of fiction, but just like novels about the Civil War or World War II, it exists in an overlay of historical truth. While all the characters are fabrications, I drew from both my internship in California, and many people I knew to develop their personalities. However, the murder of the beloved pulmonary doctor at the center of the story is true, although it occurred about five years after my internship. I tried to portray many elements of that tragic crime accurately, but since the characters of Snider, Wilson, Sam, Brent, and others are all fictitious their roles in that event are a work of fiction.

The other historical element of this novel is the portrayal of the early days and development of emergency medicine as a specialty. All the diseases are portrayed as accurately as they may have presented and been cared for in the 1970s and 1980s. There was a tuberculosis sanitarium in the Sierras named for the nearby town of Weimar, but it closed before the events in the book took place. The procedure called plombage of placing ping-pong balls into the chest cavity was done in the past, and I did care for a few patients who had it done.

The last American beryllium mine is in Delta, Utah, and the disease from breathing its dust berylliosis resembles TB. The other practices and science of emergency, trauma, and cardiology have come a long way since then, and many practices such as gastric lavage, Fogarty catheter clot retrieval, and Sengstaken-Blakemore tubes have mostly disappeared into history. Similarly, the evolution of emergency care involved the creation of trauma centers and cardiac catheterization suites, and these are described as they were evolving at that time. Emergency Medicine got its own designation as a specialty with its own residencies and certifying board exam a few years later. However, the emergency rooms in those days were staffed with a mix of doctors from internal medicine, surgery, and anesthesia. Resistance to establishing the specialty from those other medical specialties was real. I encourage today's emergency physicians to read and understand their history.

The characters in this book and their interactions with each other are all products of my imagination, but the challenges they encountered are real. There was clear prejudice, if not frank racism, then. The obstacles that Wilson faced as a highly educated black physician were daunting. I heard from colleagues how they were asked about stereotypical sports participation instead of their skills as doctors in interviews, or why wouldn't they thrive better in an "urban" environment when they interviewed in the suburbs. Similarly, while there were growing numbers of women in medicine, they still congregated in certain fields. There were boundaries to break in the procedural-based fields of surgery, cardiology, and gastroenterology. The women physicians of today should be thankful for the perseverance of their forbearers who did indeed have to shout into the "doctor's" locker room to have a set of scrubs handed out to them while they were forced to change in the nurse's locker room, and to lie about their family planning choices if they wanted to get fellowships.

In my perspective, administrators typified by Jablonski and Della Damone, always seemed to focus on the bottom line of what things would cost. They have not changed over time. Their rules and arrogance often got in the way of decent patient care. People like Brent knew exactly how to smoothly get under their skins using their own rules against them. In my mind, the administrators are still the root cause of overcrowding which has plagued emergency departments since the days of this novel. This has only gotten worse, reaching crisis proportions. On the other hand, Mayo is a world-renowned hospital. Their mantra of the 'Mayo Way' is real and represents a possible theoretical solution to many problems of turf wars, as they seem to support a community of helping each other solve problems.

Gilbert's disease is a real malady, and I felt it was an appropriate metaphor for internship. Normal people put under stress become jaundiced. A good night's sleep and food resolve the biliousness in their souls and in their eyes. It should not have to be like that, and in fact, work hours, accurately portrayed in this story, have become more humane. Like Harry, one of my fellow interns had this disorder, although he was always a wonderful person. His sunny disposition did not change with his rising bilirubin.

THE COUNTY

Finally, Sam is in a small part my literary alter-ego, an observer of the chaos around him. Like him, I went from internal medicine to a career in emergency medicine. Like him, I had many days of self-doubt and fear. Like him, my mother passed away in the middle of my internship and I was called out of my rotation in the ICU. Unlike him, I did make it home in time to say my last farewells. After the trauma of daily death, I did experience burnout, like Sam, but I got better, adapted, and stayed. In those days there were few resources for burnout, PTSD, or the trauma of intense training, but something inside drove both me and Sam to keep going. Mentors like Fish helped. Unfortunately, doctors also have a high incidence of relying on both alcohol and drugs, in an attempt to cope, to which they have easy access. I painted the characters of Harry and Corkerin to highlight that risk. Stress does other bad things to people. Some like Snider paradoxically become cruel individuals, beyond redemption, after starting as good doctors.

As I think of Sam, I think about the pear tree I have in my backyard. One year it was struck directly by lightning, nearly slicing it in half. With that thunderstorm, it became a victim of Thor's random vengeance, just like Sam feared he might be the victim of one day. The upper limbs of the tree were completely severed and the main trunk listed to one side. It was a twig of its former stature, and no fruit grew that year or the next, on the branches left hanging. Well-meaning people advised I just yank it out of the ground and replace it. But I let it be, and over time nature healed it. The upper branches grew back, and it once more was the pride of my backyard; after many years the pears returned.

I survived the institutionalization of having trained, and then training others, in the County. It did not burn to the ground like in Sam's dream, but over time did improve, like my pear tree that grew back stronger, and the County stands a much better institution than it was originally. I practiced emergency medicine for 40 years before one day I thought it was time that I fulfill a promise I made to write this book. We shouldn't think that all that has passed is behind us, we must learn from it.

CODA

Sam got a phone call at the front ER desk at the end of an unpleasant day about a patient being transferred as a "good teaching case"—a euphemism for no insurance.

At the end of the call, the ER doc from Brannon General asked Sam if he would be interested in joining their private group in a new contract they were going after, up in the mountains, up in the country. "We have heard good things about you."

Sam trying to hide his frustration, replied, "The mountains? Maybe. That's something I will have to think about."

Was it time to leave the County for the country?

Printed in the USA
CPSIA information can be obtained
at www.ICGtesting.com
LVHW041237241124
797241LV00001B/39